Deception

Books by Karen Ann Hopkins

The Temptation Novels

in reading order

TEMPTATION
BELONGING
FOREVER
DECEPTION
JOURNEY (coming in 2018)

Wings of War

in reading order

EMBERS
GAIA
TEMPEST
ETERNITY (coming in 2018)

Serenity's Plain Secrets

in reading order

LAMB TO THE SLAUGHTER
WHISPERS FROM THE DEAD
SECRETS IN THE GRAVE
HIDDEN IN PLAIN SIGHT
PAPER ROSES (coming in 2017)

PRAISE FOR THE TEMPTATION NOVELS

"I loved joining Rose and Noah during their journey in the Temptation series by Karen Hopkins."
— Katie McGarry, acclaimed YA author

"Wonderfully compelling, becoming highly emotional with an interesting ending."
— XpressoReads blog

"Temptation is a beautiful, forbidden romance . . . I highly recommend [it]."
— I Heart YA Books blog

"I completely adored this book."
— The Book Blog Experience

"I loved this book! . . . Readers who enjoy books with forbidden or secret romances will be riveted."
— Mrs. ReaderPants blog

"Belonging, the sequel to Temptation . . . places the reader in an Amish community filled with danger, suspense, romance, and mystery. The writing is addictive and fast-paced, leaving readers breathlessly waiting for more."
— Bethany Fort, Booklist Online

"I cannot say enough good things about Forever and the entire series. Karen Ann Hopkins is without a doubt one of my favorite authors. Her books and writing style are exquisite. She really knows how to capture the reader's heart and tell a heartwarming/breaking romance like none other."
— Bittersweet Enchantment Blog

"Karen Ann Hopkins captures her readers with endless descriptions of life, tragedy, healing and love. All components that make for a series that is unforgettable."
–A Leisure Moment Book Blog

Deception

KAREN ANN HOPKINS

Deception

ISBN 1548346365
ISBN-13 978-1548346362

Published August, 2017

PROLOGUE

A shiver raced over Levi's naked body as he straightened back up. He glanced down the line at the other five men, also in their birthday suits. The chill he was experiencing wasn't from being completely exposed to the inmates and the four guards in the gray-walled room, though. He was accustomed to the weekly strip searches. Any modesty that he might have had when he had arrived in the Pen was long gone. He was simply cold. But that was part of the game, and he knew it. The guards purposely lowered the temperature in the examination room to make the ordeal even worse—as if they even needed to add to the obvious torment. There was no use complaining. Levi had seen that mistake made by too many weaklings. All their whining got them was the butt end of a baton in their gut or a bucket of ice water in their faces.

Levi shrugged off the cold and focused his gaze on the certificate hanging on the wall across from him. Taking a steady breath, he narrowed his only eye to read the writing on it. *Lebanon Correctional Institution, Warren County, Ohio.* The rest of the words were too small and the cursive writing of the signatures too ornate to be distinguishable from where he stood. But the rest of the writing didn't matter anyway. What he could read was enough. It was a stark reminder that a maximum security prison had been his home for nearly a year.

Most days went by in a redundant fog for the twenty-year-old. Levi moved between his cell and the cell block cafeteria,

1

where he ate and worked in the kitchen, washing the dishes and mopping the floor, in a semi-state of denial. He was glad for the work. It occupied his time, chasing away some of the tedious boredom that his life had become. The only time the haze partially cleared from his mind was the blessed hour each week that he spent in the yard when weather permitted. He never imagined how much he would savor the feel of warm sunshine on his skin and a fresh breeze on his face. His days of resenting the hard work of tending the crops in the fields from early morning until dusk were just a memory now. What he wouldn't give to have loosely tilled, dark earth beneath his feet, and a thousand acres of farmland surrounding him once again.

Even his always stern-faced father, homely mother, and noisy siblings would be a welcome trade to the never ending stream of sneering guards and their filthy mouths. He longed to have freedom—but he'd have to wait another nine years before he was even eligible for parole. Nine more years of hell is what he had to look forward to.

"Put your clothes back on. We're done here," Chief Guard Larry said.

The sound of the man's husky voice abruptly pulled Levi from his runaway thoughts. As much as he wanted to grab up his clothes from the floor and put them on, he swallowed down the desire, and purposely slowed his movements. It was simply the need to survive that gave him such resolved patience. A show of strength and fortitude was the only thing that placed a tentative cloak of protection around him. He'd seen firsthand what happened to weak men in a place like this—and he would have none of it.

Praying hadn't hurt his standing within the cell block, either. Early on, the other inmates had noticed that there was something very different about him. The stigma that went along with being Amish carried right into the world of thieves and murderers. Levi had discovered that the others either gave him a wide berth, or sought him out for some kind of spiritual counseling. At first, he'd been amused by the steady flow of sinners telling him their darkest secrets. It reminded him of Bishop Abram Lambright and how the members of the Meadowview community flocked around him on Sunday mornings, hoping that his special standing with God would provide blessings for them.

Unwanted thoughts about the bishop filled Levi with a strange mixture of hatred and begrudging respect. After all, Abram had been the only one of his people to call on him in prison. Even his own parents had turned their backs on him. If his mind had been sounder, he would have better understood, and even accepted the reason for the immediate shunning he'd received from his family and friends after he was arrested for attacking Rose Cameron. But his mind had been twisted for a while, and his time in prison hadn't helped matters any.

As Levi pulled the orange cotton shirt over his head, his usual pale face flushed with anger when he remembered the visit from the bishop. He could still distinctly remember how his heart had raced as he'd taken the seat across from the white-bearded man who had been the hammer of authority in the community for as long as he could remember.

The bishop was a tall, thin man with deep lines of age etched on his face. Levi recalled how his heart had stopped thrumming in his ribcage altogether when the bishop began speaking to him in German. Every word he said was still seared into his consciousness, as was the entire scene.

"I have not come to hear repentance for your devilish ways, Levi. For I don't believe that you are even aware of what you've done, let alone ready to ask forgiveness from our Lord Father. You were a difficult child and evil grew in your heart as you became a man. I have no choice but to excommunicate you from our church. You will be Meidung to our people. Even if the outsiders' laws free you one day, you will never be welcomed among us."

Levi found courage at his words and calmly replied, "You invited evil into our Garden of Eden, Bishop, when you allowed an English girl to live among us. She brought the devil with her . . . and now, I've lost my life for it."

The bishop's lips became thin lines and his eyes dark pools. Levi actually leaned back again without thought, to put immediate distance between him and the holy man.

With a raised finger pointed directly at Levi, Bishop Lambright had said, "Do not dare to place blame for your deeds on any other soul. Absolution comes only with the acknowledgment of one's own sins. You should be more concerned with your eternal soul than misplaced hatred for others." The bishop took a breath and leveled an even harder look at Levi. "The time we spend living in these bodies, in this world, is but a blink of an eye to the forever we have with God in heaven, or to an eternity in the burning flames of the abyss with the dark one. You'd best remember that, Levi . . . and begin praying for the salvation of your soul."

The bishop rose from his chair and walked away. That was the last time Levi had seen one of his people.

The vision blinked away when firm hands pushed him roughly. He followed the other inmates through the door.

"Wake up, Farmer. We aren't going to wait on you all day," Larry spat out with his shove.

Farmer. It was ironic to Levi that he'd been given that particular nickname in prison. He'd never considered himself a farmer, and had always been hell-bent to make sure that he didn't end up farming. But here he was, being addressed as one on a daily basis.

Levi walked into the hallway with his head raised high and his thoughts still wandering. The gray walls continued straight into the cafeteria. There were only four small, caged windows high up near the ceiling to allow a small amount of natural light to shine through. At the moment, the sky was dark with rain clouds. The rumble of thunder vibrated menacingly throughout the corridor, but Levi ignored the sound, more intent on getting into the food line before the rest of the cell block was let in. Levi was grateful for a few minutes of relative quiet in such a place, although he was disappointed that the thunderstorm would make the yard off limits that afternoon.

As the rice and egg mixture was slopped onto his plate, a quiet conversation caught his attention. He focused on Big Red's voice, as the red-headed inmate spoke to the smaller, greasy-haired man at his side, called Snarly. Levi walked across the hall with purpose. He was the only one in the room who didn't jump at the louder boom and immediate flash of lightning, which made the lights flicker.

He sat down a few seats from Big Red and Snarly, just as the other fifty-four residents of Cell Block D began filing into the cafeteria. The shuffling of their feet and their excited voices snuffed out the silence in a heartbeat, creating the perfect environment for discussing secrets.

"Why don't you join us, Farmer," Big Red nodded at the empty seat beside him.

Levi struggled to keep the smile from spreading on his lips, rising casually to join the other men.

Once Levi was seated, he eyed Snarly and asked, "Did you read the scriptures I recommended the other day?"

Snarly nodded vigorously. "I even read some extra."

"If you ask me, it's a waste of time." Big Red snorted.

Levi had heard this argument from the large man before, but with ever lessoning conviction. Big Red wanted the others to think that he wasn't worried about his soul in the least, but Levi wasn't fooled by his bravado. Big Red had murdered his neighbor during a drug-deal-gone-bad. He was a trailer trash sort of individual, who'd had a slew of run-ins with the law before he'd even turned eighteen. But he had grown up with just enough religion to make him a little worried about the prospect of going to hell.

Because of Big Red's size, he had automatically been promoted to one of the cell block leaders when he'd arrived in the general population, just a month after Levi himself had settled in. Levi had immediately taken notice of the man, realizing that although Big Red had a violent temper when roused, he was slightly more intelligent than most of the other inmates, and a lot less demented. And although he constantly made snide comments about the power of prayer, he was always one of the first to arrive in Levi's cell for the evening scripture reading.

"That's all we have in here—time," Levi quipped in a friendly manner.

Big Red shrugged in agreement and Levi smiled back.

Levi had been working the big man for some weeks now, subtly building his confidence. When Jumper, the skinny, narrow faced man joined them at the table, dipping his head in acceptance at Levi's presence, Levi knew that he was finally in. He breathed a little easier as he shoveled the tasteless food into his mouth. He had to make a conscious effort to block the wistful yearning he suddenly felt for home-baked bread and chicken casserole as he swallowed.

The conversation drifted from gossip about the prison guards to the arrival of a couple of newbies in the block, before the moment that Levi was waiting for finally arrived. He glanced around at the four guard towers in the hall. Two guards stood watch at each one, holding semi-automatic weapons in their hands. Any one of the snipers could have easily put a bullet in Levi's head. But the irony was, that for all their power, they couldn't hear any of the conversations going on in the hall below them. And that would be their undoing.

Big Red took a look around to make sure that no one was listening. Levi worked to control the drumming of his heart while he waited.

"If you're not with us, Farmer, get up and leave now. I'd

hate to have to break your legs if you change your mind later," Bid Red said calmly.

Levi had been eagerly awaiting the offer, so his acceptance flowed smoothly from his mouth.

"You can count me in," Levi answered.

Snarly and Jumper moved in closer at that moment, close enough that Snarly's perspiration was all that Levi smelled. He ignored the unpleasantness of the scent and leaned in further still, after his own gaze swept the hall once more. His entire childhood had been filled with keeping secrets from the elders. This part of prison life came naturally for Levi.

"My brother's planning to get us out of here sometime in the next two weeks. None of you need to know the details. It's better that way. Just be ready when it happens," Big Red said with quiet authority.

Levi's head swirled—two weeks—that soon? A dozen questions shot through his mind, but he didn't speak. If Big Red had anything else to say about the matter, he would have already said it. Any kind of curiosity Levi exhibited might be taken as prying, and the last thing he needed was to undo all of the trust he had carefully built over the past months. Thunder rolled across the hall once again, but it was softer, more distant. The storm was moving away. Levi took it as a sign from God that his fortune would be changing soon.

After the lunchtime buzzer sounded, Levi rose with everyone else to go back to the cells. His step felt lighter than it had in a long time and the world around him was very distinct. He brushed his fingertips along the rippled surface of the concrete walls, touching the little bumps and nooks with familiarity. He reveled in the pumping of blood through his veins in anticipation. It had been a long time since he'd experienced the feeling.

He stepped into his cell, barely noticing the humming sound followed by the loud *clunk* of the door closing and locking automatically behind him.

Levi reached under the mattress to retrieve the leather

bound Bible that he kept safely tucked away there. He pulled it out and settled down on the bed with a satisfied grunt. Opening the heavy book in his hands, he flipped to Timothy 2:9-12. The locks of hair pressed between the pages came free and Levi brought the long, dark brown strands to his nose and breathed deeply.

He'd hidden the hair in his hand the day that the paramedics had taken him away from the suburban house in Fairfield nearly a year earlier. He'd been extra careful with the trophy, managing to smuggle it into the Butler County jail, and eventually into the Ohio State prison. And every night he slept with the hair pressed against the deep groove where his right eye used to be.

Her scent still lingered on those few strands, both arousing him and filling him with rage at the same time.

Levi licked his lips and his gaze dropped to the scripture before him.

'In like manner also, that the women adorn themselves in modest apparel, with propriety and moderation, not with the braided hair or gold or pearls or costly clothing, but which is proper for women professing godliness, with good works. Let a woman learn in silence with all submission. And I do not permit a woman to teach or to have authority over a man, but to be in silence.'

Bishop Lambright had it all wrong. Rose is the one who sinned. And her evil deeds would not go unpunished. Levi understood that God was working within the prison walls to free him from bondage so that he could do God's work. With this sudden clarity, Levi experienced euphoria.

Levi's one eye sparked with madness, and he grinned. "I'm coming for you, Rose."

Chapter 1

⮑ Rachel ⮐

I paused on the staircase to listen once more. The dark house was all quiet except for the rhythmic wheezing of Father's snoring. I smiled at the sound. Escape shouldn't be difficult. Tiptoeing across the smooth wooden planks of the kitchen floor felt nice on my bare feet. There was a soft spray of moonlight shining into the room from the window to keep me from bumping into the table or chairs. I eased the bag that I carried onto the floor carefully, and then lifted the plain, black woolen coat from the peg. I still wasn't breathing, and the lack of oxygen was beginning to become uncomfortable. Very slowly, I exhaled a small breath. I was almost free. After I slipped on the black tennis shoes, I looked over my shoulder once more. When I strained to listen, I could still faintly hear Father's snoring, but nothing else stirred in the house. *It was almost too easy,* I thought as I slowly turned the knob and pushed the door open wide enough to squeeze through. Almost forgetting the bag, I reached down and snatched it off the floor. Then I was through the door.

Lightly, I made my way down the porch steps and across the yard. As my feet pressed into the dewy grass, I absently thought that it was growing quickly and would need to be cut soon. I drew in a deep breath of the chilly night air, savoring the damp, earthy smell that was only present at the very beginning of springtime. I noticed the clusters of daffodils sprouting from the piles of dirt in Mother's flower beds as I passed by. The

9

plants were hardy, for sure. Less than a year earlier, a tornado had ravaged the farm. The storm had shredded the trees, yard and gardens until only dirt and pieces of branches were left in its wake. The two-story farmhouse that Father had built for Mother right after they were married had been transformed into a pile of debris, resembling snapped Popsicle sticks and crumpled aluminum foil. But the daffodils somehow survived all that.

I was in the basement when the tornado tore down the house—and so were my sisters, Sarah and Naomi. The sharp memory caused me to stumble. I stopped my complete fall with outstretched hands. After catching myself, I slumped down on the wet ground, sighing heavily.

My gaze wandered over the newly constructed house. I was still amazed at how quickly Father and the other men of the community had raised it. The structure was very similar to the original, with a wraparound porch, numerous windows, and a stone chimney for the fireplace. But the addition of a mudroom that jutted off the side was new, and the pitch of the roof was different, too. Mother said that she liked it even more than her first house. But I'd caught her standing in the yard on several occasions with a deep frown on her face as she stared at the building. In those moments she seemed confused—almost lost. But maybe it wasn't about the house at all. Perhaps it was because of Sarah.

The soft nudge on the back of my leg made me jump. I whirled around to see Betsy, the mixed Labrador retriever, who had shown up as a stray, cold and hungry in the dead of winter. She was now staring expectantly at me. Her tail thumped back and forth behind her black body as she impatiently waited for me to extend my hand. Once I raised my hand, the dog surged forward into my lap. She was heavy, but I welcomed the furry weight. Wrapping my arms around her, I waited a moment for her to settle down, and when her happy panting was her only movement, I thought about Sarah again.

Sarah was the good girl in the family. The perfect child who was always obedient and genuinely kindhearted. And look what that got her. Dead and buried at the age of sixteen. For a second, I felt the sharp constriction at the bottom of my throat. I swallowed it down. Sarah had been a fool. She followed the rules straight into her grave. I still hated her for it.

In a sudden motion, I pushed Betsy aside and rose to my feet. There wasn't time enough this night to be reflecting on the past. It couldn't be undone. At least my littlest sister and all my brothers were still breathing. I was finished crying over the matter.

Turning away from the house, I began to jog to the fence row, until Betsy bumped against my leg. The silly dog would surely follow me all the way to the road if I didn't do something.

"Dumm hund!" I whispered fiercely, catching Betsy's collar in my hand.

Betsy was all too pleased to have me tug her along toward the barn. When we reached the doorway, I gently pushed her through with my foot and began pulling the door closed. Just before I had it shut, Betsy's nose squeezed through the opening. I stalled for a moment to scratch it.

"You can't come with me, Betsy. It's no place for a nice dog like you," I said.

Luckily, Betsy wasn't a barker. I would have to remember to let her out when I returned, though. If Father or Peter found her shut up in the barn, questions might be raised. And that was the very last thing I needed. I wasn't going to get caught because of a dog.

Picking up speed, I ran down the far side of the yard. As I neared the road, I tilted my head to listen. Hearing the distinct sound of *clip-clop* on pavement, I moved my legs even faster. After sprinting across the road, I slid down into the ditch and up the other side. The remnants of the tornado were still everywhere, and I got poked by several jagged branches as I navigated a pile of broken trees that had been pushed off the road after the storm. The sound of the buggy was getting ever louder and I ducked behind the brush, hoping that my black clothing would camouflage me from whoever was about to pass by.

Once again, I was holding my breath as my heart pounded against my ribcage. When the buggy was almost across from me, the driver slowed the bay horse to a walk. Steam rose from the horse's flanks and I caught the scent of its sweaty hair. The voices inside the buggy were loud and animated. I recognized the horse and turned my head to listen.

"Don't you see? If Noah isn't allowed to attend our wedding, then Rose probably won't come, either," Suzanna whined in a high-pitched voice.

"I know—but what can I do about it? The elders have made their decision. Nothing short of another tornado is likely to change their minds," Timothy said in obvious distress.

"It's not fair. Rose is one of my best friends . . . I want her to be there."

"You know how it is, Suzie. We can't fight 'em. Your best bet is to talk to Rose about it. Maybe she'll come anyway," Timothy said coaxingly.

Suzanna's voice rose again. "Noah's been your buddy since you all were toddlers. Doesn't it bother you one bit that he can't come?"

"Of course it does! But there's nothing I can do about it. So why should I get stressed over it?"

The buggy was pulling away and it was getting more difficult to hear. With some apprehension, I left my hiding place and followed it, staying behind the brush, to hear more.

"There are other options . . . " Suzanna said.

"No. We're not having this conversation," Timothy argued.

"Well, what about the dress shop?" Suzanna implored.

"That's another business altogether. Please don't start any trouble before we're even married, Suzie, please . . . "

At that moment, Timothy flicked the reins and his horse surged into a trot. I never did hear Suzanna's response.

Untangling the branches from my coat, I shook my head. Suzanna and Timothy were just like everyone else in the community. Well, Suzanna at least showed some spirit, but Timothy was a dolt. He'd never stand up to the bishop—not in a million years.

After I climbed out of the ditch, I wiped my muddy hands on the sides of my coat and began walking. Overhearing the conversation between Suzanna and Timothy had been useful, though. I'd learned that Noah was indeed being fully shunned by the community, and the dress shop idea that the girls had been making plans for would not be happening. It was ridiculous they even thought that the elders would agree to it in the first place.

I was walking in the opposite direction of the buggy, but I could still hear the clopping sound in the distance. If Suzanna had any sense at all, she would withhold her Sunday evening kisses from Timothy when he dropped her off at her house. I knew firsthand how brain dead people got when they officially began courting. They were suddenly allowed to spend a few hours together after Sunday evening church—alone. I couldn't resist smirking when I thought about how stupid Jacob and Noah had acted when they were still courting. All that sloppy excitement over the possibility of a few stolen kisses. The smirk on my face turned to a frown when I thought about the fact that they had both been legal adults at the time—almost two years older than I was now. I would never grovel for a slightly longer leash, that's for sure. I would cut the damn thing in half.

Hearing a car's engine, I glanced over my shoulder. It was a silver mustang. I stepped aside and waited.

The car stopped beside me and the passenger's side window rolled down.

"Come on. It's only ten-thirty—the night is young," the blonde girl said with a wide grin. Charlotte had recently had all her hair whacked off and now sported a spiky, boy type 'do' that prettily framed her pixie face.

Avery leaned over the steering wheel and acknowledged me with an inviting tilt of his head. He smiled briefly before the back door swung open.

Sadie slid over, making room for me. I didn't hesitate slipping into the backseat beside her. I eyed her sparkling mini skirt with envy, just before I took my jacket off and pulled the navy blue frock over my head. I dropped the ugly dress to the floor.

"Ooh, I like it!" Sadie said as her eyes slid over my outfit.

Charlotte turned around, hanging over the seat to check me out, too. "Wow, you don't look Amish anymore," she said slyly.

I glanced out the window for a moment at my house on the hill, watching it grow smaller as Avery sped down the road. The smell of the cigarette smoke that filled the cab didn't bother me anymore, and when Sadie offered me a smoke, I took it. Settling into the seat, I took a puff and listened to the loud music. I relaxed for the first time in hours and it felt good. But I wasn't able to completely enjoy the moment. I had the miserable prospect of the rising at five o'clock in the morning to do the laundry by hand.

CHAPTER 2

I strained for a moment, trying to free the rototiller from the chunky, brown dirt. When the machine didn't budge and stalled instead, I groaned in frustration.

"Here, let me do that," Ruth said irritably.

The old Amish woman yanked the handles from my grip and bent to pull on the cord. The engine revved back up and with a great shove, the tiller was freed and surged forward with Ruth still holding on. She traveled down the row at an impressive speed before she stopped and hit the turn-off switch.

I rolled my eyes at Suzanna, who only laughed loudly. Sarah Ann seemed to enjoy the sudden jostling movement of Suzanna's body. My four month old baby, who had been named after my sister-in-law, Sarah, and my dead mother, Ann, made her own squealing noise that sent Suzanna into near hysterics.

"Why, Sarah Ann has my kind of humor," Suzanna declared.

The sun was shining for the first time in what seemed to be several weeks. As I shook my head in mock annoyance, I lifted my face to the warm rays. Moisture was making my underarms and beneath my breasts sticky, but I didn't really care. After the long, cold winter I wasn't about to complain about sweating.

With my eyes closed for a moment, I listened to the sound of Suzanna's horse, Wynn, rustling in her harness at the side of the garden and the birds chirping in the maple trees beside the farmhouse. The air smelled like earthworms and the light, southerly breeze was mild. It was almost a glorious day—*almost*.

My eyes popped open. I jumped when I found Ruth standing close beside me.

"I don't get it, Ruth. Why does it matter if Noah goes to their wedding?" I said it harshly, not able to keep the resentment from my voice.

Ruth sighed heavily. She took my hand between her own, squeezing tightly. "I've already gone over this a dozen times with you. You aren't listening."

I simply shook my head, too exasperated to say anything. I came from a world where almost anything was negotiable. The stubborn ways of the Amish were beyond maddening. I pulled away from Ruth and flopped down on the ground beside Suzanna. Since my friend appeared to have a death grip on my baby, I didn't even attempt to pry Sarah Ann away from her.

"Maybe we could arrange a meeting with Bishop Lambright—" Suzanna offered in a determined voice, but was silenced when Ruth interrupted her.

"This isn't just a matter of Abram changing his mind, young lady. It's a part of our *Ordnung*. The rules can't be changed for this wedding, without affecting all those in the future." The wrinkle lines on Ruth's face were still set grimly, but she continued speaking with a softer, more prodding voice when she looked between me and Suzanna. "Your husband joined our church . . . and then left. Rose, dear, your in-laws have been very welcoming of Noah in their lives, more so than most of our people would be in the same circumstances. But make no mistake, there can be no exceptions regarding our community events when it comes to his shunning."

"But why am I allowed to attend then?" I asked angrily.

Ruth took a deep breath, probably to calm her own rising temper. She said steadily, "Because you're English . . . and you have always been so."

"But Rose joined the church!" Suzanna exclaimed.

Any patience that Ruth may have had left vanished in a rush of words. "She was never one of us to begin with. I think

Abram is being extremely generous on the matter by allowing Rose to be present at all." She paused and narrowed her eyes on me. "Or do you want to make such a fuss, that your own invitation is rescinded?"

Ruth didn't wait for me to answer. She swiveled abruptly and headed for the house.

Feeling immediately bad about riling the woman who'd always been so kind to me, I shouted over my shoulder, "I'll finish up the tilling for you."

Ruth waved her hand in acknowledgment, but kept on walking.

"I think I've really pissed her off," I said quietly. Turning to Suzanna, I stroked Sarah Ann's tiny hand in my own.

"Oh, she'll get over it," Suzanna said absently.

I immediately picked up that she was distracted by something else. "What's going on, Suzanna?" I asked tentatively, fearing that something more serious than Noah's shunning was on the horizon.

Suzanna faced me with a measured sigh. She paused for a moment, seemingly gathering her words—or a strategy. With Suzanna, the later was more likely.

"Miranda and I want to open a dress shop," Suzanna stated flatly.

I absorbed her words, more confused than before she'd said them.

"You mean . . . like a store or something?" I fumbled with a response.

Suzanna nodded. "Exactly. One of my aunts lives up on Route 48. She has a shop near the road that she used to sell baked goods in. She doesn't have time for it anymore, now that she's taking care of my grandmother who's been sick."

Suzanna paused to catch her breath and I motioned her with my hand to continue, filled with sudden curiosity.

"Well, Miranda and I . . . and Summer, too, want to open our own shop."

"Summer?" I shrieked. "What could she possibly have to do with such an endeavor?"

Suzanna laughed. "You underestimate Summer. She's really good with numbers, so she can do the recordkeeping. Plus, even though she doesn't have her own car yet, she does have a driver's license and we'll need a way to get to the supplier."

My mind was whirling. "Are you really serious about this?" I asked skeptically.

"Why, don't you think we can do it?" I tried to interrupt at that point, fearing that I'd offended her, but she plowed on, "You're no better than those stuffy-headed elders!"

"You've actually mentioned it to the bishop?" I immediately had a vision of the tall, Abraham Lincoln looking man, with his long, bushy white beard and stern eyes. I couldn't help inadvertently shivering.

Suzanna handed Sarah Ann to me and stood up. As she talked, she went to her horse and buggy that was parked only a short distance away. I readjusted the baby on my hip and followed her.

"Yes, we had a meeting with the elders last week. They didn't even take the time to discuss the matter before they shut it down. There won't be a vote, either. Basically, the entire idea was dead in the water before it even got started."

The obvious disappointment in Suzanna's voice cut right to my heart. The problems that Noah was dealing with were nothing compared to what Suzanna and Miranda would have to face their entire lives. I had to admit that there were some wonderful things about the Amish lifestyle, like the closeness of the community and always having people around to help out. The simple lifestyle was nice, and I certainly couldn't complain about the food. But completely giving up your freedom was a terrible burden to bear. In the end, when I'd been faced with the same prospect, I couldn't do it. I had always known deep in my heart that I'd never be happy with a group of grumpy old men telling what I could and couldn't do.

But just like I wasn't able to take defeat about Noah going to Timothy's wedding, I wasn't willing to accept that Suzanna and Miranda couldn't follow their dreams. There had to be a way.

"Wait, Suzanna." Suzanna stopped and turned back to me, a slight frown still on her face. "Did they say why you guys can't do it?"

I considered how many of the Amish had their own businesses. They were actually quite entrepreneurial. It seemed to be in their blood—to run their own bakeries, grocery stores, birdhouse factories and butcher shops. Noah even had his own construction business, as did his father. For the first time since the conversation began, I didn't get what the problem was.

"The bishop and the ministers don't think it's proper for young women of childbearing age to be starting up a business. And then, Bishop Lambright also said that if women were able to buy their dresses already made, they wouldn't have to do it at home."

I knew my face must have turned beet red, I was so angry. "And that's a bad thing?" I growled.

"I guess he's worried that we won't have time to make babies and be good wives to our husbands if we're running a business." Suzanna snarled the words out.

Before I had a chance to rant, a maroon minivan pulled in. It was Tonya, one of the Amish drivers. She was also Summer's mother, and the woman who had arranged my kidnapping from the Amish community. Even though it had turned out to be the best thing for me, I still couldn't shake the extreme resentment that I felt every time I saw the middle-aged redhead.

Luckily, I didn't have to talk to Tonya this time. Ruth climbed into the minivan at the same time that Summer jumped out and ran toward us. As I watched the minivan back down the driveway, I muttered, "I don't understand why Ruth pays that woman to drive her around."

Suzanna bumped into my side and said with little humor,

"It's the Amish way—forgive and forget—at least when it comes to outsiders."

"Oooh, let me see that little bug," Summer said delightedly when she skidded to a stop in front of us.

I handed Sarah Ann over to Summer without thought, noticing how my baby girl immediately wrapped her fingers into Summer's hair. The bright strawberry red color seemed to mesmerize Sarah Ann. And I was certainly glad for the extra pair of hands that my baby accepted so readily.

"So I hear you're wanting to get into the dress-making business," I teased Summer.

"I'm more than ready. I need my own car something fierce, and I can't imagine a better career than working with my best buds," Summer said excitedly.

Suzanna immediately doused Summer with cold water when she said, "It isn't happening. The elders said no."

Summer hunched over, rolling her head back and forth dramatically. "I thought it was too good to be true."

"Now wait a minute. Are you ready to give up so easily?" I said.

Summer straightened back up while Suzanna gazed at me doubtfully.

"There might be a way that it could work . . . " I offered at the same time that my mind was still figuring out the details.

"What are thinking, Rose?" Suzanna asked in a conspiratorial way.

I was insane to even consider it, but seeing the look of hope that now shimmered on the girls' faces, I gave in to the madness. "What do you think would happen if me and Summer *supposedly* owned the shop . . . and you and Miranda worked for us?" I directed the question at Suzanna.

A smile spread on the Amish girl's face, and her eyes twinkled. "That might just work."

Summer began softly bouncing in place to Sarah Ann's delight.

"Suzanna, if you can help me get this stupid tilling done, we can start making plans. I don't think Ruth will mind if we have a business meeting in her kitchen while she's gone," I said grinning.

Chapter 3

······ Justin ······

"You need to get out more, bro," Sam said as he smacked the back of my head for no good reason.

I rolled my eyes and glanced over at Mason and Gavin, who were both leaning back against the kitchen counter. Gavin was quite a bit taller than Mason. I couldn't stop myself from smirking each time I saw the two standing side by side. I dropped my face to my bowl of cereal to hide the expression.

"Come on, Justin. We have tomorrow off from school for teacher recuperation day." Mason laughed at his perceived wittiness and added for good measure, "We can sleep in."

"What's wrong with you anyway?" Sam growled. "When I was your age, I never missed an opportunity to go out."

I chuckled. "What, was that like, a few months ago?"

"Don't be a smart ass, dude. I'm only trying to help you out." Sam's tone changed to coercion when he went on to say, "Besides, Noah and Rose need some downtime. Summer and I are on babysitting duty tonight. We'll probably take the little bug out for some greasy food."

"I'm being kicked out of my own house . . . *why exactly?*"

"You moron—they're still practically newlyweds. They need some time alone," Sam said angrily.

"I won't bother 'em. I'm in the middle of a serious level. I don't get many opportunities for an all-nighter to advance my civilization," I replied.

"The entire damn world doesn't revolve around Xbox. You really need to reevaluate your priorities," Sam huffed.

I lightly shook my head, looking up at Mason and Gavin once more. Yeah, I was going to be better served going out with the two of them for the evening. I wonder what Sam would say if I told him how much weed Gavin smoked or that Mason couldn't keep his Honda under eighty miles an hour. Or the fact that if I went with them, I'd more than likely end up in a bar. Hah, it would serve Sam right if I ended up arrested or dead in a city gutter.

I met Sam's hard stare, and said extra sweetly, "This is about Summer, isn't it? She's the one orchestrating this clearing of the house."

Sam grunted and shrugged. I was so glad at that moment that I wasn't a slave to some irrational woman.

"You'll have fun . . . I guarantee it," Mason spoke up.

I rolled my neck, popping the joints, and then faced Sam. I was in a giving mood—and it certainly wouldn't hurt to have Sam in my debt.

Rising from the chair, I deposited the empty bowl into the sink. "Give me ten minutes to shower." I pointed at Sam. "You owe me one."

• • • • ● • • • •

The only reason we even got into the place was because Gavin's uncle was the owner and bartender. The guy was pretty squirrely. It was common knowledge among the high school students in Meadowview that the bartenders at Dewey's Bar served underage kids—especially if they were pretty girls.

After I faked a friendly return wave at Dewey, who was pulling a draft at the bar, I followed Gavin and Mason to a corner booth. Once I was seated, I surveyed the room that was dimly lit and smoky. I counted a total of twenty-two patrons, equally divided between rough looking biker-type dudes and overly bleached, tattooed and skanky looking women. It certainly wasn't a wholesome place.

"What can I get you boys?" the waitress asked.

She had a flushed, round face, and her light brown hair was pulled up in a high ponytail. With a quick glance, I decided that she wasn't as scary looking as most of the other woman in the bar. I wondered if she'd card us.

I listened as Gavin and Mason each ordered a bottle of beer before the waitress turned her red face on me.

"I'll just have a cola, thanks," I said.

Mason laughed, and Gavin persisted. "What are you doing, man? You're supposed to be loosening up."

I just smiled. "Yeah, I'll let you guys get loose and then I'll drive your sorry butts home."

"Good man," the waitress commended, flashing an admiring raised brow at me.

I winked at her. "I try."

After the waitress walked off, Mason whined, "For such a backward person, you're pretty smooth with the ladies."

"It doesn't hurt that I resemble an Abercrombie model," I said.

"You're so full of it," Mason chuckled with a crooked smile.

Actually, I wasn't joking, but laughed along with him as if I was.

The waitress returned with the two beers and my cola a moment later. I sipped my drink slowly. It was going to be a long night, and I only had a five dollar bill in my pocket. I listened to the other guys' conversation as it became ever more animated with every swallow they took of their own drinks. I contemplated why a seemingly nice woman, like our waitress, would resort to serving underage kids booze. It certainly wasn't for the great tips.

Glancing back towards the bar, I had my answer. I spotted

a couple of girls from school sitting on stools, along with a guy who looked to be in his twenties, and another girl who I didn't recognize, but was kind of familiar in some way.

Most of the other guys in the bar had noticed the three girls, too, and realization dawned on me what Dewey's game was. He let the girls in to attract more of the paying drunkards. I grimaced at the thought of what might happen to a teenage girl in such a place, taking a larger gulp of my soda in an attempt to erase that train of thought.

"Hey, look, it's Sadie and Charlotte," Mason said at the same moment glass could be heard shattering.

We all followed the noise with our gazes. Near the pool table, a very tall man with a close cropped beard and wearing a gray jacket with cutoff sleeves was wielding a pool cue. An equally large, heavier built man in a black T-shirt and a blonde woman in extremely tight fitting jeans and a cleavage revealing shiny metallic top were dodging the tall dude's thrusts.

"You think you can proposition my woman right in front of me like that?" the man said with another slash of the cue, which came frighteningly close to the other man's head.

My companions were laughing and pointing, but I simply watched with rapt interest. The two men and the woman darted and danced around as if they were characters in a movie—or a video game. I was imagining how I'd play the game just when one of the bouncers finally intervened.

The bald headed newcomer was larger than either of the other men. He had no trouble at all grabbing the cue from the man's hand and tossing it to the ground. He then got a firm grip on the attacker and put him into a bearlike hold.

I thought at that point, the party was over, but nope. The man who'd been fleeing the cue a moment before, drew his arm back and punched the restrained man squarely in the gut.

The bouncer yelled for the other man to quit, but the man either didn't hear in his rage or didn't give a damn. This finally brought the other bouncer, a short, but very stout, buzzed-headed man from the front door. As the two bouncers subdued the two instigators, the rest of the patrons hooted and hollered.

On the TV screen, the action would have been a lot of fun to watch, but in person, it was mostly just barbaric. As the two men were dragged by our booth, toward the door, the wailing woman trailed after them. I caught a whiff of a mixture of sweat and blood. The woman's face was a wet mess, smeared with mascara. Obscenities flowed from her mouth like a dirty river.

"Disgusting," I commented, moving further back into the booth.

"Oh, come on, that was amazing!" Mason declared. His excitement must have made him braver. The next thing I knew, he was shouting across to the bar. "Hey Sadie, why don't you guys join us?" Mason leaned in and whispered, "Wait until you see her friend . . . she's really hot."

Oh, great, I thought. I'm barely in the mood to be sociable with these dimwits, let alone having to make small talk with some ditzy, drunk girls, too.

I watched Sadie whisper to the other two girls and the guy. A moment later, the girls were walking toward us, but the guy remained at the bar. He was talking to Dewey and nursing a half-full glass of amber liquid that I guessed to be some kind of whiskey.

Sadie slid in beside Mason and Charlotte directed the new girl into my side of the booth. I caught the fresh scent of spring flowers in the thick, smoky air and turned to the girl at my side.

"You smell nice," I said without thinking.

The other girls immediately giggled, but the girl who I'd complimented turned four shades of red. Her light brown eyes widened in what I can only say was freaked-out recognition. I continued to stare at her, ignoring Sadie who introduced the girl as Jewel, and Mason's incessant background chatter.

Jewel had long, brown hair with blonde highlights that fell

in soft waves around her oval face. My gaze lingered on her slender neck and the smooth place above her collarbone, before it drifted up to her ears that were absent of any piercings at all. That struck me as very odd, but I just filed the information away and glanced down at the girl's athletic frame and the classy black and white dress she wore. She definitely stood out in the room full of denim and stretchy tank tops. The dress was still sexy, the hem just shy of her knees. But whereas Sadie and Charlotte's outfits pushed up and out each curve they had, and looked to be amazingly uncomfortable, this girl's dress fit her like a glove, displaying her perfection without shoving it down anyone's throat.

"Hello," Jewel said carefully. Her left eyebrow raised in silent warning. Once again, she seemed to know me, although she was being very cautious not to let the others in on her secret.

Curiosity pierced my mind. I stared harder, frowning at Jewel for a long moment. Our eyes were locked. I thought I saw a fleeting look of fear pass through hers.

Something about the shape of her eyes—the color of them and the odd brindle affect in the strands—was very similar to someone else I knew. Noah. Realization struck me the same as a slap to the face. I leaned back in astonishment. I was sitting in a bar, looking at none other than my brother-in-law's younger Amish sister—Rachel Miller. She was dressed in sexy street clothes and holding a bottle of beer in her hand.

The night suddenly became extremely interesting. Finally, a game I could actually play.

I dipped my head, hiding the smile. When I looked back up, my face was a mask of ignorance.

"It's nice to meet you, Jewel."

CHAPTER 4

⤜⤏ Rachel ⤎⤛

I looked away, trying desperately to control the smile from erupting on my face. There hadn't been many opportunities for me to speak to Justin, but when I had, I'd seen how quickly the gossip spread among the other girls in the community. I became very careful, avoiding any contact with him all together, fearing what would happen if Father and Mother believed the lies. If they had thought that I was showing Justin any attention whatsoever, I would have been severely punished. The threat of Father's switch on my bottom hadn't been my only concern.

No, it was the splintering bench in front of the church congregation that I'd feared. If I had been caught having a conversation with the English boy, without strict supervision from an adult in the community, it would have been a sin. I would have paid the consequences by being forced to sit in front of all the church members while Bishop Lambright recited my wrong doings. If the bishop and the ministers deemed the offense to be minor, I had only a couple of weeks of shunning to look forward to. But if they thought it was more serious, I might be shunned for a month or more.

Temporary shunning as punishment was even worse than a beating in my opinion. You lost the few freedoms you were usually allowed, such as going to the ball games on youth nights and after Sunday services. You weren't allowed any social time whatsoever, only long days of work, with extra chores piled on. It was enough intimidation to keep most of the Amish kids in line. An outsider wasn't worth the risk—in most cases anyway.

Noah, my older brother, had deemed a secret relationship with Rose worth the dangers. They were now married and had a beautiful baby girl. But he was permanently shunned from the community. The outcome was life changing, even when all seemed to work out in the end.

As for me, I was way too stealthy to get caught. I'd been sneaking out of the house for about six months now, and no one was the wiser. I was careful not to get emotionally involved with any of my so-called English friends. They were no more than a means to an end. I'd always found the Amish way lacking in something. I couldn't exactly put my finger on it. In the past, I was mostly content to be alongside Mother and Sarah as we did the laundry, worked in the garden or prepared the meals. But after Sarah died, everything changed. All the little feelings of resentment I might have had about the way of life before multiplied a thousand fold. Nowadays, it seemed well worth the risk to go out and have some fun.

Now that I had my face under control again, I glanced back up at Justin. He was still staring at me without shame. He was definitely a rascal. I'd sensed that about him the very first time he'd come to the farm with Rose and the rest of his family. Back then, things had been simpler—happier in a way. For a second, I remembered how Sarah and I had hurriedly cleaned the house to make it perfect for the English visitors.

"What's the weird look for?" Justin asked casually.

I blinked and looked around. Sadie and Charlotte had left the table with the other two boys without my noticing. They were now gathered around one of the pool tables, attempting to play a game.

I was thankful that Justin hadn't given me away to his friends, but I wasn't ready to trust him just yet.

Meeting his gaze, I said, "Look, I appreciate your discretion.

I really do. But you need to forget you ever saw me here. I could get into worse trouble than you could even imagine."

Justin leaned back and rested his arm on the back of the booth. He glanced around the room, seemingly looking for eavesdroppers, before his voice dropped a little lower and he said, "I get it. Your secret is safe with me."

"That's it? You're not going to ask me what I'm doing or why I'm doing it?" I asked in surprise.

Justin shrugged and took a sip of his cola. He swallowed and said, "I'll listen if you want to talk, but it doesn't take a rocket scientist to figure out what's going on."

As if I was seeing Justin for the first time all over again, my heart rate sped up. I felt my checks flush with heat. I'd always thought he was devilishly good looking, but his nonchalant attitude about life made him much more appealing. He had the same dark brown hair and wide-spaced, light blue eyes that Rose possessed. He was tall, lean and muscular, but I could tell that at sixteen, he still had some more growing to do. Actually, Justin resembled Rose and his father more than his older brother, Sam, who was fair-haired. Sam probably looked like his mother. That thought made me sad. He wasn't that much different than me after all. Justin had also lost a family member.

I usually wasn't comfortable talking to just anyone, but I suddenly felt the pulsating desire to get Justin Cameron to open up to me. There was something very mysterious about him.

"Do you come here a lot?" After the words were out my mouth, I realized how stupid they sounded.

Justin laughed, but he didn't mock me.

"No. This is the first time. A lovely establishment—don't you think?"

He was working hard to keep from laughing again. The side of his mouth twitched and his eyes sparkled. I couldn't keep my own mirth in. When I laughed, he laughed right along with me.

For the first time in forever, I felt at ease. After I took a sip from the beer, I winced a little. "It even smells bad in here."

Justin nodded in agreement and then confessed, "Besides the exhilarating conversation that I'm having with you, I'd rather be home empire building."

"What's that?" I asked, not even trying to hide my interest.

While Justin went into an animated description of several of his favorite video games, I listened patiently. His enthusiasm was contagious and by the end of his speech, I envied his freedom to play such games.

"Is this Xbox your favorite thing to do?" I asked.

Justin thought for moment and said, "It's a close tie between gaming and reading."

I felt light headed with happiness. The alcohol might have contributed to the euphoric feeling I was experiencing, but I doubted it. None of my siblings, including Sarah, ever read anything. And besides the Bible, neither did my parents. Whereas, I was a voracious reader and for the very first time, I'd met someone who felt the same way.

"I love to read, too!"

Justin looked at me quizzically and then leaned in. "What kind of books?"

"Oh, I'll read just about anything . . . but I especially like historical fiction books. You know, the kind that are based on real life events, but the characters are mostly made up."

"That's really cool. I read westerns sometimes. My favorites are fantasy, though."

"The kinds with dragons and warlocks, and such?" I ventured.

Justin grinned. "The more dragons, the better."

"You're the first person I've ever met who actually likes to read," I said in wonder.

"Seriously?"

When I nodded, he snorted.

"What, is it against the Amish rules or something?"

"No, not exactly. But our reading materials are monitored." I took another sip of the beer. "I got in trouble once for reading a romance novel."

Justin raised his brows in mock shock and I giggled. "It wasn't *that* kind of romance. There was hardly any kissing at all, in fact. I was more interested in the time period. It was set during the Civil War, and since we aren't taught your history in our schools, I didn't really know anything about it."

"My history *is* your history, Rachel," Justin said in a bit of a scolding way.

A small burp erupted out of my mouth unexpectedly, and I said, "Excuse me."

I was horrified at my bad manners, but the sudden wave of nausea and light-headedness worried me even more.

"Are you all right?" Justin looked concerned as he squeezed my shoulder.

I knew that the familiar touch wasn't a big deal to an English boy, but I still shivered at the intimacy of it. An Amish boy would never touch me in any way unless we were already courting, or at least if he planned to court me.

"I'm fine. I just felt a little dizzy there for a minute," I lied.

Justin smiled in a knowing way and disagreed. "I think you're drunk."

Anger flared inside of me. "I am not drunk!" My voice rose higher than I expected or wanted. I consciously brought the level down when I spoke again. "This is only my second beer."

Justin didn't even try to look convinced, but he remained silent.

"Well, and the other drink that Dewey gave me," I admitted.

Now Justin was angry. "That jerk gave you a mixed drink?" When I nodded, he asked, "What was it?"

I thought for a moment, feeling fuzzy-headed again. Finally, I was able to locate the words in my brain.

"Something iced tea, I think," I said.

Justin ran his hand through his hair and groaned. When he

glanced back up, he said, "That's not good." He shook his head softly and blew out a breath. "Why *are* you doing this?"

"What—I don't understand."

"Hanging out in a trashy place like this, drinking poison?" Justin said. His mouth was puckered as if he'd bitten into something sour.

"I only go out once or twice a month. It's not a big deal. Besides, isn't this what English teens do?"

"Ah, no. I'm pretty much a hermit myself, so I probably don't count in the percentages, but Rose never went out drinking. And even though I know Sam used to party a lot, most of his friends back in Fairfield didn't drink."

My head was spinning. I swallowed down the foul liquid that rose in my throat. The sick feeling wasn't something new to me, and I actually didn't mind it that much. It was the wonderful heavy-minded sensation that I felt when I returned to my bed after one of these excursions that I loved. On nights like these, I slept as if I was a baby—no nightmares filled with black funnel clouds tearing up my house or visions of Sarah's rotting face in the window. The alcohol was the only thing that shut my mind down.

The high and mighty look on Justin's face began to annoy me greatly. Pushing the fog away, I muttered, "Don't pass judgment on someone unless you've walked in their shoes."

Justin was about to respond when Sadie and Charlotte returned with the two boys. Even in my own diminished state, I noticed that the other four were even worse off than me. Their overly loud voices banged in my head and seeing Sadie sitting on Mason's lap and his hand rubbing her bottom filled me with even more queasiness. I rubbed my face, worrying after the fact, that the makeup I'd put on in the car had smeared.

"Are you girls ready to take this party elsewhere?" Avery said brightly, appearing out of nowhere.

Avery's eyes were wide and clear and his voice sharp. I wondered if he'd drank anything at all.

"Aw, do you have to go?" Mason whined to Sadie.

"I'll see you in school in a couple of days," she drawled and then kissed him on the lips.

My eyes widened a bit at her friendly display, but I wasn't surprised. Sadie always hooked up with someone when we went out.

The other girls stood up and joined Avery at the end of the booth. But when I rose to join them, Justin's hand snaked out and grabbed my arm, stopping me.

"Hey, I'll drive you home," he insisted.

"You don't have a car to drive," Mason joked.

Justin rounded on him, shutting the shorter guy up promptly. "If you think that I'm trusting my very valuable life in your hands, you're delusional. I'm driving."

Before Mason could argue, Avery spoke up, turning to Mason, "Yeah, dude, you're in no shape to drive. Let your buddy here do the right thing." A small smirk appeared on the corner of Avery's mouth as he faced Justin. "You're a good kid. Don't worry about Jewel. I'm sober—she's in good hands."

Causing me to catch my breath, Justin released me and rose in the booth, taking a step toward Avery, who was about six years older and twenty-five pounds heavier than him.

In a sharp whisper, Justin said, "That's what I'm afraid of."

Avery laughed loudly, probably thinking that Justin was just playing around, but I knew better. The grim line of determination on his face told me that he was ready to fight, the same as if he was one of his video game heroes.

I placed my hand on Justin's arm. "It's all right. Avery's a friend. I'll be fine."

Confliction passed over Justin's eyes as I looked into them. *Please, please, don't make a scene,* my mind begged him.

After an agonizing moment, Justin stepped aside. With a sweeping hand, he waved me in Avery's direction.

I hurried past Justin and followed the girls who were close on Avery's heels. Before I went through the door into the chilly nighttime air, I glanced back over my shoulder. The look on Justin's face made me catch my breath.

His expression was one of complete disgust.

CHAPTER 5

Rose

When Noah walked through the door, he went straight to the baby swing and picked up Sarah Ann. I sipped my cup of hot tea, a drink I'd grown quite fond of living among the Amish, and watched Noah as he cuddled our baby. He rubbed the prickles of the day's growth of stubble on his jawline against Sarah Ann's soft cheeks. She made a shrieking noise, thoroughly enjoying the attention. I cringed a little at Noah's work clothes, sweaty and dirty from a long day of framing a house, knowing full well that the smell would be immediately transferred to Sarah Ann. I didn't say anything, though. That's why I always bathed her in the evening, after Noah had showered himself. I sat back and smiled, feeling as if I was a very lucky woman.

"You're going to have that little girl spoiled rotten," I said.

Noah grinned at me. He then began rapid-fire kissing on Sarah Ann's neck. The sound and touch made her squeal. When he finally stopped, he looked over at me with a twitching grin and teased, "Oh my, sweet daughter. I do believe that your momma is jealous."

A second later, Noah rushed over, and while holding Sarah Ann on his side, he leaned down and began kissing me the exact same way. At first the kisses tickled. I giggled and pulled away, but Noah followed me. The next kiss was on my lips. When his tongue slipped into my mouth, I surrendered. He finally meant business and even after almost a year of marriage,

I couldn't resist him. Warm honey spread out in my belly and lower, and I almost couldn't stand it.

Noah broke away just long enough to whisper in my ear, "Sweetheart, how I missed you today." His mouth was back on mine before I could answer.

A small part of my mind heard Sarah Ann gurgle, and I was impressed that he was able to balance her and make me squirm at the same time. But I didn't dare ask how he was doing it—I just didn't want him to stop.

The loud throat clearing was followed by Sam saying, "Dammit, don't you two ever take a break?"

Noah broke away from me in a hurry and turned around to greet his not-so-favorite brother-in-law. Noah definitely had a soft spot for my younger, less critical brother. Although he wouldn't admit it out loud, I knew Sam irritated the heck out of him.

"No, actually, this is the first time all day that I've been able kiss my beautiful wife," Noah said in a controlled voice. His Amish training did come in handy sometimes.

"Aw, how sweet," Summer cooed. She swept around Sam and hurried over to Noah. "Now hand over my little bug—pretty please." Summer held out her arms, not at all shy about begging.

Noah stepped back and put out his hand to stop Summer. "Wait a minute, I just now picked her up myself."

"But it's your date night . . . " Summer began. I rose from the chair and silenced her.

"Quiet, Summer, I haven't even told him yet!" I said, irritation flooding every inch of my body.

"Sorry, cat's out the bag," Sam said. "We're going to take the bug over to Dad's and Tina's for the evening. We'll be back by midnight, so you better get to it—that carriage is turning back into a pumpkin on the twelfth gong." Sam graced Noah with a lopsided smile and added, "You don't have to thank me. That's what brothers are for."

Noah looked at me in confusion and a touch of fear. I shrugged, and he implored, "And you're all right with this?"

"Well, we haven't had a date night since Sarah Ann was born—" I searched for the right words "—Sam and Summer spend a lot of time with her, and she's comfortable with them." When his facial expression didn't change, I spoke more forcefully. "Look, they take excellent care of her and they'll be with Dad and Tina most of the time. We need a night to ourselves . . . I need it."

I puckered my lips into my best pout and even forced my eyes to tear up. Deep down, I didn't have a doubt that Noah would say no, but if he did, I really would begin crying. Hope had trotted into the room when she heard my raised voice and was now sitting on my foot. I absently reached down and rubbed her black and white fur. Even the dog felt sorry for me. I was that good.

Noah faced Summer. "Do you know how to feed her?"

Summer rolled her eyes and Sam barked out a laugh. "Of course I do, silly. I do it all the time when I'm visiting Rose."

And for good measure, Sam threw in, "If you haven't noticed, I live here, too. I've been on diaper duty since day one."

Noah took a deep breath. We all waited, holding our own. Sam and Summer looked truly worried, and I was putting on my best fake-worried face. But inside, I was becoming a little annoyed that Noah was dragging the suspense on so long.

"Where's Justin?"

That wasn't the question I was expecting from him. Since Sam had made all the arrangements, I glanced at him for the answer.

"He's out with some friends," Sam stated flatly.

"Justin has friends?" Noah asked in a truly perplexed manner.

Summer giggled and Sam grunted, "Yeah, a few. And it wasn't easy getting him to evacuate his gamer chair, so you better not mess this deal up. We've all gone to extreme lengths to give you two lovebirds a night alone together. The least you can do is say thank you and go get yourself cleaned up."

Noah actually blushed and his lips tightened. Sam was even better at manipulation than I was.

"You're right. I'm sorry." He planted a kiss on the top of Sarah Ann's head and then handed her over to Summer. "It just took me by surprise, that's all."

"So we're going on a real date?" I asked as the bubbles of excitement began spreading inside of me.

Noah's smile nearly took my breath away. "Yes, we are my dear. Just give me twenty minutes to get ready."

"I'll be waiting."

Noah jogged out of the room with more energy than I'd seen from him in quite a while. It occurred to me then that he might be looking forward to it as much as I was.

When Noah was gone, Sam turned to me and growled, "Why does everything have to be so damn difficult with that guy?"

I ignored the comment and focused on giving Summer some last minute instructions and filling the diaper bag. But to myself, I had to agree with Sam for a change.

I pushed the plate away and sat back uncomfortably. My belly was bloated from the ravioli, but I wouldn't have had it any other way. The little green lantern in the middle of the table reminded me of the lanterns that lit Ruth's house in the evenings. I sighed contentedly, remembering how much I enjoyed watching the flickering lights when I'd lived among the Amish.

"A penny for your thoughts," Noah said softly.

I looked up and met his gaze. The Italian restaurant was

dimly lit and there was a classical melody playing quietly in the background. The linens were either green or white and expertly pressed. The utensils were shiny, even in the low light. Antoinette's was my favorite place to eat, even though I didn't get to dine here very often.

I hadn't stopped smiling since we'd arrived. "Thank you, Noah. This is a perfect date."

"Hey now, we're only halfway through the night. There's still the movie and an ice cream cone to go," Noah said.

"Are you having a good time?" I asked tentatively.

"Of course I am. Why would you ask such a question?"

I decided to be honest. "You used to be Amish. Sometimes, there are little things that remind me of your old world—like these cute lanterns." I motioned at the lantern on the table. I hesitated, searching for the right words. Noah could be overly sensitive about his heritage. I didn't want to do anything to ruin the night. Carefully, I prodded, "Do you miss it?"

Noah breathed and looked away for a moment. When his gaze returned, he looked tired. "You ask me that question at least once every week. And I always tell you the same thing— there are some things I miss, but I wouldn't trade my life with you and Sarah Ann, and even your crazy brothers, to go back. I'm perfectly content where I am now."

I felt the sting of regret for having brought the subject up again. Noah wasn't lying. I did make a career of asking him the same question. But it was because deep down, I worried every day that Noah *would* begin to miss his old life, and then he'd begin to resent me. Maybe even hate me for taking him away from it.

I should just let the matter drop and enjoy the evening, but I couldn't let it go just yet. It was wreaking havoc with my mind.

"I talked to Ruth today. She said there isn't any way that Bishop Lambright is going to allow you to attend the wedding."

Noah lifted his shoulders and looked confused. "Yes, we already know that. So what's the problem?"

My cheeks warmed. "The problem is that Timothy is one of your best friends. And it also means that when Matthew marries Miranda the following month, you won't be able to go to that wedding, either."

"So . . ."

"Doesn't it bother you in the least that those grumpy old men are keeping you from going?" I nearly shrieked, barely managing to keep my voice level under control.

Noah chuckled. He reached over the table and took my hands in his own. "Rose, sweetheart. I was brought up to follow rules and not question authority. I knew when I left the church, I'd be shunned, and I fully understood the consequences. I've watched a lot of other young people go through the same thing before me. I never expected to be treated differently from any of the others. I'm certainly no better than them." Noah took a breath and then smirked. "Besides, weddings aren't really for guys—they're for the girls. I see Matthew every day on the work crew, and several times a week we take our lunch with Timothy. They understand and accept why I can't go to their weddings. The only ones having an issue with the matter are you and Suzanna."

"And Miranda," I added for good measure. Searching Noah's face, I realized that he was being completely honest with me. Some of my angst over the situation disappeared. "Tell me the truth—how do you feel about me going to the weddings without you?"

I held my breath, afraid that he was going to go all Amish on me and tell me that he didn't want his wife going anywhere without him. I really hoped that wasn't his reaction. I didn't want to get pissed at him on our first date night in many months.

When he simply smiled and brought my hands to his lips, I regretted having doubted him at all.

"Of course you can go to the weddings. They're your friends and it's obviously very important to all of you. If you're willing to sit on a hard bench for three hours, who am I to stop you?"

I grinned back. "It's worth it for the food afterwards."

Noah nodded. "Yes, I guess it is."

The waitress showed up at that moment and asked up if we wanted dessert. I politely declined, acting very much the lady, but Noah ordered me a piece of four layered chocolate cheesecake anyway. He knew me all too well, and I adored him for it.

We were halfway through our desserts when I worked up the nerve to mention the other thing on my mind.

"Has Timothy or Matthew said anything to you about the girls wanting to open their own dress shop?"

Noah swallowed. "As a matter of fact, that's all Matthew talked about today. Seems Miranda is giving him fits over it."

"What do you think about the idea," I asked carefully.

Noah didn't hesitate to answer. "Sounds like an interesting idea to me. Both girls are savvy sewers. I'm sure there are times of the year when the women folk are too busy in the fields or caring for the children to make their own dresses. It might be quite lucrative, actually."

The aggravation that I'd been experiencing all day vanished. "So you're all right with it?" I asked excitedly.

Noah's eyes widened and he held up his palms to slow me down. "Whoa, it doesn't really matter what I think. Abram and the ministers are against it and I don't have a dog in the fight."

Before I even began to speak, Noah's face turned down in a worried frown.

"Uh, that's not exactly true," I said sweetly.

"Rose . . . ?" Noah was definitely terrified now.

"Summer and I are going to be business partners with the girls. We're calling the shop Stitches—N—Stuff." Once I started talking, excitement shimmered through me and I couldn't stop. "We'll sell cloth and sewing supplies, too, and Sarah Ann can spend the day right there at the shop with me. It will be perfect."

"You're not a seamstress and you certainly don't know anything about sewing supplies. Why do you want to get involved in such an endeavor?"

I let his words slide off my back, more intent on convincing him what a grand idea it was and not so worried about my pride at the moment.

"Noah, don't you see? It's nearly impossible for me to go back to school right now with Sarah Ann so young, and even if I could work it out somehow, I wouldn't want to leave her. And I certainly don't want to go to night classes when that's the only time I get to see you." I paused and tucked my hair behind my ear, collecting my thoughts at the same time. "Even though I love being home with Sarah Ann . . . I get a little lonely . . . and bored sometimes. I think I need something to do—to build— if you know what I mean."

Noah thought for a moment, and then his face softened. "Rose, sweetheart, if you really want to do it, I'll support you wholeheartedly. Matthew and I can even convert the building from a bakery into a clothing shop—put up racks and shelves and such. But you still have Abram to contend with, and frankly, that's a huge obstacle."

"We have a plan to deal with the bishop. I don't think he'll be a problem after all."

Noah looked at me with raised brows. I pursed my lips and said, "You know, I was thinking that I don't really feel like going to a movie."

Noah's expression changed to anticipation. "What do you want to do, wife?" he asked in a smooth voice.

I looked at my cell phone and saw that there weren't any messages or missed calls. "It looks as if Sam and Summer are going to survive until midnight. That gives us a few hours to do anything we want. Seems like a shame to waste a big, old empty house on a movie."

"I agree." Noah leaned over the table and without any modesty at all, kissed me full on the lips. Sometimes Noah shocked me, and this was one of those times. If I hadn't known better, I wouldn't have believed that he'd grown up Amish.

I trembled with anticipation as his mouth closed over mine. The kiss was a promise of better things yet to come.

CHAPTER 6

······ Justin ······

Micah handed me the box, and I grimaced at the unexpected weight of it.

"It's heavier than it looks," Micah said, smiling in a friendly way. He picked up the remaining box and joined me on the short trek to my car.

"Who would have thought that chicken legs weighed so much," I said conversationally.

Micah laughed, convincing me that he was the most jovial of all the Amish I'd met so far.

"Thank you for driving on such late notice. When Rose called and said that the baby wasn't feeling well, I figured I'd have to harness up the horse to make the trip to town myself," Micah said.

I thought back to the choice Rose rudely gave me at eight o'clock that morning when she barged into my room and flicked the lights on, blinding me. *"I need your help, Justin. Please say you'll do it!"*

I groaned at the memory. Her complete inability to remember anything since Sarah Ann had been born bordered on frightening. Her latest dilemma was that she'd forgotten all about how she'd agreed to drive the Schwartzes to town. They had to pick up eighty pounds of pre-ordered chicken from the supermarket for some shindig the community was having at the schoolhouse that evening. Something about a dinner and then a secret voting event that I couldn't care less about.

I had dropped off Gavin at his house the night before at about midnight, but I had no choice but to bring Mason home with me. After he'd thrown up on the side of the road several times, he'd passed out in the car and I'd left him in our drive-way to sleep it off. He was still there when I'd pulled away an hour earlier, and I wouldn't be surprised to find him asleep when I returned.

"It's not a problem. Trust me, I'd rather be here, driving you around than back home taking care of a fussy baby." I aimed the keys and unlocked the doors just as we arrived at my dumpy little blue car.

Micah paused, holding the box he carried on his hip, and waited for me to drop mine into the back first.

"Do you actually babysit for your sister?" Micah's voice held a hint of awe when he asked the question.

"Unfortunately, quite frequently. I guess you could say that I'm a man of many talents."

Micah laughed. "Do you mind if we stop at the drive-thru for some fast food?"

"You were reading my mind," I said, climbing into the driver's seat.

The drive home was filled with a lot more conversation than I expected from the Amish kid. We were close to the same age, but for some reason he seemed younger. Maybe it was the ultra-innocent vibe swirling around him. Whatever it was, he seemed really happy to have another guy to talk to. In between bites of his hamburger, he was asking questions. Usually, such nosey pestering would have driven me crazy. But today I was happy to have the distraction. Without it, I'd be thinking about Rachel. And that was one place I didn't want to go to.

"Is it strange to live with your sister, brother and brother-in-law?" Seeing my raised brows, he added, "I mean without parents to supervise you?"

I looked out the window at the passing scenery. The weath-er had turned cool once again, and the buds on the trees that had been bursting to life a few days earlier were back to droopy hibernation. There was a carpet of rich, green grass everywhere, though, signaling that spring would be in full swing soon enough.

"Mom died a few years ago . . . and since my dad's a doctor, he's a pretty busy man. Sam and Rose have been taking care of me for a while, I guess you could say. Now that I'm getting older and driving, I don't need much attention," I said simply.

"It must be wonderful to be able to do whatever you want—like those other communities that allow rumspringa. In Meadowview, we don't." Micah had a faraway look on his face and I wondered what he would do if given the same freedom.

"You got it all wrong, dude. Rose and Sam are *worse* than most parents when it comes to rules." I stopped and thought for a minute and then said, "Well, I'd wager, I still have a lot more freedom than you do."

Micah seemed glad for the opening and immediately said, "Do you talk much with Noah about the Amish ways?"

I shook my head. "No, not really. I get the feeling that it's a sore subject for him . . . like he still has issues about it. I don't want to stress him out or anything. But I've made my own observations since I've lived here, and honestly, I don't know how you survive."

"Yes, it is difficult," Micah said wistfully. There was silence in the car for a moment and then he added, "It's been even more troublesome here lately."

Micah lapsed back into awkward silence and I glanced at his stoic profile. I already had an idea why the kid was so depressed, and I got the distinct impression that he wanted to get something off his chest. I squirmed on the inside at the thought of getting on a more personal level with an Amish kid, but the pull of sympathy—and curiosity—was too much.

I sighed and asked, "Want to talk about it?"

He looked relieved.

"You know that Sarah was killed in the storm, right?"

I nodded.

"Well, she wasn't just any girl. I was courting her," he said the words in such a cautious way, you'd think he'd just told me that he'd slept with his third grade teacher. The news didn't surprise me. I'd heard bits of information here and there, enough to know that the two had been hooking up. And I'd seen him at the debris of what used to be the Miller's house, after Dad had pronounced Sarah dead. It wasn't a pretty sight. No guy showed that much emotion unless he *really* cared for a girl—maybe even loved her.

But I played along as if I hadn't a clue. "Wow, that's tough. How are you holding up?"

Micah shrugged, hesitating for a moment. I could tell by his fidgety demeanor that he really wanted to say something more, but was conflicted for some reason. My curiosity grew as I waited.

"My father wants me to begin courting again—and he has a girl picked out," he said forlornly.

Already knowing that the Amish world revolved around getting hitched young, I figured that part probably wasn't the problem. Carefully, I ventured, "And you don't like the girl?"

"She's very pretty, actually—bright red hair, green eyes like mine. She has a pleasing disposition also; she reminds me a lot of Sarah."

I thought back to all the schoolhouse dinners I'd attended and I might have remembered the girl he was talking about. She was pretty hot, for an Amish girl.

"Then what's the problem?" I asked, as I made the turn onto the main road leading into the Amish community. The bright yellow sign with a black silhouetted horse and buggy stuck out like a sore thumb on the side of the road. Almost every time I saw one of the signs, I shook my head, feeling as if I'd entered an alternate universe. This time, I barely noticed it, waiting expectantly for Micah to spill the beans.

Pristine white farmhouses and barns dotted the landscape, and we passed fields full of cows, corn stumps, and occasionally horses. I was beginning to think Micah was finished talking when he said in a rush of words, "There's another girl that is special to me. She's the complete opposite of Sarah and Wendy. She has a short temper and she's aloof. I don't think she cares for the Amish way of life one bit."

"What's the attraction, then?" I was only asking for his benefit. Noah had fallen for Rose for the same reason—some guys liked a challenge.

"She's just so different than the other girls. And she's really smart. Her quick wit impresses me."

"Why don't you just go for it then? Surely if you tell your dad how you feel, he'll let you date her. Noah did say once that your kind is allowed to pick your own wives—unless of course, she's English?" I laughed, but when he didn't immediately respond, I looked back at him questioningly.

"No, she isn't English, but my father will have issues about us being together. There's bad blood between our families. Besides, this girl doesn't even know I exist." Micah took a deep breath and dropped his head back on the headrest.

My mind was racing at the information, putting all the pieces together as quickly as I could. By the time I pulled into the schoolhouse parking area, I was going only a couple of miles an hour, following a procession of several buggies. I drove slowly, keeping my eyes pitched for any children that might dart out in front of the car as I wove in and out between parked buggies and boys leading horses to the hitching rails behind the schoolhouse. I was shocked to see so many people already gathered to begin cooking the dinner, but I was even more shocked at what I'd figured out.

I knew what families were feuding—and I knew an Amish girl that matched Micah's description to a T. After I'd parked and cut the engine, I turned to Micah. "Rachel Miller is the girl you're crushing on."

KAREN ANN HOPKINS

Micah's face went ashen white and his mouth dropped open. "How did you know?"

"That's not really the issue you need to worry about." I motioned with my chin out the window and Micah's gaze followed. "She just got out of that buggy over there, and she's walking straight toward us."

CHAPTER 7

❧ Rachel ❧

What was he doing here? And with Micah Schwartz nonetheless. My mind raced with all kinds of horrible scenarios as my eyes darted left and right to see if anyone was paying attention to my altered course. Instead of following my sister-in-law, Katie, up into the schoolhouse to start peeling potatoes for the annual community dinner, I set a course straight for Justin's small, blue vehicle. I didn't worry too much that Katie would come looking for me. She was fairly easy going and wouldn't miss me for a little while. She also had her baby boy to distract her. When I reached the car, I turned to look at the schoolhouse again. Katie was just going through the doorway, with the baby on her hip. The door closed behind her. I wasted no time in walking up to the driver's side window. As the window rolled down, I was greeted by Justin's grinning face. I became flustered for a second, worrying that I'd made a mistake approaching the car, when I noticed Micah staring at me.

I thought quickly. Swallowing, I forced a smile. "Justin, would you care to drive me back to my house? I forgot the bag of taters that I was supposed to bring." The lie came easily. The words just popped into my mind and out of my mouth. As Justin's brow furrowed in concentration, I thought about what I'd just done. Mother would be home, so I'd have to act as if I thought that I needed the potatoes, when in reality, I already knew they'd been delivered the day before. I could probably trick Mother on that one. Katie might notice I was missing,

51

but then she might not. And if I showed up with a bag of potatoes, what could she or the other women do? Punish me for bringing more potatoes? All in all, it was a good plan. Except for Micah. Unfortunately, he'd have to come along or it might look suspicious if I was alone with the English boy.

"Uh, what do I look like an Amish driver or something?" Justin said, frowning.

"Isn't that what you're doing with Micah, here?" I asked tartly.

Micah spoke up. "Justin is doing me a favor today. Rose was going to drive me to the store, but her baby wasn't feeling well. Justin filled in for her since he doesn't have school today."

"Is Sarah Ann all right?" My own problems vanished at the thought of my dear little niece being sick.

"She's probably fine. Rose and Noah went out on an impromptu date last night. I think it was a combination of Sarah Ann's fussiness over missing her mother, and Rose being Rose, not wanting to get up early to drive an Amish kid around."

"Gut," I said, slipping into my birth language. I glanced at Micah to see his reaction to what Justin had said at the same time Justin did.

Justin quickly said, "Sorry, it's not you. My sister is spoiled."

"I'm the same age as you, Justin. So why call me a kid?" Micah asked calmly.

I studied Micah for a moment. I understood why Sarah had fallen for him. His light brown hair was thick and wavy and he wore it a bit longer than the other boys. But it was his large, clear green eyes that were beautiful. He wasn't quite as tall as Justin, but he was taller than most everyone else. What made him special, though, was his kind personality. I still remembered quite vividly how he'd followed me out into the rain at Sarah's wake. He'd briefly and unabashedly taken my hands into his own and told me how sorry he was. Then he ran off in the rain to who-knows-where. That was the last time I'd spoken to him. And I couldn't recall ever talking to him before then, either. But that one episode had been enough for the gossip mill to label us as a possible couple. I didn't know what Elijah Schwartz thought about the rumors, but my own Father had given me a stern lecture about how difficult such a relationship would be, and that he advised against it. I had laughed and cried at the same time over the absurdity of his tirade.

"It's just a saying. Don't take it personally," Justin finally responded to Micah. He turned to me. "I'll take you home, but first, I have to help Micah with the chicken."

"Micah, do you mind coming along with us. I wouldn't want to get into trouble." Micah understood exactly what I meant, and being the sweet boy he was, he quickly said he'd be happy to. I watched Justin and Micah walk up the hill, side by side, and couldn't help comparing them to each other. One was English and the other Amish, but even without knowing either one very well, I thought they were similar in temperament. They were both friendly and laid back. And each had a hint of restlessness in him. If it weren't for their different cultures, they might have been good friends.

Justin arrived back to the car before Micah did, and he wasted no time leaning up against it, beside me, and saying, "How are you feeling this morning?"

Strangely, the way he asked sounded more concerned than sarcastic. I glanced down at my feet and then back up. "I have a headache, but other than that, I'm fine."

"I'm surprised," Justin said.

"I wasn't *that* drunk," I smiled, meeting his gaze with challenge.

"Maybe you're getting too much practice," Justin said in a particularly probing way.

"It's really none of your business. Your sister is married to my brother—and that's the only connection we have," I said firmly, trying to convince myself of the truth of the words.

Justin chuckled. "Isn't that enough of a connection to make us pretty close. All the Romeo-Juliet drama we suffered through with those two gives us something in common."

I wasn't sure if he was just being pleasant or if he was flirting with me. I wanted desperately to figure it out, but Micah was jogging down the hill and I knew I'd lost my opportunity.

I dropped my voice. "Micah can't know anything about me going out. He isn't like us."

Justin's eyebrows furrowed, and then he shrugged.

The ride to my house was quiet and awkward. Justin stared straight ahead and Micah was too shy to say anything at all. Both of them went into the house with me to help with the potatoes, since the only bag we had in the pantry was a fifty pound one. I still worried about what Mother would say if she saw Justin and Micah with me, but it turned out that I didn't need to worry after all.

"Peter, where's Mother?" I asked my thirteen-year-old brother when I met him in the kitchen. He was eating a sandwich and his hair was mussed up as if he'd just gotten out of bed. Ach, it irritated me to no end that my three little brothers could sleep in while I had to get up so early to begin the laundry most days. Even little Naomi, who was only five, had to rise before sunup to help with the chores. Jacob, the oldest of the Miller children, had always been an early riser, like Father. Noah was somewhere in between them all.

With his mouth still full, he said, "She went to Saretta's to quilt—took Naomi and the little boys with her." Peter noticed that Justin and Micah were standing behind me. His eyes widened and I wasn't sure if it was because of Justin's presence in the kitchen or Micah's. Even though the Schwartz-Miller feud had softened since Sarah's death, some things couldn't be completely undone.

God must be taking care of me, I thought, letting out a great sigh.

"We're getting the potatoes and taking them to the schoolhouse," I said squeezing by Peter. "The bag is in the pantry. This way," I motioned to Justin and Micah.

"Wait," Peter stopped me. "You should look in on Maisy.

I think she might have colic. I called Father and Noah, but I don't know if they got the messages."

I couldn't ignore the worried look on Peter's face, but the thought of having Justin and Micah here when Father returned made my heart rate speed up. Father would be beyond furious. But Maisy was the most dependable old horse in the world. I had to check in on her.

"Peter, please take the big bag of potatoes out to Justin's car, while I run and check on Maisy," I said, not waiting for his response.

I really did turn and run out the door and through the yard. Justin and Micah kept up with me, one on each side. Even Betsy ran with us, probably wondering what the urgency was. We finally slowed to a walk when we entered the stable. I headed straight for Maisy's stall.

"What is this colic we're talking about?" Justin asked.

I glanced over my shoulder to see his face genuinely curious. Micah already knew obviously, and he looked grim.

"It's kind of like a really bad stomach ache in a horse. Sometimes they get over it with medication, other times they need surgery or they'll die," I told him as I opened the stall door.

Maisy was lying flat on the ground. Her sides were wet with sweat and pieces of hay and shavings clung to her. With a quick glance, I saw that her breathing was more rapid than usual and I heard her grinding her teeth. She looked up at me, making a half whinny-half groaning noise.

"Justin, please use your cellphone to call Rose. Tell her to contact Dr. Springer and ask him come out to the farm as soon as possible for a colicky horse," I said, kneeling down beside Maisy's head. I stroked her face, taking a shaky breath.

"Sure thing," Justin said. He had his phone in his hand and was walking down the barn aisle.

Maisy pulled away from my hand and began to roll.

"We should get her up." Micah appeared at my side with a halter and lead rope in hand. As Maisy thrashed, Micah agilely dodged her striking hooves, fastening the halter onto her head. He motioned me aside, before he tugged on the lead rope. He touched his free hand to her shoulder at the same time and showing his experience with horses, he had the mare on her feet quickly.

"I don't like the way she's rolling. She might twist her intestine, if it isn't already." Micah paused to look at me, and asked, "Do you mind if I walk her in the yard a bit? It might help."

For a moment, I was without words, truly surprised that Micah had even thought to ask my permission to do something with the horse. I nodded and he *clucked* to Maisy, getting her moving. I watched him leave the shady interior of the barn. I was about to follow him when Justin's hand appeared on my shoulder.

"She's calling him right now." His face still looked worried, but he seemed to have regained his composure with the phone call.

I was opening my mouth to answer, when Father appeared in the doorway of the barn. The shock on his face when he saw Justin, quickly turned to red-faced anger. He barely hesitated before he strode toward us.

"Rachel, was warden sie tun?" Father asked me, what are you doing? His voice was terse and loud. I glanced at Justin, assuming that he got the gist of it and then turned back to Father, answering in English.

"Justin was kind enough to drive Micah to the supermarket to pick up the chicken for tonight's dinner. He was still at the schoolhouse when I realized I had forgotten to bring the potatoes when Katie picked me up earlier. He offered to drive us to the house to save time." I took a quick breath and went on to say, "Then Peter told me that Maisy was colicky, so we came to the barn to help."

I watched Father's expression turn from outright anger to suspicion and I began to relax a little. I'd take suspicion over a whipping any day.

Father glanced back and forth between Justin and myself, his chestnut-bearded face scrunched up in concentration. He was obviously suffering from some kind of serious inner conflict. I waited patiently, knowing that I had given a plausible excuse, with the potatoes being the only possible kink in my story. Hopefully, Father wouldn't concern himself with the vegetables, and delve any deeper into that part of the story.

When he finally collected his thoughts enough to speak, I swallowed down the knot that formed in my throat, seeing from the look in his eye that he wasn't about to let the matter rest.

Tilting his head to Justin, he said, "I have suffered much because of the relationship between your sister and my son, Justin Cameron. Even though I accepted the inevitability of their union, I never have condoned it in my heart." His finger jabbed in Justin's direction and he lowered his voice to a menacing level. "But Hell will freeze over when I allow my daughter to become involved with an Englisher."

"Father, you are mistaken," I interrupted.

He silenced me with a stern look and a wave of his hand.

He returned his gaze to Justin. "Rachel is *not* allowed to ride in the car with you, or be around you under any circumstances. There will be consequences if this happens again." Father straightened up taller and narrowed his eyes. "Do I make myself clear?"

Justin never had the chance to answer, because at that very moment, Rose marched into the barn with Sarah Ann in her arms. It was obvious from her flushed face and the tightness of her features that she'd heard enough of Father's rant to be extremely upset with him.

"Now, you listen here, Mr. Miller, while I make *myself* clear."

I held my breath and chanced a look at Justin. He was grinning from ear to ear.

CHAPTER 8

······ Justin ······

I was pretty happy to see Rose right then. I'd never enjoyed confrontational situations the way she and Sam did. Frankly, I was much better at diplomacy before things went over the cliff. This time however, I didn't have enough time to charm the frighteningly large Amish man before he went ballistic.

I took in my sister's appearance, noting her tangled hair, sweatpants and face lacking any makeup. She must have hurried out of the house right after she'd gotten off the phone with me. Sarah Ann was still in her footy pajamas, but unlike her mother, she was smiling at everyone.

Rose was glaring at her father-in-law with an intensity that made the large man take a step back. He began to speak, but she cut him off immediately.

"I'm the one who was supposed to take Micah to the store to get the stupid chicken. But your granddaughter here—" she thrust the baby forward gently in Mr. Miller's direction "—was being fussy, so I asked Justin to do it for me." Again, Mr. Miller was going to speak, but Rose's voice rolled over his. "He was generous enough to get out of bed early on a day off from school to drive a member of your community into town so the Amish could have their dinner tonight. And you have the audacity to accuse him of trying to make out with your daughter? You should be ashamed of yourself!"

Mr. Miller's face turned beet red and he cleared his throat loudly. He looked at me and Rachel, standing beside each other, and I took a step closer to Rose out of pure survival instinct.

"It appears that I have made a mistake." He looked at me. "I do apologize for making assumptions, but what I told you still holds firm. If I catch you with my daughter again, there *will* be consequences."

"Are you kidding me . . . ?" Rose began, but it was her turn to be interrupted by Mr. Miller.

"Rachel, go get the horse from Micah. He needs to be on his way. I'll be there in a moment," Mr. Miller ordered.

She didn't hesitate, hurrying out of the barn. I really doubted that even Rachel, with all her stubborn rebelliousness, would ever think to argue with her father the way that Rose had just done. Actually, I don't think I would have, either.

Mr. Miller regained his composure and faced Rose again. Only this time, he was half grinning. He held out his arms to Sarah Ann. "May I hold the baby?"

Rose's eyes became thin slits as she contemplated whether she was going to relent. Besides Sam, Rose was the most stubborn person I knew. After a long moment of Rose and Mr. Miller staring each other down, Rose finally gave in.

"Just because Noah and I snuck around, doesn't mean you have to be paranoid about Rachel and Justin. I don't appreciate you yelling at my brother that way. If it happens again, there *will* be consequences," Rose threatened Mr. Miller's with his own words.

I realized at that moment that my sister was more jaded with the Amish than I'd originally thought. Especially, with Noah's father.

Mr. Miller nodded curtly without speaking, and that's when Rose handed Sarah Ann over to him. The man kissed the baby on the forehead and began talking softly to her in his own language. We followed him through the barn door and out into the sunlight, which was brightening with each passing minute. I avoided looking at Rose and instead shielded my eyes from the rays as I glanced at the sky. It was almost a cloudless day and the light breeze on my skin was warm and dry. I smiled, realizing that I wasn't used to so much drama before ten o'clock in the morning.

Mr. Miller's long strides began to separate us from him as he went directly to the veterinarian's truck that was now parked in the driveway. A tall, gray-headed man was beside the truck. He was pressing a stethoscope to the horse's stomach. I watched as Mr. Miller passed the baby off to Rachel in exchange for the horse's lead rope. Micah was nowhere to be seen. I did a quick scan and discovered him sitting in the passenger seat of my car. He must have immediately responded to Rachel's instruction from her father. Smart kid.

"Wait up," Rose said, touching my arm. I stopped, and turning my back to the scene with the horse, I faced my sister.

I was mentally preparing myself for whatever direction the conversation would go, when Rose began her tirade in a hoarse whisper.

"Are you freaking nuts? I was told months ago that you and Rachel had something going on, but I didn't believe it. I thought you had more sense."

Months ago? "What are you talking about? This is the first time I've said a word to the girl since her house was destroyed by the tornado. Sam and I came over here to help with the cleanup in the following days. I had a couple of conversations with her. After all, she'd lost her sister and her home in one sweep. I was just being nice. That's it. I haven't seen her since, until today when she asked if I'd drive her back here to get potatoes," I said as convincingly as I could manage.

And it was almost entirely true—except for the part about not seeing Rachel until today. That was a lie made to protect a promise. So it didn't count in my book.

As I talked, Rose listened intently. But I could tell by her raised eyebrow and tightly pressed lips that she'd been thinking the entire time. I knew her well enough to be very aware of her active mind.

"Are you telling me the whole truth, Justin? This is important. I just chewed out my father-in-law to protect your butt, and I'd feel a whole lot better if I didn't have to worry about any future surprises." Rose looked up at me sternly.

I loved my sister. She was almost as clever as me. But not quite. I nodded and for effect, sighed tiredly. "Why would anyone say that Rachel and I were involved?"

Rose's mouth set in a grim line and her eyes sparked. "Because that's what the Amish do—gossip. It just makes me so mad that a rumor got started, and all because you were being helpful." Her expression changed to contemplation and she added, "I wonder if it's the same in Micah's case."

I raised my brow questioningly and she went on to say, "When I heard about you and Rachel, I was also told that she was messing around with Micah."

"Really . . . " I said it in the least interested way I could possibly muster while I pondered the news. Micah and Rachel? I already knew that Micah had a crush on her, but never gave it much thought that those feelings might be reciprocal. Unfortunately, when I met Rose's gaze, her eyes were narrowed all over again, and I knew that I had made a mistake.

Rose took a step closer, our toes nearly touching, and she said in a low, threatening voice, "Don't even go there, Justin. I'm warning you. She's trouble with a capital T. Even before her sister died, she'd been a moody, difficult girl—a manipulating type." Rose took a breath and her eyes moistened. My attention switched from fear for my own discovery in a lie to Rose's intense feelings. She said, "Look, I know firsthand how hard it is to have a relationship with an Amish person. I love Noah with all of my being, and we're happy, but it was an awful journey to get here. And we're still dealing with fallout in the community. Noah is shunned, Justin. I guess I didn't really grasp the meaning of it all until he wasn't allowed to go to his best friend's

wedding or eat dinner at his parent's house." Rose wiped the
tear away and sniffed. "I don't want you to go through the same
thing. I love you too much for that."

I pulled Rose into a brief hug. "Don't worry, sis. I'm a lot
smarter than you."

Rose swatted me across the stomach and laughed at the
same time she dabbed her eyes with her fingers. "You better get
out of here before Amos gets his beard in a wad again."

"Yeah, good idea. I have to take Micah and those potatoes
back to the schoolhouse anyway."

We walked side by side down the driveway in silence until
we reached the small group surrounding the horse. Peter was
now holding the rope.

"Is Maisy going to be all right?" Rose asked as she walked
up to the horse and rubbed its forehead.

"I've just administered some mineral oil and I detected gut
sounds. I reckon the mare is on the road to recovery," the vet
told her.

Once I'd heard the good news, I started walking again, but
Rachel called out. "Wait, Justin." I stopped, and she turned to
her father after she handed Sarah Ann back to Rose. "I have to
get back to the schoolhouse."

"Rose, would you mind taking Rachel up the road?" Mr.
Miller said.

"Yeah, I'd be happy to. I need to talk to someone over there
anyway," Rose said.

I glanced back to see Mr. Miller's quizzical look, but I kept
on walking. I'd had enough drama for one day. I didn't even
look Rachel's way, trying desperately to forget the Amish girl.
But as I walked to my car, I couldn't stop thinking about her.

Was it possible that Rachel and Micah had something going on behind the scenes? Perhaps all his talk about having a
crush on her was made up for my benefit—a trap of some sort.
If he'd heard the same rumors that Rose had, he might have
been worried that I was involved with her. But he seemed like

such an honest person. And you can't fake that kind of depression. Was it just a coincidence that Micah wanted Rachel and the rumors were already flying? Images of Rachel sipping from the beer bottle and leaving the bar with that squirrelly-looking dude flashed in my mind as I got into the car and started the engine. I really pitied Micah if he did fall for Rachel. Rose was right—she was trouble.

"I heard Amos' raised voice coming from the barn. What was that all about?" Micah asked with a mild frown.

I decided to be truthful and hoped that he'd return the favor. "He was upset to see me and you with Rachel. It seems that he's worried that one of us might be hooking up with her on the side."

"Hooking up . . . ?" Micah said in confusion.

Even though he was wearing suspenders and had an old-fashioned haircut, I had forgotten that he was Amish for a moment. I searched my mind for terminology that he'd understand.

"You know, secretly dating or courting or whatever," I said, pulling onto the roadway.

"Why would he think such a thing?" Micah's eyes were wide with surprise.

I really felt sorry for him. He was definitely clueless and probably terrified that I was after Rachel for myself.

"It's just community gossip as far as I'm concerned. What about you?"

Micah's face visibly relaxed, but then became tight again. "I've only spoken to Rachel a few times. Once was after Sarah's wake. I guess you could say I offered her condolences. That's about it."

"But you want it to be more?" I asked, glancing over at him. The windows were partially down and the warm wind whipping through the vehicle made everything seem less urgent in a way.

He shrugged. "I don't know. I'm not sure if the connection

I feel to Rachel is real or just my desire to be with someone who in some ways reminds me of Sarah." He took a deep breath and met my gaze for a moment. "It still hurts, losing Sarah."

"I'm sure it does" was all I could manage to say.

I pulled into the schoolhouse parking lot for a second time, noting that the activity level had increased. A large grill was smoking and there were four black clad, bearded men hovering around it. Women were bustling back and forth from buggies to the schoolhouse, and children ran everywhere.

When I finally parked, I glanced at Micah, who didn't seem to be in any hurry to exit my car.

"All things considered, you might be better off going for the sweet little redhead," I said honestly.

Micah's face was sad. "I know."

CHAPTER 9

Rose

"Thanks, Sam, for babysitting Sarah Ann," I said, flattening the long black skirt down with my hands in a nervous fit. The shirt I'd chosen to wear was crisp white and buttoned up the front. All in all, I thought I looked pretty drab—perfect for an Amish meeting.

"Do you think I'm underdressed?" Summer asked worriedly.

I appraised her from head to foot, taking in her large, hoop earrings, denim jacket and faded blue jeans. In any other place, her casual attire would have been acceptable, but the Amish didn't believe in jewelry or women wearing pants. I thought for a moment and decided the heck with Amish dress protocol. Summer was English. She shouldn't have to dress to their standards.

"No, you're perfect," I lied.

"You guys are wasting your time," Sam said with his usual negativity.

"I have a plan. It's going to work," I told him with a sureness that I wasn't entirely feeling inside.

"Why do you want to get involved in the Amish intrigue anyway? You escaped that nonsense last year," Sam said.

He had a point. It certainly wouldn't be easy. But then I thought about Suzanna and Miranda and how much they wanted a dress shop, and it made sense all over again.

"You wouldn't get it, so why should I bother trying to explain," was all I said.

"Well, I'm not afraid to tell you why I'm doing it," Summer said. "I need a job and I need a car. Besides, working with Suzanna and Miranda will be fun."

"Until you have to get up at four o'clock in the morning." Sam laughed.

"It isn't like that. This is a dress shop, not a bakery. We'll have regular business hours," Summer insisted.

"Anything involving the Amish means early morning rising," Sam countered.

Before the two of them could get into a knock-down, drag-out fight, I intervened, saying, "We need to get going, Summer."

Summer smiled at my distraction. "Sure thing." She then skipped up to Sam and gave him a kiss on the lips. He was immediately responsive and she pulled away, laughing, "Later, stud."

"If you're lucky, Sarah Ann will sleep the entire time," I told Sam, grabbing up my car keys from the countertop.

"I'm never that lucky," Sam said with a mock frown.

When we turned into the schoolhouse driveway and were stuck behind a buggy, I finally had enough.

"You have to calm down, Summer! Or you're going to scare the bishop and ministers," I told her firmly.

"Aren't you at all worried? I just found out Amos Miller has taken Marcus Bontrager's minister position. And here you are, telling him off this morning—we are so screwed." Summer slumped into the seat, thudding her head onto the headrest.

"Nice to know you have so much faith in me."

"It's not you—the whole idea is insane. Bishop Lambright will never go for it, and he'll probably give us a lecture besides,"

Summer said the words with such theatrics that that I had to chuckle.

"It won't be that bad. I promise."

Summer was silent while I parked, but before we got out of the pickup truck, she said thoughtfully, "Why are we here early? I thought the meeting began at 6:30?"

"You can help Suzanna and Miranda with the cleaning up from dinner. I have someone to talk to. And I need to do it alone," I said.

"Stop being so mysterious!" Summer demanded.

I shook my head lightly. "Sorry, I can't. It will just freak you out, and if Suzanna and Miranda realize what's going on, they'll kill me for sure."

"Then why are you doing whatever you're doing?" Summer asked.

"Because it's the only way the girls have a chance of having a dress shop in this community."

"I *do* have faith in you. Good luck with whatever it is," Summer said. She squeezed my hand and then flung the truck door open. I took a moment to breathe and to think before I did the same.

I was trying to be inconspicuous as I skirted the outside of the gathering room in the schoolhouse, but it was impossible. Every few steps I took, someone said hello to me. Mostly they were women and children, but James Hershberger stopped to chat for a moment, and I ignored Amish propriety to give the old man a hug. He didn't seem to mind and recovered quickly enough to ask about Noah and Sarah Ann. He was Ruth's husband and had been my temporary foster dad when I'd lived among the Amish. He was extremely easygoing for an Amish man, and he'd always been fair to me. I missed our talks about the history of his people and their culture in general.

But I was on a mission and politely left James, keeping my eyes pitched for the person I was looking for. When I finally spotted her, I stopped and reconsidered what I was doing—and if it was the right thing. A couple of little girls in matching maroon colored dresses and white caps squeezed by me and a table, but I paid no attention to them. I was suddenly filled with indecision.

I watched the object of my scrutiny as she bustled around with the other women. She balanced a large, gray plastic tub on her hip and was carefully depositing dirty glasses from the table into it. I could see that many of the glasses were partly filled with water, so I knew the tub was heavy, yet the woman didn't let the strain show on her pretty face. Her doe-like hazel eyes were focused on her work, except for the occasional comment she made to the younger girl who followed behind her with a black garbage bag for the crunched up napkins and plastic plates.

The young woman wore a sky blue dress that was brighter and more eye-catching than any of the other women's dresses in the building. Even Suzanna, who I'd spotted when I'd first entered the building, was wearing a simple green dress—being cautious about her attire. But not this woman. She didn't really have to be. Her Father was Mervin Weaver, one of the ministers. And that was the main reason that I sought her out.

Taking the color of her dress as a sign that I *was* doing the right thing, I left the safety of the wall and headed straight toward her before I could change my mind.

I had to swallow down a ball of distaste rising in my throat when I said, "Hello, Ella. Can I help you with that?"

Ella stopped and stared at me shrewdly. I could hardly blame her. The last time I'd spoken to her, she'd been trying to apologize for nearly getting me killed by providing her sicko Amish friend, Levi, with my aunt's address in Fairfield.

I'd stayed there after my dad's forced removal of me from the Amish community. Katie, Ella's sister, and my sister-in-law, had assured me that Ella hadn't understood what she was doing— that Ella would never have given Levi the information if she'd known that he would eventually hunt me down and attempt to rape and kill me. Somehow, I'd managed to fight off Levi, jabbing his eye out with my car keys in the process, and shooting him in the end. Levi was now living far away in a maximum security prison. He'd pled guilty to have a life sentence reduced to fifteen years. Part of me still wished the bullet had killed him. Then I wouldn't have nightmares most nights, fearing the eventual day that he'd be released from prison.

A shiver ran down my spine, and I took a quick breath to push the rush of fear aside. Finding the courage, I repeated myself. "Do you need help?"

Ella continued to balance the tub on her hip. She mumbled something in German to the girl patiently standing behind her with the garbage bag to go on past her.

When the girl was out of earshot, Ella's eyes narrowed and she said in English, "What do you want, Rose? If I remember correctly, the last time we spoke, you told me that you would never forgive my sins or something to that effect. Why now do you seek me out with friendly words?"

I had to give her credit. Ella was straight forward if nothing else. The Amish woman had been a thorn in my side since the first youth gathering I'd gone to. She had been in love with Noah at the time, and didn't take kindly to me supposedly stealing him away from her. If truth be told, Noah had never cared for her much anyway. The only reason I thought that my insane idea might actually work was because Suzanna had told me that Ella was courting Elijah Schwartz's oldest son, Paul, who also happened to be Micah and Constance's brother. The Amish community was incredibly interconnected to a point that I often got headaches thinking about who was related to whom, but one family I didn't have any trouble with at all were the Schwartzes. They'd created an amazing amount of turmoil because of Noah's breakup with Constance Schwartz. The two had been engaged at the time, and Elijah had gone crazy with vengeance when it happened. It was because of me that Noah called off the wedding and was subsequently the reason that Mr. Schwartz wouldn't allow his son, Micah, to court Sarah Miller. It had been a nasty mess that only her tragic death had ended.

Now, standing here before Ella and her cautious gaze, I felt guilty for the way I'd responded to her attempt at friendship. Who could blame her for falling in love with a guy like Noah? And if I really trusted Katie, who'd always been a faithful friend, Ella hadn't seriously intended me harm. A vision of Sarah sprang across my vision and I knew what she would encourage me to do. Kind Sarah would ask me to genuinely forgive Ella.

"Can we talk?" I leaned in and whispered.

Ella continued to frown, but interest sparked in her eyes. After a pause, she called out to one of the other girls in German and deposited the tub onto the table.

"Follow me," she said, winding her way between the tables. Right before we went through the back door, I caught Miranda's shocked gaze from across the tent.

I tried to smile reassuringly to the slender, mousy haired Amish girl, but feared I had failed miserably. I was glad to close the door behind me and block the wondering face from view. I'd deal with her and Suzanna later, after my talk with Ella.

Once we were clear of the building and standing on the slope above the playground, Ella turned. "So, what do you want?"

I glanced around. Some children were swinging and others were running around in the grass. A few younger teenage girls were setting up the volleyball nets beside the parking area, and a couple of mothers with small babies in their laps were sitting on the opposite knoll. Otherwise, we were alone.

"It was wrong of me to hold such a long grudge against you and I'm sorry for that. I realize now that you can't be held responsible for Levi's actions." I searched her eyes for some kind of softening in her demeanor.

"You know, he's sent me letters from prison." Her words caught me off guard, the breath caught in my throat and my heart pounded in my chest. Seeing the obvious shock on my face, she hurriedly went on to say, "I've shown them to my parents and we've thrown them away. I want absolutely nothing to do with him."

"Why is he still trying to contact you?" I asked, afraid of her answer on too many levels to count.

She shrugged a little, but her eyes were sharp. "Either he wants to find out information about you or he's stalking me—either way, it's scary." Anticipating my next question, she said, "He doesn't say anything in the letters that would incriminate him. He mostly talks about the weather or his job mopping the floors of the cafeteria."

"Why didn't you mention this to me sooner?"

"You made it quite clear that you didn't want anything to do with me. Besides, at the time, I didn't want to upset you," Ella said, frowning. "But I've always wanted to talk to you about it. No one else knows better than you what an evil person he is. I felt dirty every time I found one of his vile letters in the box—and I wouldn't sleep properly for days afterward."

I felt a kinship with Ella that I'd never experienced before, and never in a million years expected to. Ella got it. She shared the same fear that I had been living with since the bastard attacked me.

"You know, if you talk to the post office, I think they can return the letters without forwarding them to you," I suggested as my mind swam in the murky waters that were Levi Zook.

"It's already done. After the third letter, Da talked to the mail carrier. But it still upsets me that Levi is thinking about me at all."

"I totally understand." I stared at two little girls chasing one another around the swing set. I envied their innocence.

After a moment of us standing quietly side by side, Ella said, "What did you want to talk to me about in the first place?"

I looked back at her, my mind in a fog. Blinking, I tried to forget about Levi. He was in prison and no threat to me or anyone here in the peaceful Amish community. We were all safe.

"Have you heard anything about the dress shop idea floating around?" I asked carefully.

Ella smiled a little. "I thought you stayed with our people long enough to know that all business here is everyone's business." Her eyebrow lifted. "Yes, I know of it."

I took a breath. "Any chance that you'd be interested in being a partner in the endeavor?"

Ella's smile disappeared as her mouth dropped. "Suzanna and Miranda would never have me as a partner. They hate me."

Again, Ella's straight forwardness was moving the conversation along quickly.

"Summer and I are partners, too. I think I can talk them all into accepting you, if it's something that you'd be interested in."

"Why me?"

I motioned at her dress, "Look at you, Ella. You're one of the best dressed Amish girls I know. You get away with wearing shades of color that the other girls wouldn't dream of, the cut of your sleeves is different than the others, and your hem is a bit shorter. You're a trailblazer when it comes to Amish fashion."

"And, my father is one of the ministers," Ella said bluntly.

I grinned. "Well, that too."

Ella tilted her head considering. When she spoke, her face relaxed into what I could only describe as great relief.

"I'm so glad you came to me with this offer. Even if it's only to help bolster your chances of the elders allowing it. I still really appreciate it." I held my breath when she swallowed. "I would love to be a part of it. I've never been close to any of the girls. It didn't matter to me when I was younger, but lately here, it's bothered me. Perhaps this will give me a chance to build friendships. And you're right, Rose." I waited for her to elaborate. "I'm sensible when it comes to style. Even though our options are limited being Amish, I've discovered ways around the rules. And many of the women in our community and the neighboring ones are so busy with their family businesses and caring for their children, they don't have as much time to sew. If we play our cards right, it might be very prosperous, indeed."

I returned Ella's smile. I'd definitely made the right decision.

"The meeting is in a half hour in the back classroom," I told her.

"I'll be there. If you'll excuse me, I had best go finish the cleaning," she said. Ella half turned and then came back to me, giving me a brief hug. I was taken by surprise too much to properly respond, standing rigidly in her arms. She released me and whirled away.

I had to admit that I was touched by Ella's enthusiasm and affection. Maybe in my own jealousy, I'd judged her wrongly from the very beginning. Or maybe she'd changed. Either way, I'd know for sure in the days to come.

The sun was setting in a brilliant burst of pink and red on the horizon. A rush of colder air made me shiver. But it wasn't the chilly breeze that caused my goose bumps. An image of Levi appeared before me. His carrot red hair was cropped short and his pale skin was even whiter. The black pool that was his only eye looked at me with madness—and I was terrified.

"You're a very clever, clever girl, Rose."

The sudden voice behind me made me jump. My heart was beating madly when Martha Lambright squeezed my shoulder.

"What do you mean?" I asked her, fearing that I already knew the answer.

"I overheard part of your conversation with Ella Weaver. It must be difficult to mend fences with Ella for your own purposes." Martha said it in a friendly way, but I wasn't deceived. She was a complicated woman.

Martha was Bishop Lambright's wife. She was about twenty years his junior and the couple had no children of their own. She was an attractive woman in her fifties, the light spray of gray at her temples the only sign that she was even that old. Her skin was relatively wrinkle free, except for the creases at the corner of her eyes when she smiled. The Amish woman had been an enigma ever since the time she'd come to my aid when Summer and I had tricked Levi into showing his true colors. After that incident, Martha had always been friendly, but in a creepy way that kept me on edge. Could she really be that nice, or did she have her own agenda?

Glancing sideways at her smiling face, I suddenly had the feeling of an ambush.

CHAPTER 10

❧ Rachel ❧

I caught Constance looking at me as I handed her the glasses. She never said much, so her silence as we worked alongside each other wasn't out of the ordinary. Still, I was more aware of her today than usual. Constance was Micah's older sister and she'd almost been my sister-in-law. Rose had stolen Noah from Constance, and a bitter feud between the Schwartzes and Millers ensued. That was all history now. For the most part, there was peace between the families, and it seemed that both Father and Mr. Schwartz felt that it would stay that way as long as none of their children intermingled again.

I hadn't really cared about the situation until today, when Father had so rudely lumped Micah into the same off-limits category that the English boy Justin was in. It's not that I *wanted* to get involved with Micah. It was more the resentment that Father was willing to declare him not worthy just because of what happened with Noah and Constance. Sarah had dealt with the exact same thing, except that at the time, she'd been secretly courting Micah, and the families had been in the middle of a war, which included Mr. Schwartz buying up land and a horse that Noah had been interested in, just to spite our family.

Constance continued to look quizzically at me as she waited with an open hand for the next glass. I quickly handed her one. She smiled briefly, then went back to work. Micah favored his sister, with his wide spaced eyes and the light sprinkling of freckles over his nose. But where his hair was a sun-kissed light brown, hers was a dark auburn.

"How are you doing, Rachel? I haven't really spoken to you since Sarah's passing. How are you handling it?" Constance asked, while she swished the glass in her hand in the sudsy water.

For a moment, I was taken aback. I couldn't recall Constance ever speaking to me on a personal level before. Her tone was kind, though, so I tilted my head in her direction and replied, "I'm quite all right, thank you."

"I lost a baby sister. She was only two—fell out a second story window that had been left open when Mother was distracted caring for my youngest brother, who was only a newborn at the time. I was ten years old and even though I was at school and not in charge of little Samantha at the time, I still carried the weight of guilt on my shoulders for many months afterwards." She paused to meet my gaze and her eyes were moist. "You see, I'd been sick that day, but I'd gone to school anyway, fearing that if I did stay home, I'd be stuck caring for the younger children. But the truth is, if I'd only stayed at the house, Samantha would be running around with the other twelve year olds right now."

As I listened to her story, many emotions passed through me. Constance must have understood my own guilt of having survived the collapsing house that had killed Sarah. I understood that her openness was an attempt to comfort me, but in actuality, she was the one who was still broken due to circumstance. At that moment, Constance needed me more than I needed her.

"Don't be foolish," I scolded lightly. "Of course you should have been in school. You were a child yourself, and it certainly wasn't your responsibility to care for the babies."

Constance paused, searching my eyes, "You really think so?"

"It was a tragic accident. My younger brothers have broken

many bones falling out of the hayloft, off of horses, and off of the trampoline. I've often thought that my own mother didn't watch them well enough—always busy with a younger child or the house cleaning."

Constance's eyes widened in shock, and I smiled inwardly. It always felt good to rant a little.

A moment later, she was recovered and seemed thoughtful when she said, "It is true that most of our women have their hands full with younger children and chores." She paused as if remembering something and then rattled on, "Have you heard about the special meeting that was called for this evening?"

I shook my head. I was really out of the loop, too sleep deprived for any kind of gossip as of late.

Constance glanced around the small room in the corner of the schoolhouse to make sure we were still alone. Except for the occasional girl entering the room to set salt and pepper shakers or tubs of glasses on the table, it was just us.

She lowered her voice even more and leaned in close. The strong scent of soap on her skin invaded my senses. "Your sister-in-law, Rose, has asked the elders to allow her, Suzanna, Miranda and the English girl, Summer, to open a dress shop on Route 48, where Mary Yoder's bakery used to be."

I absorbed her words, feeling an immediate stab of envy that I wasn't involved in such a scheme. Sewing wasn't my favorite thing to do, but I was genuinely good at it. And the chance to spar with Bishop Lambright over the details would be highly entertaining.

"Aren't you engaged to Mary Yoder's son, John?" I asked, trying to figure out Constance's interest in the news."

"Yes, I am. But we've decided to hold off on the wedding until next year." She saw my raised brow and added, "I learned my lesson with Noah. I'll not be rushing into anything so soon again."

I grinned back. "Good idea. Why your interest in this dress shop business?"

"Don't you see? If our women are able to buy some of their family's clothing, instead of making it all, they'll have more time on their hands for other things. Some of us are blessed with a love of sewing—I for one am not one of them. I suffer through sewing my own dresses. I can only imagine how tedious it will be to sew a husband's pants and shirts and all the children's outfits, too."

"Do you think the bishop will allow such a thing?" I asked with strong doubts myself.

Constance shrugged. "There's no telling. But I do hope they succeed." Constance glanced at the wall clock. "The meeting's going on right now."

There was a hint of nervousness in Constance's voice and I felt sorry for her. She truly wanted the girls to be able to have their dress shop. It was a great idea, but I wasn't delusional enough to think that group of stubborn old men would ever agree to it.

We finished the washing up without further conversation, and when I left the kitchen, squeezing through a crowd of women, I heard that the talk was all about the dress shop and whether the girls would succeed. It seemed everyone had an opinion on the matter. As I passed Ruth Hershberger and her daughter, Emilene, I overheard them quietly arguing about the very idea of it. Emilene was all for the shop, which made sense since she had twelve children to care for. Ruth was more traditional, asserting that the addition of such a business would change the core values of our people too much.

The building was crowded with almost all church members either already gathered or filing in. I spotted Mother standing across the room with Katie and Naomi, but I didn't join them. Even though Amish were considerably quieter than the outsiders were, the crowd gathered here today was so large, that the mixture of voices and shuffling of feet caused the room to be filled with noise. Children scampered around legs and men flattened down their beards with anxious hands. I assumed the meeting was taking place in one of the classrooms in the back of the building with a closed door. And the entire community was waiting for word of the elders' decision.

The press of bodies was too much. I needed fresh air and time alone. I made my way through the crowd with my face downcast, hoping to avert any attention before I reached the back door. I slipped through it, closing it behind me with relief.

The sky was almost completely dark with only a hint of dull light on the western horizon. My eyes adjusted from the room that was lit with dozens of gas lamps to the growing inkiness of approaching night. Finding my favorite spot beneath the wide trunked maple tree, I sat down, leaning back onto its bumpy bark.

I closed my eyes and rested. I had made plans with Sadie and Charlotte to go out with them that night, but was doubting whether I could pull it off again so soon. The exhaustion I'd felt when I'd climbed out of bed at five o'clock in the morning to begin the laundry was returning. And then there was Avery's odd behavior the previous night to think about. For the very first time, he'd requested that I sit in the front seat. The girls had giggled and taken the backseat without argument, forcing me into the front seat with him. When he had leaned over and placed his arm against mine while he drove through town, I'd immediately tensed. As the city lights were replaced with the darkness of country roads, Avery's hand had become bolder, moving to my thigh. The weight of his hand still lingered there and I rubbed my thigh to erase it. When it had happened, I'd been at a loss for what to do.

I'd met Sadie at the schoolhouse dinner the previous autumn. She was there with her grandparents and without any shyness at all, she struck up a conversation with me. That one fateful meeting had led to many late night, secret get-togethers. In time, I was introduced to Charlotte and Avery. Avery had always been polite and respectful in the past, never showing any romantic interest toward me. But now, I worried what he might do at our next encounter.

The pricking sensation of a headache began to develop on the right side of my forehead. I pressed it with my fingers and sighed. And then there was Justin *and* Micah. Justin was easy to talk to, but didn't understand my people's ways much at all. Micah was very sweet, but his previous love for my dead sister was an obstacle in my mind, along with the issues of his family. They were both good looking and athletic. And they were dreamers, like me.

The quiet clearing of a throat nearby made me bolt forward and look to the side. I squinted into the shadows.

"Who's there?" I whispered. My heart was pounding madly.

"It's only me," Micah said as he stepped into the moonlight. "May I sit with you?"

For a second, I thought about saying no, but I just couldn't get the word out of my mouth. Feeling the blood pumping through my veins in both fear and exhilaration at being alone with Micah, while so close to the rest of the community, I said, "If you're willing to risk it."

Micah sat down close to me, but didn't dare a look in my direction. I watched the side of his face as he gazed at the stars. The only sounds were the croaking of a few early season frogs and the occasional car passing by on the road. It was nice to sit in silence with someone, not feeling the urgent need to fill the air with conversation. Somehow, it was just comfortable being around Micah. Maybe it was because he was filled with the same depression that was always with me.

"Do you think Sarah is up there among the stars?" Micah asked absently.

The question wasn't exactly unexpected, but it did raise the warning signs once again. I certainly didn't want to court a boy who was still in love with my sister. It didn't matter to me that she wasn't around anymore to compete with. I wanted to be the greatest love of a man's heart—not second best.

"Yes, she's up there. I think she keeps an eye on me. Sometimes, when I'm doing something I know she'd disapprove of, I feel her staring and shaking her head," I said.

"Hmm," Micah mused.

I remembered the time that I'd gazed out the window from the kitchen at Micah talking to Sarah while she hung the laundry. I had felt the irritating swell of hot jealousy at the sight of Sarah being shown so much attention from the handsome new boy in the community. At the time, I'd thought it was so unfair that everyone loved Sarah and no one seemed to like me at all. Now, I dragged around a heavy guilt that I'd ever begrudged my sister anything. She'd deserved to be treated special—because she was. She was the good girl and I was the bad one. It had always been that way.

And here, the boy who I held a secret crush for was sitting beside me in the dark. But instead of being thrilled, I felt sick to my stomach. What would Sarah think? Or maybe she *was* watching right now, shaking her head.

"Do you like being Amish?" Micah asked, facing me.

That question did take me by surprise and I had to pause for a moment to think before I answered.

"I'm not like Noah. He never broke the rules, but he questioned everything about our ways. He used to argue with father all the time about whether Mr. Denton, our driver, was going to heaven. Father seemed to think that he wasn't, at least not the same heaven that our people were going into. Noah disagreed. He said that Mr. Denton was a good Christian man, and although he was divorced and seldom went to church, his kind deeds would secure him a place with God." I chuckled. "And these arguments took place long before Noah ever met Rose. It's almost as if he was destined to walk another path from the beginning. But I'm not so sure. There are some things that I love about being Amish and other things I hate. I imagine that it's the same for the outsiders, too."

Micah seemed to be absorbing what I'd said. "What about you?" I asked.

"I guess my thoughts are similar to yours. I enjoy working on Da's building crew and farming the land. I have many friends here and besides the problems we've had with your family, our place in the community is peaceful. But there are times when I question things." Micah turned back to me and his voice grew in intensity. "Like this matter with the dress shop. I don't see why most of the men feel it's such a bad idea. Why shouldn't the women be able to go out and buy a dress occasionally when they need one? Why should we care at all?"

I smiled into the darkness. Micah was unique among the Amish. I guess it was something that I'd noticed a long time ago. He had a mind of his own.

"What are you smiling about?" Micah asked sharply. "Do you disagree?"

"No, I agree wholeheartedly. I'm just happy that you feel the way you do."

Micah's expression changed from chagrin to something else. My heart skipped a beat and I swallowed. When he leaned in, I didn't pull back. I just waited. Boys and men had flirted with me on outings with Sadie and Charlotte, but I'd never kissed any of them. And never had my stomach done somersaults at the anticipation of someone's lips on my own. I wondered if my body's reaction to Micah meant something important.

Just as Micah's lips were about to brush mine, and his pleasant scent of horses and leather filled my nose, a voice called out from the schoolhouse.

"A decision has been made. Abram is making the announcement in a few minutes!"

Micah grunted and pulled back. I laughed. There would be more time for kissing later. We couldn't miss this speech.

CHAPTER 11

Rose

I experienced the very unpleasant sensation of deja vu when I stared back at Bishop Abram Lambright, who was seated at a table at the front of the classroom. Amos Miller and Mervin Weaver were seated on either side of him, and James Hershberger was at the end of the table. In a chair in the corner was Martha Lambright.

James looked bored, fidgeting with his fingers and gazing off into space, but the other three men were alert and Amos seemed borderline agitated. Martha wore the same tight smile that she had earlier. My heart pounded as my gaze passed over the Amish authority.

Bishop Lambright sat in his usual upright, commanding pose. His white beard was long and his white eyebrows were bushy. He had a slender face that resembled Abraham Lincoln. He was a terrifying figure to look at, but I had learned from experience that he was a fair man most of the time.

Even though Summer sat on the other side of Suzanna, I felt her tapping foot vibrating the table where we sat. Miranda was on my other side and next to her was Ella. Without looking, I knew that Suzanna still glared at me, but I ignored her. She'd understand soon enough why Ella had been included in our business endeavor. Thankfully, both Miranda and Ella sat calmly, with no emotion showing on their faces, just as I expected from them. Miranda was extremely resilient to sudden change, and Ella had always had the capacity to put on a good show when needed.

The sky beyond the windows was dark, and I wondered how Sam was doing with Sarah Ann. Surely the baby had woken from her nap by now. Noah was probably home. Between the two of them, they should be able to care for her. I pushed aside the encroaching anxiousness and focused on the matter at hand.

Behind the elders was a chalk board and at each side of it, drawings from the students were crammed on the wall. My gaze flicked over the images of barns, horses, cows, silos, and buggies, reminding me once again where I was. Reasonableness didn't apply here.

"Who is speaking for your group?" the bishop asked in his no-nonsense way.

I glanced at Suzanna and with a thrust of her chin, she motioned for me to take the stage. I swallowed down the butterflies and rose from my chair. The bishop's brow raised in irritation that it was me about to speak. Mr. Weaver's face was blank, while Amos's was red with annoyance. I didn't glance either way to gage Martha or James's reaction.

"Hello, everyone." I nodded. "It's especially nice to see you, Bishop Lambright. It's been a while."

The bishop interrupted me. "We haven't got all day, Rose. Get on with it."

I felt satisfaction that the man had remembered my name, but irritated that I even cared, and that he was so rude.

I disregarded Summer's snort. "All right. I'll get to the point, then." I paused, sweeping my gaze over the elders and then continued, "You all know that Suzanna and Miranda would like to open up a dress and sewing supply shop where the Yoder bakery used to be. It's my understanding that there are questions about whether young women in the community should be starting up such a business venture, instead of . . . " here I faltered, " . . . having babies and doing housework."

Suzanna's soft groan sounded in my ears, but I continued, "I have a proposition that might be a compromise."

"We have no qualms about the girls selling sewing supplies. I even checked into the possibility of them working part-time at Mast's general store. I think that would solve the issue quite nicely," the bishop interrupted with a prodding tone.

Suzanna stood up beside me, her arm brushing mine, and said forcefully, "That's not our interest." Bishop Lambright's eyes widened and his mouth tightened. Suzanna must have feared his expression for she went on to say in a meeker tone, "We want to open a new business in the community. One that serves both the women of our church with competitive prices for their sewing supplies, and those who might not have the time to make their own dresses and other clothes for their families."

The bishop's hand came down hard on the table. "That is against the Ordnung. Our women are not allowed to purchase clothing, they must make it!"

"Excuse me, Bishop. But I don't believe it states that precisely in our Ordnung," Ella said in a friendly way.

I looked between Ella's face and her father's. Surprisingly, Mervin Weaver's face continued to show no emotion.

The bishop swiveled in his seat to face Mr. Weaver. "And you knew of this—that your daughter was in on these shenanigans?"

Mr. Weaver shrugged a little and said quietly, "I just learned of it a few minutes ago."

"Actually, the girl *is* correct," James chimed in, making me love him even more. "We made an allowance some ten years ago that our women could purchase their caps from Amish supply stores, instead of having to make them themselves. The wordage from that section was completely taken out."

"But the caps are different. They are more difficult to create without special material and tools," the bishop argued.

"I agree." Amos had finally found his voice. Now I knew on

which side he stood. "Our women have been happily sewing their frocks since our beginning. It's part of our culture that the young ones are taught the skill from their mothers. If they can go out and easily buy a dress, the ability will be lost . . . and so will a large part of our heritage."

"Not true," I countered. Taking a deep breath, I gathered my thoughts, only sparing a quick glance at my father-in-law. I spoke directly to Bishop Lambright. "Just today, I talked to a dozen different women, asking them if they would purchase a dress from the shop. The answer I got from all of them was that they would continue to sew most of their clothing at home, but would greatly appreciate the opportunity to be able to buy an occasional garment when their time was limited." Again, I let my gaze follow each of the elder's faces and even rest for a moment on Martha's. The woman was still smiling, but with an expression more of admiration than giddiness.

"Don't you agree that during the planting season and the harvest, and when women are having babies, it would be nice to allow them to have options?" I asked.

"And what is your purpose in all of this—and the other English girl's? Neither one of you can sew. What can you contribute and why do you even care?" the bishop said.

I glanced at Summer and saw the hurt on her face that the bishop still didn't remember her name. That angered me. But his statement about me not being able to sew is what sent me over the edge.

"For your information, I can sew quite nicely. I made my own dress while I lived with Ruth and James and I even mended his pants." I pointed at James.

James nodded. "That she did."

"I'd like to be involved with this business for many reasons. It would be nice to have a job that I can take Sarah Ann to. And, I worked at the veterinarian's office so I'm really good at bookkeeping. I have access to the internet for ordering, and I can drive the girls to pick up supplies to sell at the shop. I believe this business will be successful and I want to be a part of it." I nodded to Summer, urging her to say something.

"Well, I need a car . . . and I a job to pay for it." The bishop rolled his eyes. Summer swallowed when she saw his reaction, but continued anyway. "And I want to help my friends."

Bishop Lambright's expression became unreadable and Amos frowned. Mervin was still blank-faced and James was smiling.

"And what of you Ella—why are you here?" the bishop asked her impatiently.

Ella didn't hesitate. "Sewing is a passion of mine. Right now, I work part-time at the butcher shop, and honestly, I despise the job. This sounds like a wonderful opportunity for me."

The bishop leaned forward and stared at Ella for a moment, then he said, "You haven't always gotten along with these girls . . . do you really think you'll be able to work together?"

Ella took a measured breath and glanced down the line. I forced a smile to reassure her.

When Ella turned back to the bishop, she looked resolute. "Why yes. I hope that friendships will grow right along with the business."

We all faced Bishop Lambright again, waiting for his response.

There was a long moment of scary silence while the bishop thought. His face was still void of emotion, but I wasn't fooled. He was wrestling in his mind with the pros and cons, and his own prejudices on the matter.

It seemed like everyone in the room was holding their breath when the bishop finally spoke.

"You girls have made some interesting points, and I can see the allure of working together in the creation of a business. But I can't condone such a drastic change of our ways. Whether for good or bad, this is not a box I wish to open. My vote is against."

My heart fell into my stomach and I sat back down, sagging

in the chair. Suzanna had been right. We'd lost before we ever got started. But Suzanna remained standing and I glanced up questioningly at her. She continued to look straight ahead and my attention went back to the bishop.

He motioned with his hand at James. "What say you on the matter, old friend?"

The realization that the Amish had some sort of democracy system hit me like a breath of fresh air. With sudden energy, I rose beside Suzanna and followed her gaze to stare at James.

"I am an old man. And I've witnessed firsthand how our people have stayed true to our way of life, even as the rest of the world left us behind. But, I've also witnessed change in our community. Such as when we voted so long ago to accept chainsaws into our toolshed to keep the men from laboring long hours with handsaws. I also remember when we voted to allow our members to own Bobcats." James chuckled and wagged a finger at the bishop. "You remember how strongly some opposed us. And look at us now—every family has one. In order to survive, we must occasionally be open minded to a little bit of change. It hasn't destroyed us in the past, and I doubt that it will in the future. I say give the girls a chance to have their shop. They may decide that it's more trouble than it's worth. But let them make up their own minds."

A hint of a smile appeared on Suzanna's mouth and Miranda let out a breath. Ella was more reserved and Summer was beaming. I realized it wasn't celebration time yet, and turned my gaze to Amos.

"In most things we see eye to eye, James, but not this time. Some kinds of change are too drastic. And this is one of those. Regardless of what the women told Rose, I believe more and more of them will use the services of an outside seamstress. This will cost our families more money . . . and for what? A little more relaxation time for the women? Idle time breeds all kinds of mischief. We already know that to be the case with our young people." Amos's gaze landed squarely on me. I stared right back at him. "I vote nay as well."

A tried to remain hopeful, but Mervin was the last to go. The wildcard. I met Ella's gaze, searching for her own hope, but found nothing. Maybe I'd misjudged Ella's ability to get her father to do what she wanted.

"And that leaves you, Mervin. What is on you mind," the bishop asked.

Mervin Weaver had a quiet voice anyway, one that seldom rose above a hoarse whisper. I was expecting to strain to hear him, but was surprised when he immediately spoke up. "I think the girls have made a good argument. And I sympathize with my daughter about her work at the butcher shop. Just last month, one of the Mennonite girls cut her hand badly. She required twenty-six stitches. That is not the type of work I desire for my child. Ella is an excellent seamstress, and what she said about developing friendships is also correct. We can't forget that those of our people who leave for the outside are generally the ones who do not forge strong relationships within the community. If this dress shop keeps all these girls content, then they will stay. And I think we can all agree *that* is our biggest priority—to keep our children within our ways." Mervin glanced at Amos, but the redheaded man continued to stare straight ahead. "Our women enjoy their sewing. They would never give it up entirely. My vote is yes."

Everyone's gaze shifted back to the bishop.

"It appears that we have ourselves a tied vote." Bishop Lambright smoothed his beard and looked at Mr. Weaver, saying, "I'm surprised. I didn't think this would happen. I guess the old saying, to expect the unexpected, is appropriate." He exhaled loudly and faced us again. "I was prepared in any case, which is our blessing, since the last thing we need is for this matter to be brought before a vote of the entire congregation."

The layers of Amish politics was more complex than I ever dreamed. The idea that the community might have voted on whether or not we set up a dress shop would be absurd any-where else. But in this instance, I was just happy to know that there were situations when all the people had a say in how their lives were run.

The bishop continued, "In this case, Martha will be the deciding vote. She is not one of the elders, but she frequent-ly represents the women in matters pertaining to them." He flicked his hand at his wife for her to come forward, and she did. "What are your thoughts?" he asked his wife.

Martha stood between the two groups—one, the older men and the other, five young women. I held my breath, terri-fied that all my worries about Martha Lambright were correct. I even remembered when Ruth had warned me not to trust the Amish matriarch. I knew it my bones that Martha was about to throw us under the bus.

Her eyes briefly met mine, but I couldn't read anything in her businesslike manner. Ella rose from her seat and was fol-lowed by Miranda. Summer took an extra couple of seconds to get the gist, but then she stood with us as well. Somehow, the fact that we were showing a united front made me feel a little more confident.

"The best interests of our community are always in my thoughts, and as a woman myself, the women's concerns are even more so." Martha glanced between the two groups. "I've listened to everyone's passionate pleas, and agree with both the men and the girls on certain points. I'm not sure if there's a right or wrong answer here—only time will tell for sure. But I must say, that I'm pleased to see the way of grace among our young people and the burying of ill feelings. Mervin is right about that. Having strong ties between our children is important for our growth." Martha paused and looked at me, considering. She finally spoke again. "My main concern is that this a joint Amish—English project."

I couldn't stop myself from speaking up right then, fearing that we were about to lose our case.

"I'm sorry, but what about all the English drivers that your people hire on a daily basis? And then there are several building crews who have drivers that also work alongside them with the construction." Grasping at straws, I threw in, "And Katie used to clean English homes and babysit their children for extra income."

Martha smiled and the hairs rose on the back of my neck. The other girls were completely still.

"Very true, Rose. And our society could not survive without those interactions, and of course all of our English customers who buy baked goods, meat, and crops from us are essential to our well-being as well. But selling our wares to the English or building their houses is very different than entering into a business agreement with them," Martha said in a kind voice.

"But how so?" Summer asked, turning all of our heads. Her cheeks reddened and she shrugged innocently.

"For one thing, this type of business would require a lot of contact between the five of you. And I wonder if that much exposure would be detrimental to our girls?" Martha paused again. She took a deep breath and looked out the window. The room was quiet enough to hear a pin drop.

Miranda's dove-like voice broke the silence, surprising me even more than when Summer had spoken. Martha was jarred from her thoughts and she looked at the petite Amish girl in the plain navy-blue dress with much interest.

"Please, Mrs. Lambright, this is so important to us. We all need this dress shop for different reasons. Suzanna wants a goal in life to keep her busy, and Ella needs friendships and an opportunity to show off her sewing skills. Summer has to have a job where she feels safe and secure. Rose wants to be with Sarah Ann and still feel that she's being productive. And I . . . I need something to bring happiness into my life. And this dress shop will provide these things for all of us." Miranda then said a few sentences in her own language before she was finished.

Miranda's impassioned plea brought tears to my eyes and

I had to wipe them away with the back of my hand. I noticed Ella doing the same thing, and even James's eyes were moist. The bishop and Amos looked a little less annoyed, and Mervin blew his nose in his handkerchief.

But Martha's expression was more of curiosity than anything else while she studied Miranda. I was so proud that Miranda didn't flinch at the intense look directed her way. I reached over and took her hand into mine, squeezing it in solidarity.

Martha's brow raised at the action. Finally, she spoke. "My vote is—in favor—but under one condition."

Suzanna asked tentatively, "What is that?"

"That I'm a silent, non-profiting, partner for one year. After that time, if everything is going smoothly, by our standards and in a Godly manner, the business will be all yours," Martha said, a small grin erupting on her mouth that appeared to be genuine.

Summer high-fived Suzanna and Miranda hugged Ella.

I just smiled. We had won. Stitches—N—Stuff would be a reality.

Chapter 12

❧ Rachel ❧

When I stepped into the kitchen, I was surprised to see Father and Mother already seated at the table with mugs of coffee in their hands. I rubbed my eyes and glanced out the window. It was still dark. Usually, I was the first into the kitchen and the one to brew the coffee. I always had a few minutes of peace and quiet before the rest of the house began stirring. Not this morning, though.

My heart raced as I said, *"Gut mariye."*

Mother sighed and didn't say a thing. Father took a sip from his cup and scratched his beard. The strange silence made me worry all the more. I caught a glimpse of Peter stumbling into the room behind me.

Father spoke up loudly. "Back up to your room, son. You may have a few more minutes of rest this morning."

Peter looked at me with the confused face of a person who still wasn't quite awake.

"But why, Da? I thought we needed to be at the house site earlier this morning?"

"Plans have changed. Take advantage of a little more shut eye. Now off with you," Father grumbled.

Peter didn't stay to pester Father further. The thirteen year old turned and left the room in a hurry.

Father nodded at the chair across from him. "Have a seat."

I sat down without question. Father bowed his head in silent prayer, as did Mother. I joined them, but did no praying in my mind. I was too busy wondering what was going on. Had they somehow discovered that I'd been sneaking out of the house for months? No. If that were the case, Father would be screaming. And the night before, I'd been a good girl, too tired to meet up with Sadie, Charlotte, and Avery. I'd gone straight to bed when we'd arrived home from the schoolhouse. I thought harder. Perhaps, Father was upset that I didn't help unhitch Juniper and groom him off. It might have been my turn to do so, and I'd forgotten?

"After the meeting last night, I realized that it might not be a good idea for you to remain in the house during the day, helping your mother with her duties," Father said in a level voice.

My gaze swept to Mother. She shook her head sadly, but said nothing.

"I don't understand. What have I done that has angered you so?"

"No, child, I am not upset," Father hurriedly said. "I just want to nip this in the bud before it becomes a problem."

I waited, not breathing. My entire world seemed about to crash down around me.

"You are different than Sarah was. She had a milder spirit, more obedient and content with the simplicity of being here alone with Ma and her younger siblings all day long. You're more like Noah—I sense rebellion stirring in your heart."

"But, Father," I began, only to be cut off.

"Hear me out. I trust that you haven't crossed the line—yet. But I fear for you. I will not lose another child."

I realized that he wasn't only talking about Sarah's death. He was also referring to Noah. When Noah had gone English to be with Rose, he had been shunned, not only from the church, but also from our family. In a way, he was no longer Father's son.

"I've decided that you'll begin working at the Fischer's birdhouse factory next week. It's about time that you brought some income into the household, and it will keep you busier than you are here at the house." He must have recognized the look of distress on my face. I felt as if I was going to throw up. He quickly added, "It won't be so bad. You'll have the opportunity to make friends among the other girls who work there. You've always kept too much to yourself, drawing your pictures and taking walks alone. It isn't natural—and you might be corrupted if you don't begin fitting in with the other young women."

"But what about Mother? How will she take care of the laundry, cooking, and cleaning all by herself? We barely mange to get it all done each day as it is," I said, my voice gaining volume. I had to change his mind—I had to.

"Ma will be fine. School will be let out soon for the crop planting, and the little boys will be around to help out. And Naomi is five and old enough to begin learning how to do the laundry." Father turned to Mother. "Tell her, Rebecca, that it will be all right."

I looked at Mother, taking in her moist eyes and defeated manner. She wasn't supportive of Father's decision, but there was nothing she could do about it. Very rarely did Mother argue with Father.

Images of tiny Naomi struggling with a basket of wet clothes out the door to the clothes line and sweeping the kitchen floor invaded my mind. She was still a baby in my eyes, and way too young to begin the hard labor that Sarah and I had started doing when we were close to her same age. And then there was Mother. She was a frail woman, slender and fine boned. I feared it would be too much work for her with five children still living at home.

When Mother spoke, she sounded resolute, and my heart plummeted into my stomach. She would not help me or herself.

"Your Father is right. It's about time that you began interacting more with the other girls your age. Since you finished school in eighth grade, I don't recall you ever spending time with any of the girls in the community. If it hadn't been for

Sarah, you wouldn't even have talked to anyone—and now she's gone. I only want what's best for you."

"But it's not my way to be sociable, Momma, you know that. I enjoy my art and spending time alone. It's just the way I am." I tried to convince her, ignoring Father's red face and growing anger.

"If given the chance, you might discover that you're more sociable than you think," Mother said gently.

She reached across the table to pat my hand, but I snatched it away.

Forgetting the switch that Father might use on my backside if I pushed him too far, I said, "I'm not like Noah. I'm happy to stay here with Mother and help her with the house and the younger ones. It's silly for me to do otherwise."

Father let out a deep breath. "It is out of your hands. You must trust your parents to decide what's best for you. I'll talk to my friend, Merle Fischer, today. I'm sure he'll put you on the payroll." He pointed his finger at me. "And you will be friendly to the other girls and obedient and hardworking for Merle."

I stood up. "Or you'll do what, Father? Beat me?"

Father rose from his chair and looked down on me. His hair and beard were still disheveled from sleep and his face was set in stony wrath. I guessed that he had voted against the girls opening a dress shop, and since he couldn't punish them, he was taking it out on me. But it didn't matter. Looking up at him in all his quiet fury, I knew that I had no choice but to obey.

When my head had rested on the pillow the night before and my eyes had finally closed, I had come to the decision that I wouldn't sneak out of the house to gallivant around with Sadie and Charlotte any longer. Especially with the way Avery had behaved. I believed that it had been a sign that I was on the wrong path—that maybe Micah really was my destiny.

But in a blink of an eye, everything changed. Father could order me to work at the birdhouse factory, working with the machines and the gossipy, shallow girls by day, but he couldn't control my nights. I was too clever for him. And I almost didn't care if he did discover my deception. I would not be told what to do, by him or anyone else.

Just as the sky beyond the window brightened to a buttery yellow, I wiped a tear from my eyes and feigned contriteness.

"I'm so sorry, Father. I didn't mean to speak harshly." I sniffed and wiped my nose. "It's just that the idea of leaving the house frightened me, and I worry about Mother. But I'm all right now. I can be brave."

Father swept me up in a bear hug and for a moment I felt safe in his arms. He patted the long braid that fell down my back, not yet pulled up into a bun.

"It will be fine, daughter. You will see that it's for the best," he said brightly.

I pulled back and nodded up at him. "I'll begin the washing now."

"You may go then," he said.

As I took the first step of the staircase leading to the basement, I heard Father say to Mother, "Why must raising children be so difficult?"

I didn't hear Mother's response. It didn't matter. Because Father had no idea just how difficult it would become.

CHAPTER 13

······· Justin ·······

Rachel kept invading my thoughts. I was barely able to focus in any of my classes throughout the day, and now that I was home, sitting at the table in the kitchen, it was even worse. Rose was putting Sarah Ann down for a nap, and the house was too quiet, forcing my mind to wander all over the place. It had been a week since I'd last seen her. An entire week. I'd dated a few girls in the past—never anything serious, and none of those girls had taken a hold of my mind the way this wild Amish girl had. And we weren't even dating. And never would. It was completely implausible, even if Rachel was interested. Rose was right. What a disaster it would be to go down that road.

The problem was that no matter how my brain rationalized the information and pounded it into my head, I still couldn't get the girl out of my mind. What was she doing? Was she still hanging out with those slutty girls and that squirrelly twenty-something-year-old guy? Even though she was bent for sure, she'd exhibited more intelligence and depth than any of the girls I knew—except my sister and maybe Summer, but she was annoying as all get out.

I ran my hand through my hair. I was used to being in control of my life and I didn't like feeling this way.

I didn't notice when Sam walked through the doorway, and his voiced startled me.

"Hey man, do you have a headache or something?"

Glancing up at Sam's mildly concerned face, I inwardly thanked him for the plausible excuse.

"Yeah, I've had one all day," I said weakly.

"You need to drink more water . . . and get more sunshine. You're like a vampire, going from building to building," Sam said as he crossed the room and began rummaging through the refrigerator. "Rose needs to stock this thing better."

"Why don't you ever bring groceries home?" Rose snapped as she waltzed into the room. She pushed Sam aside and began pulling out the deli meat and cheese. "Make a sandwich."

"I'm kind of sick of sandwiches," Sam dared to say.

Rose's eyes narrowed. "You are such an oaf. Working part-time at a building supply store and taking a few classes at the community college, you have no right to be complaining about the food."

"Hey, Dad agreed that I shouldn't overdo my class schedule this semester. And he's the doctor." Sam smirked, but he began building one of his usual giant subs anyway.

"That's only because you didn't want to be separated from Summer and refused to go away to college as planned. Dad figures you can't handle a job and a full course schedule." Rose chuckled.

"He never said that," Sam insisted.

"Yes he did," I chimed in.

Sam shrugged. "I didn't stay around here because of Summer. I did it for you, Rose. I knew you'd need my help with the baby. I did the chivalrous thing."

Rose took the pain reliever jar off of the shelf and put two pills in my hand. Then she filled up a glass of water and gave that to me, too.

"Thanks," I said.

"You look like crap," Rose said, sitting down across from me. She tried to feel my forehead, but I flinched away. I wasn't going to be treated like I was her other infant. "I'm fine. It's just a headache."

Rose seemed satisfied with my answer and turned her attention back to Sam.

"You are such a jerk. Why won't you admit that you love Summer?" Rose said in a tired voice.

"Because I don't," he said.

"You don't know what love is," I said.

"And you do? Come on—you've never even had a girlfriend," Sam growled the words out.

"I've had several," I said smugly.

"Name 'em," Sam demanded.

Rose interrupted, "It doesn't matter, Sam. We're talking about you. If you don't get you're act together, you're going to lose that girl. And she's the best thing that ever happened to you."

"Why? Has Summer said something to you?" Sam was suddenly on high alert, his eyes wide with concern.

"No . . . but if I was her, I'd want a verbal declaration that you loved me."

"Luckily, she's not you. We're taking it a hell of a lot slower than you and Suspenders did." Sam grunted and then took a bite of his sandwich.

Listening to my siblings argue about inconsequential things had distracted me for a few moments. Only half listening to the drone of their conversation, I thought back to the night I'd run into Rachel at Dewey's. She'd looked like a normal girl in regular clothes. Rather hot, actually.

Hearing Rachel's name, my head snapped up. "What did you say?" I asked Rose.

Rose's eyebrows rose. "I don't trust you. There's something going on between you and that girl," she accused.

"The most I ever talked to her was last week. She's got issues. I'm just curious," I said as convincingly as I could.

I could tell by Rose's suspicious looking frown that she wasn't fooled, but she let it go.

"Suzanna told me yesterday that Rachel has started working at the birdhouse factory—and she hates it."

"I thought she stayed at home, helping her mother do the laundry and cleaning," I said nonchalantly.

"She did . . . but I think she's a casualty of the dress shop fallout." Rose frowned.

Sam bellowed, "It's insane if you ask me. A dress shop is a legit business. I still don't get the hoopla."

"Didn't Summer explain it to you? Basically, it's all about the men maintaining control over the women. Some of them didn't care, like James and even Mervin Weaver. But Amos opposed the idea from the get-go. I think he went home angry and took it out on Rachel. He wants to make sure that she's too busy to dream up criminal activities, like sewing dresses." Rose rolled her eyes and shook her head.

If Amos Miller only knew what his daughter was really into, I thought.

"What's the big deal with the birdhouse factory?" Sam asked.

I turned to Rose, wondering the same thing.

"Miranda worked there for a year. She said it was terrible. The girls only had a couple of fifteen minute breaks in an eight hour work day. And even though the money was good, Miranda had to give ninety percent of her income to her parents anyway. Then there were all the injuries—one girl nearly cut her thumb off on the equipment a while back."

"She wasn't allowed to keep her own money?" Sam asked, his eyes popping out.

Rose shook her head. "And neither will Rachel. It was the same with Noah. Until kids are about twenty and engaged, their parents take most of their income."

"That's not fair," I said angrily.

"No kidding. Since Suzanna and Miranda are almost married, they're able to keep their profit from the dress shop, but Ella will have to fork over a large portion of hers," Rose said.

"Why work at all then?" Sam asked, taking the seat beside me.

"They have no choice in the matter. They finish school at eighth grade and either stay at home, helping with the house and farm chores, or go into the work force. Most of the time, they're happy to get out. They do get to keep a small amount of earnings, which is better than nothing at all. And they see their friends."

"Rachel doesn't seem very sociable to me," I commented offhandedly.

"Bingo. That's why she's so pissed. She's a loner—enjoys drawing pictures and reading books." Rose's eyes narrowed once again as she looked at me. "That's why it isn't unimaginable that you might find her attractive. She's a lot like you."

"What?" Sam's voice rose even higher. "Are you kidding? Leave the kid alone. He's got more sense than that," Sam scoffed.

"Thank you, Sam," I said, smirking at Rose.

Rose stood up and pushed the chair in. "I don't have all day to chat with you dorks. I'm meeting the girls and Noah at the shop this afternoon. We're going to begin cleaning and building racks."

I noticed that Rose was more relaxed than she'd been in over a year. Her smile was wide and her eyes were bright. She was truly happy. I couldn't help smiling back at her.

"What?" she asked suspiciously.

"I'm glad you found something to focus on. It seems to be just what you needed," I said.

"Thanks—you're right. It's the best thing that's happened to me in a long time." Then she pointed at Sam, "And you better take my advice about Summer."

Stunning me, Sam nodded. "Maybe I'll take her out to dinner at Antoinette's tonight. Do you think she'd like that?"

An even bigger smile spread across Rose's face. "She'll be thrilled."

When I was finally alone again in the kitchen, my thoughts drifted back to Rachel, and I began to wonder about what the Amish girl would do if she was really upset with her circumstances. Rubbing my forehead, I didn't have to stretch my imagination. She was going to blow.

CHAPTER 14

Rose

Sighing, I wiped the damp hair off of my forehead and glanced at Sarah Ann in the playpen. Thankfully, she was still asleep. If I was lucky, I had twenty more minutes before she woke. The late afternoon sunlight shining through the windows clearly illuminated the drab section of the wooden floor I had missed. I wrung the mop out again and got back to work.

Miranda was still humming the same lullaby that had put Sarah Ann to sleep earlier, and I paused from my mopping to glance in her direction. She was standing on a footstool, attaching the curtain she'd made to the rod above the window. The pattern of the cloth had dainty yellow and white flowers on a light blue background. The curtains, combined with the dark hardwood floors, gave the place an appropriately cozy, country look. Listening to Miranda humming along reminded me of how much this dress shop meant to her. It was as if she was a different girl altogether—one who was finally filled with hope.

"You know, your speech is what saved the day," I commented.

Miranda stopped humming and looked over at me. "Do you really think so?"

It amazed me that she hadn't already realized the obvious. But then again, of all of my Amish friends, she was the least confident. The first time I'd met her, I had noticed that she wasn't only shy, she was very troubled. Later on, I discovered why. Her brother, Levi, had molested her when she was younger, leaving permanent psychological scars. Other than me, she was the only other person I knew of who was one of Levi's victims. One of the reasons he came after me was because I'd stuck up for Miranda when no one else would.

Looking at Miranda's frail form, large brown eyes, and pale skin, I understood why she wasn't able to stop Levi. But there was no excuse for her family. They should have protected their daughter. Instead, they shielded their son. The entire business made my blood boil.

I wondered if Miranda had nightmares about her brother. Did she fear his possible return someday the
way I did?

I glanced back at the doorway leading to the backroom and listened. I could hear Ella shuffling boxes around and organizing shelves. Summer had borrowed my truck to drive Suzanna into town to purchase bolts of cloth to begin working with and to sell, so it was only the three of us in the building at the moment.

Even though Ella had been a strong ally in getting the dress shop vote to go our way, and she'd proven herself to be a hard worker and an enthusiastic one as well, old habits die hard. I still didn't completely trust her, as much as I wanted to. We were on the road to true friendship, but it would take some time for me to count Ella on the same *friend* level that Summer, Suzanna, and Miranda were on.

I lowered my voice and asked Miranda, "Do you ever think about Levi?"

I really hated bringing his name up with her, knowing it might open old wounds, but he had been on my mind a lot lately. And my nightmares were getting worse. Just the night before, I dreamed that I awoke in the middle of the night to hear Sarah Ann crying. In the dream, I'd left Noah in bed and crossed the room, walking through the closet that adjoined our bedroom to the nursery. The moonlight was shining through the window, illuminating the room in an eerie, gray light. My heart had stopped beating when I'd seen Levi standing beside the crib. He held a knife in his hand and bright red liquid dripped from it. My baby wasn't crying anymore. Levi had smiled at me sickly and I'd awoken, screaming in my bed.

Noah had held me for some minutes, gently rubbing my back and whispering all kinds of calming words. When I could finally speak, I told him about the dream. He had looked worriedly at me and said that it was my mind playing tricks on me—that there was nothing to fear—that Levi was locked away in prison and wouldn't possibly be out until Sarah Ann was a teenager. After an hour of shivering in fright, I finally had fallen back asleep, my wet face still pressed against Noah's chest.

I got it. He was right, there wasn't anything to freak out about. I was just suffering from some kind of post-traumatic stress disorder. Sam had suggested that I talk to Tina, our future stepmother, who just happened to be a shrink, and Noah agreed that it might be a good idea, since I wasn't getting much sleep these days. But I wasn't ready for that talk just yet.

"Why do you ask?" Miranda's face visibly paled even more than her usual ashen complexion.

I shrugged and decided to be honest. "I've been having really awful nightmares about Levi lately, and Ella said that for a while there, she was receiving letters from him in prison." Our gazes met and I could tell that she was holding her breath. "Has he contacted your family at all?"

Miranda climbed down the ladder and crossed the floor. She picked up my hand that wasn't holding the mop and squeezed it. "No, Rose. He has made no contact with any us—and nor will he." She lowered her voice to a whisper. "Bishop Lambright visited Levi in the prison some months ago. He told him that not only was he shunned forever from our community, but that he was never allowed to enter any Amish settlement again."

The thought of the bishop sitting in a prison and talking to Levi sent a shiver over my skin. But the fact that he'd made the effort gave him major brownie points in my book. He must have thought that it was really important to hire a driver and travel so far to have the conversation in person. But the bishop just didn't get it. Levi didn't care about the rules or being officially welcomed back to Meadowview. He did whatever he wanted.

"I hope the bishop made a lasting impression on Levi" was all I could say.

Miranda nodded solemnly. I saw fear in her eyes, too.

Suzanna and Summer chose that moment to burst through the door. It jingled from the little bells that Ella had attached to it earlier.

"You'll never believe the sale price we got on this material!" Suzanna exclaimed. Her arms were full of large bags and Summer was dragging in a huge box.

Forgetting Levi for the moment, Miranda and I rushed over to help the girls with their bundles. Ella soon joined us at the counter where everything was piled high. Originally, the glass case below the countertop had been filled with all kinds of Amish made pastries. Now it would showcase handmade aprons and baby clothes. The transition from bakery to dress shop was proving smoother than I originally thought it would be.

Suzanna tore through the bags, making neat piles of the different kinds of material. Ella and Miranda oohed and ahhed over the colors, but I was more interested in the prices per yard. It turned out that Suzanna had been right. The prices were low enough that we would have a nice profit once the cloth was turned into dresses.

"You did well, Suzanna," I said.

Summer cleared her throat loudly and we all turned to her.

Suzanna laughed. "Summer helped with the negotiating. Without her, the deal wouldn't have been so sweet."

Summer beamed. "The lady at the supply store turned out

to be an old friend of Gram's. She said she'd be happy to work with us on prices and she can order just about anything we want."

"Good work," I said, knuckle bumping Summer.

Sarah Ann's cry got my attention and I went to the crib, which was placed strategically out of the way. The baby girl's face was already red with frustration at my slowness. I smiled. Dad said that I'd been the same way.

I picked her up and nuzzled her cheek. Her coo of happiness was the sweetest sound. "Is everyone being too noisy for your liking?" I mumbled against her neck.

"She is such a good baby," Ella said. She turned to Suzanna and added, "She slept nearly the entire time you were gone."

"She favors her English momma that way—loves her sleep." Suzanna grinned.

"Yes, I do. I won't deny it—which makes me wonder where Noah is. I thought he'd be here by now," I said as I pulled my cell phone from my pocket and checked the time.

"Matthew said that they had some errands to run after they left the site. They must have gotten a late start," Miranda said. She didn't seem to mind that her fiancé was late, more intent on neatly stacking the bolts of material.

The rumble of Noah's diesel work truck could be heard, and Summer ran to the window and looked out. "Speak of the devil."

Even now, after being with Noah for so long, I still experienced an explosion of butterflies in my stomach when I saw him after a long day of separation. He walked through the door with Matthew and Timothy in line behind him. The breath caught in my throat when his warm brown eyes met mine.

Noah came straight toward me and placed a light kiss on my lips. He then kissed the top of Sarah Ann's head. When he pulled back, I looked up at him questioningly.

"We have a surprise for you girls," Noah said with a huge smile.

"What is it?" Suzanna asked with wide eyes.

Noah looked over at Timothy and Matthew. "Why don't you bring it in."

Timothy grinned as broadly as Noah, and Matthew's face was flushed. My curiosity was on overdrive as they left the building. Glancing over at the girls, I saw impatience on their faces as well.

There was a knock on the door and Noah ran over and opened it. My eyes widened in hopeful understanding, but the large object was covered with a brown sheet.

Noah made a show of wiggling the sheet teasingly in front of us before he finally pulled it off with an extravagant *swoosh* of cloth.

I heard several of the girls draw in their breath and Summer shouted, "It's perfect!"

I couldn't say anything. Tears began rolling down my cheeks.

It was a sign that read, *Stitches—N—Stuff.* The words were written ornately in script on a white, wooden background. There were paintings of a needle and thread, a buggy, and a dress placed neatly around the words.

"We built it together—" Noah motioned to Timothy and Matthew "—but Justin painted the artwork on there." He shrugged. "Now that it's official, we wanted you to have a proper sign for the shop."

"It's beautiful . . . thank you." I sniffed, attempting to hold in the surge of emotion. Noah wrapped his arms around me and Sarah Ann.

From under his arm, I peeked at the other girls. Suzanna and Miranda were both hugging their men, and Ella and Summer had walked over to the sign to take a closer look. The two girls jabbered excitedly as their hands brushed over the wood.

I swallowed the giant lump in my throat, trying desperately to get my act back together. I was so happy at the way things had turned out for all of us. But even for the tears that wet my cheeks and the smile on my face, there was a shadow of worry that I couldn't quite erase.

I'd learned from experience that just when things were the best, something terrible always happened to ruin it.

CHAPTER 15

✎⟶ Rachel ⟵✎

I glanced longingly at the wall clock. Only fifteen minutes to go and I could finally leave.

"Hey, be careful with that!" Ingrid said, as she grabbed the piece of wood that I was about to push over the table saw.

"Why did you do that?" I demanded.

Ingrid reached for the on/off switch and cut off the motor. Ingrid's family powered all the cutting equipment off of generators, and thus were able to stay within the Ordung's rules to have their birdhouse factory. The tall girl was only a few years older than me, but her plain, serious face made her look like she was in her thirties. She acted like a matronly housewife as well.

Ingrid sighed heavily when she turned around. "How many times today have I told you to be careful with this particular saw—eh? Two, three times now?" She touched the side of the machine. "The metal guard is missing here. If you are not careful, your hand could easily slip over the blade with the wood. There is nothing to stop it from happening—except for you."

"I *was* being careful," I grumbled, not able to keep from frowning.

"Ach, you were daydreaming, staring at that silly clock," Ingrid pointed at the wall. Then she stepped in closer. "This is not the place for idle thoughts. You must pay attention at all times."

I stared at Ingrid and thought of several cuss words I wanted to say to her. And after I'd told her off, I would pull the smock off and throw it down. Then I'd walk out the door. Of course, this was only the scenario that played out in my mind. But the image was very vivid, and for an instant, I thought I'd actually do it. My mouth opened and the words were about to fly out when the bell rang, announcing quitting time.

Snapping my mouth shut, I swallowed the resentment down. Ingrid still waited my acknowledgment of her lecture.

"I'm sorry. I'll be more vigilant next time," I said in feigned meekness.

Someday, I'll tell Ingrid what I really thought, but not today.

"All right then. You better be off with the other girls or you'll miss your ride." Ingrid left me without a goodbye.

I unbuttoned the smock and laid it on the work table. I passed by a table full of finished feeders that were colorfully painted with flowers and birds. I glanced longingly at them, wishing that Ingrid's father had put me in the much coveted artistic department. When I had asked about it, Mr. Fischer laughed at me and said something about paying my dues first.

It was absurd, really. I could paint better than any of the other girls, but that didn't matter to anyone here. I would begin on the cutting line and then progress to the building tables. I groaned inwardly as I picked up my lunch box from the shelf and snatched my jacket off the peg beside the door. The sky was cloudy and the air heavy with threatening rain. Tonya's minivan was already starting to pull away when I stepped out.

"Wait!" I cried.

I ran down the driveway and reached the van just as the first few raindrops struck.

The door slid open and the other girls squeezed in further to make room.

Tonya said, "I don't have time to wait for you. You better get your butt in gear next time."

Without any thought, I replied, "It's your job to wait."

Tonya swiveled around in the driver seat to stare back at me with pure venom. She looked a lot like her daughter, Summer, with bright red hair and green eyes, but that's where the similarities ended. Tonya was a bitch.

Tonya's expression changed to a sly smirk and I became nervous.

"Just wait until your father hears how you sassed me. I'm betting he'll be pretty upset with you." Tonya was satisfied with the impact of her statement and turned around.

The van lurched forward. I ignored the other girls' sideways glances in my direction and looked out the rain streaked window. The world was quickly turning misty and glistening wet. It matched my mood perfectly.

I walked through the quiet kitchen, glancing around. The smell of roasting meat wafted on the air and the water was bubbling over from the pot on the stovetop. I rushed over and turned the gas burner off. I poked the potatoes with a knife and discovered they were very much over-cooked.

"Ma?" I called out

"Down here," she replied from the basement.

When I reached the bottom step, I saw that Mother had only just begun the washing. She was standing in the middle of four large laundry baskets that were overflowing with dirty clothes. Her hands were immersed in sudsy water and she was vigorously scrubbing the garment. She didn't even look up when I joined her.

"You haven't done the laundry yet?" I stated the obvious.

"No, no. What a day it's been. That old cow got mastitis and I had to bottle feed her calf this morning. It put me behind with the cleaning and mending. Reckon, I'll be its nurse maid for the next few months." She dropped Father's pants into the tub with the rinse water and picked up another pair to wash.

I rolled up my sleeves and began sloshing the pants around to rinse them.

"You don't need to do that, dear. You've been working at your job all day—I don't expect you to help with this. By the way, how was it?"

"But it's almost four o'clock and you have four loads to wash, rinse, wring, and hang. You'll never get it all done before Father returns home," I said as I squeezed as much water from the pants as I could with my bare hands before I put them through the crank wringer.

"That is so." She paused to look at me with a small smile. "Maybe I do need your help."

"There's no way you'll be able to take care of the house, washing, cooking, and animals without my help. Having me work at the birdfeeder factory is ridiculous," I complained.

Mother grasped my arm with her wet, sudsy hand. "You must be respectful, Rachel. Your father means well. He only wants what is best for you."

"And this is best for me—and you?"

"Sometimes we don't always see the reasons why at first, but later on, they become obvious. I'll mange all right. I did it before you girls were old enough to help me. I just need to manage my time better," she said in light voice.

I marveled at her optimism.

"Now, tell me how work went. Were the other girls nice to you?"

"They were nice enough. Father will be sorely disappointed that I didn't get any time to socialize, though. I worked on the cutting machines all day. I've been strictly instructed that it's dangerous to be chatty." I finished pulling the pants through the wringer and dropped them into the basket, then began rinsing another pair.

"Oh my, I had hoped they wouldn't put you on those

things. You're much better suited to the painting. Did you tell Merle about your artistic talents?"

"Yes, Mother. But he didn't listen. You have to work through the entire system before you're allowed to paint the stupid boxes."

Mother sighed. "I'm sorry. I was hoping it wouldn't be so bad. Have faith and say your prayers. It will all work out. The Lord will take care of you."

Mother was soft spoken, kind, and obedient. I'd only remembered her raising her voice on a few occasions, and that was when one of the little boys was in danger of being injured by their reckless behavior with horses or on the trampoline. She meant well, but her words still angered me. I felt abandoned by everyone, including God.

I only half listened to Mother as we worked side by side to get the laundry hung before Mr. Denton brought Father and Peter home from the worksite. My mind was revisiting my day at the factory and my altercation with Tonya. I thought about Micah's kind words and his warm breath on my face, and Justin's easy laugh and penetrating gaze. I also remembered Avery and his unexpected advances.

But most of all, I planned my next getaway. I was ready for another night out with my English friends. After the day I'd had, I definitely deserved it.

CHAPTER 16

······ Justin ······

I hated smelling Gavin's cigarette smoke. The only reason I'd swung by his place earlier to invite him along was because I wasn't sure if I'd be able to get into Dewey's by myself. He was my insurance.

We drove beneath the street lamps, listening to the radio and not saying too much. Gavin wasn't like Mason who never shut up. Gavin was awkwardly quiet. But it didn't matter. He had his purpose. I could put up with the smoke and dead-air silence for the chance to speak to Rachel.

I had little doubt that she was at the bar. It was just a gut feeling, but it was a strong one.

I certainly didn't know her very well, but it felt as if I did. Rose was right—Rachel was a lot like me. And it wasn't just the books and her artistic abilities. She was a loner. She was using the bar as an escape from her workload at home, not because it was her thing. And I knew what it was like to lose a family member. It totally sucked.

After I cut the engine, I followed Gavin up to the door. The rain had finally stopped, but the pavement and the Bradford Pear trees lining the city street were still dripping. The humidity all around created a pleasant "welcome to spring" smell in the air.

I didn't have long to savor the sudden change of season. The muscled, bald bouncer, who I'd seen the week before breaking up the fight, opened the door for us. The man's broad arms were heavily tattooed and his square face was covered with thick stubble. He was a frightening-looking dude, even though he smiled at us in a friendly way. He even said a few words in passing to Gavin.

Once through the door, I commented, "It must be nice to know the right people.

Gavin smiled slyly. "Sure is."

I took a seat beside Gavin at the bar and absently listened to him order a beer from a female bartender. I vaguely wondered where Dewey was while I requested a cola, ignoring the exaggerated roll of Gavin's eyes. He hadn't outwardly mocked me the night before, just commented at one point as I drove Mason's car home that it was nice to have a chauffeur on binge nights.

Gavin wasn't a bad kid. His grades were all right and he played soccer. He was about my height and baby-faced, with blond hair and blue eyes. His main problem was that he always went with the crowd. No independent spirit lurking around inside of him. And the fact that his uncle owned a bar had made him a delinquent.

I searched the room twice, and was disappointed to discover that Rachel wasn't even there. I was sullenly sipping my drink, thinking about how I'd traded a relaxing evening at home with my video game system to be sitting inside a smoky bar, filled with questionable people, when I spotted her.

Rachel, and the two girls I barely knew from school, came out of the narrow hallway that led to the restrooms. My eyes took in all three girls as they crossed the room and sat in a booth that was occupied by the squirrely-looking guy, Avery, and another dude I didn't recognize.

Once again, Rachel was the best dressed of the girls, wearing a cream colored dress that just reached the top of her knees. The high heels she had on sparkled, and one side of her long hair was draped down over the side of her face. Compared to the other girls, one wearing an extra short red miniskirt and the other a pair of torn jeans, she looked as if she was a fashion model. I could only imagine how much she enjoyed dressing up after wearing a frumpy Amish dress all day long.

Gavin also caught sight of the girls. He picked up his beer. "I'm going to hang with them for a while."

The fact that he didn't ask me to join him didn't bother me in the least. I'd rather sit alone in silence—or talk to Rachel. But since she was surrounded by losers, I didn't feel like approaching her at the moment.

I stared at the glass shelves across the bar from me. They were filled with bottles of every imaginable type of liquor. The mirror behind them shined from the recessed lighting aimed straight at them. The tune that was playing on the jukebox was an old eighties hit, and I started to think that the bar probably hadn't changed much in the past thirty years.

"A penny for your thoughts."

I looked up and there was Rachel, standing beside me. She motioned at the stool that Gavin had left and I nodded. I was a little surprised that she'd come over to talk to me, but I tried hard not to show it.

"So, how are you tonight, Jewel?" I asked grinning.

Rachel laughed lightly and then sighed. "I'm much better now. It's been a rough day." She pushed her hair behind her ear and eyed me seriously. "I didn't think I'd see you here again."

"Hah, fooled you." I held up my glass of cola. "I'm a real party animal, beneath this sophisticated exterior." Since I was wearing dark denim jeans and a T-shirt, it was clearly a joke.

Rachel ignored what I said and leaned in. She touched my hand and pulled my drink to her face. I watched with wide eyes as she sniffed it.

When she leaned back, she was smiling. "That's only cola."

"Duh, I'm only sixteen, like you. And I'm fond of that whole law-abiding-citizen thing." After I spoke, the lady behind the bar asked Rachel what she was drinking, and Rachel ordered a Long Island Iced Tea.

"I thought you'd learned your lesson the other night about those," I said frowning.

Her smile deepened. "It proved to be just the kind of drink I wanted."

Rachel was in need of a serious intervention. I wasn't even sure that I was up to the challenge. Between the Amish thing, a new job, and the dead sister going on, there were almost too many issues to address. I didn't even know where to begin.

I ended up just shrugging. "Well, I guess if you enjoy being mentally and physically diminished, that's the drink for you."

I almost laughed at the sudden change of expression on her face. It went from smirking to quite offended in a heartbeat. I guess I'd chosen the right thing to say.

There was heated silence between us for a long moment, before Rachel finally cracked and said, "I started working at the birdhouse factory today. Do you know of it?"

"Only in name," I answered truthfully.

"I work there from seven in the morning until three in the afternoon, with only two fifteen minute breaks," she said matter-of-factly.

"That's probably illegal for someone your age," I offered.

"I don't know about that. The length of the work day isn't what bothers me." She took a quick breath and hurried on, "It's the standing in the same place, all day long, cutting blocks of wood that makes it so unbearable." She met my gaze. "The boredom is torturous."

I felt her pain and was filled with my own indignation. "Are you using machine saws?" She nodded. "That's definitely illegal."

"It doesn't matter about your laws. We follow our Ordnung and it's perfectly all right for young people like me to work with cutting devices. I guess I'm blessed that I'm not employed by the butcher shop." Rachel took a mouthful of her drink with a gulp.

I sighed. Her life really was screwed up.

"Is there anything you can do to get out of it?"

"No." She paused, thinking, and then looked at me. "Father was furious over your sister and the other girls winning the vote to have their dress shop. He's taking it out on me."

"That doesn't make any sense." I thought about Mr. Miller and the times I'd been around him. He didn't seem diabolically evil to me.

Rachel shrugged. "I guess he's afraid if I have too much time on my hands, I'll get into trouble." She glanced at me with a slight smirk and a raised eyebrow. I smiled back.

"Maybe he should have forced the job on you earlier," I teased.

Rachel swatted me with her hand and then took another swig of her drink. After she swallowed, she asked, "What about you . . . do you have a job?"

Rachel's face was flushed and she made a popping sound when she said *job*. She'd already drank too much, even though she was only a few sips into it.

"Nope, at the moment, I'm career school," I said.

"What about when you graduate? Are you going to college?" Rachel propped up her head with her hand and stared at me intensely.

I wasn't sure if she was that interested in my life or was too drunk to stop herself.

"Of course. I'm going to be a video game designer. I already have my school picked out."

Rachel frowned. "Are you going far away?

"It's in California." Her face dropped even more and I hurriedly said, "But that's not for another year."

"I'll be sad when you leave," Rachel said. She took another, more thoughtful sip of her drink.

"Really—why?"

"Because you're my friend. And I don't have many of those." She stared straight ahead.

"What about them?" I thumbed toward the group in the

booth. The two girls were laughing loudly, and I realized that they were also toasted.

Rachel smiled sadly. "They aren't my friends—just entertainment."

The strong emotion of desperation flowed through me and I leaned in, speaking with conviction. "Rachel, you're way too good for people like that and places like this. There are other ways for you to vent." I paused to think. "Like going to the movies or roller skating or something."

Rachel sat up straighter, her eyes full of sudden hopefulness. "Would you do those things with me?"

I wondered what I'd gotten myself into. Rachel definitely intrigued me—but the entire Amish thing was terrifying. I'd seen what Rose went through, and it was even worse for Noah. It would have been a lot easier if they'd both hooked up with people from their own cultures.

Pushing the selfish part of me aside, the one that wanted to explore a relationship with Rachel—and really wanted to kiss her—I had to consider what was best for her. I wanted to do the right thing, if such a thing existed in a situation like this.

Ignoring her question, I asked, "What about Micah? He's into you. Have you thought about hanging out with him?"

Her reaction startled me. With a raised voice that I feared would draw attention from the other patrons, she said, "That's a problem where I come from—we can't just hang out and explore the possibilities! First we have to join our church, making a lifelong commitment to our faith and way of life, and then we'll only get a little bit of unchaperoned time each week to be together. There won't be any movies or skating for us!"

I shrank from her wrath at the same moment that Avery and his companion, who was about the same age and build as him, only scruffier looking, arrived by our bar stools.

"Jewel . . . is this dumb shit bothering you?" Avery asked, his voice dripping heavily with feigned concern.

I stood up. "Hey, who are you calling dumb shit? Your

IQ can't be much higher than a soccer game score added together."

Avery puffed out his chest and bumped into me with it. The rooster behavior was a little startling, but I held my ground. For a moment, as the song changed to a real headbanger one and the dim, smoky interior of the bar was in my periphery, I imagined myself in one of those hardcore cable TV shows. The kind where all the characters always acted irrationally.

The bald bouncer appeared out of nowhere. "Take it outside, boys," he ordered.

I was about to argue the sense of doing such a thing, when the large man recognized my desire to question his authority. His brow raised at the same time he grabbed up the loose material of my T-shirt at the shoulder.

"Don't touch me," I exclaimed.

"Leave him be. He didn't do anything wrong." It was Rachel. The sentiment was nice, but since I was still being shoved toward the door, I wasn't very hopeful that her protest would make any difference at all.

And where was Gavin? I managed to swivel my head around just enough to see him wide-eyed and useless by the other girls. I did catch Rachel's panicked face, and I was suddenly as worried for her as I was for myself.

"Don't come back," the bouncer told me, pointing a finger in my face when we crossed the threshold.

"Like I'll be missing anything," I shouted at his backside. The door closed in my face and I was alone on the sidewalk.

That was interesting, I thought, as I walked to my car. By the time I was seated and had the key in the ignition, I was feeling stubborn. Rachel was already intoxicated. What might happen to her if I left her here in that condition? And with those people? Maybe something horrible that I'd read about in the newspaper the following morning. Then I'd have to live with the guilt for the rest of my life—and I'd never get the chance to kiss her, either.

I dropped the keys onto the console and waited. Call me crazy, but I wasn't about to let that jerk intimidate me.

I only had to wait about fifteen minutes before Avery, his friend, the two girls, and Rachel exited the bar. I watched Rachel lagging behind the group, hugging her stomach. Her head was down. I took a steadying breath and gripped the door handle. Before I could talk myself out of it, I swung the door open and jumped out.

"Hey, Rachel. Do you want a ride home?" I called out across the small parking lot on the side of the building.

Her head popped up and her face instantly brightened. "That would be swell—" she began, but got immediately cut off by Avery.

"She's riding with us," Avery told me in no uncertain terms.

"But I want to go with Justin. He lives right next door to me," Rachel argued.

"Quiet! You arrived with us and you'll be leaving with us," Avery said. He took a few steps back to Rachel and grabbed her arm.

Rachel tried to pull away and one of the girls said, "Rachel, stop it! You're acting like a bitch."

Before I even realized I'd moved, I found myself a foot or so away from Avery and Rachel. "Let her go," I said threateningly.

Avery stopped struggling with Rachel. He pushed her toward the other two girls, who caught hold of her from both sides. Avery's companion walked up behind me, straight into my personal space.

"I don't think this newbie understands the way things work around here." He took a step closer and I could smell the alcohol on his breath. I wondered if he'd gotten the tattoo of a spider below his left ear in prison.

Taking me completely by surprise, Avery shoved me—hard. I stumbled back into the other man's hands. His fists closed around each of my arms, and even though I fought against the restraint, I couldn't pull free.

"Hold 'em, Jasper," Avery ordered.

"Oh, I got him," Jasper said, squeezing even tighter.

"Stop it!" Rachel yelled. But when she tried to escape her captors, the strength of the two girls combined proved too much for her.

I saw it in Avery's eyes and knew that the fist was coming before it even hit my face. I braced for impact, but that didn't help much. The pain that shot through the side of my face was worse than anything I'd ever experienced before. I immediately tasted the blood running from my nose into my mouth.

I thought that would be it—a lesson of sorts by a demented redneck. But they weren't even close to being finished with me.

Five more punches followed, two to my face and three in my gut. My right eye was swelling shut and my entire face was puffy. Blood ran freely down my chin and my stomach felt like jelly. If it weren't for Jasper holding me up, I probably would have fallen down already.

Rachel was sobbing in between the profanities she yelled at Avery and the two girls. It seemed as if it took ten minutes for me to receive the beating, but in actuality, it went down in only about one minute. The street in front of the bar was quiet. I could vaguely hear the traffic on the busier, parallel road, and I could see the brighter lights of the center of town shining in the distance.

I tried to swallow, but it hurt too much, and when I did, some of the blood from my nose got into my throat, making me gag. It tasted awful. And every part of my body was stinging. Jasper finally let go, without orders from Avery, at least not that I heard. I stumbled and my knees hit the ground. I reached forward and braced my hands on the damp pavement to keep me from completely going down. For a moment, my head swam with dizziness. I took a shuddering breath to stop the spinning. My head rested against the pavement. I didn't know how it got there.

The voices around me were muffled, distant sounding. And

then they were gone. I heard the engine start up. A moment later, a vehicle swerved frighteningly close to my skull as it peeled out of the parking lot.

I laid there in the parking lot for a while, grateful to feel the warm breeze on my sore skin. My head cleared and my vision gradually sharpened. I reached into my pocket and pulled out my cell phone. With numb fingers I began touching the screen, but nothing happened. Then I felt the crack and looked harder at it. When I'd hit the ground, I'd landed on the phone, breaking it. It was an irritating loss, but what really had me barely breathing was that Rachel was gone.

I tried to rationalize as I stood up shakily, that she'd been hanging with the group for a while and she'd come to no harm. But deep down, I knew better. Avery had taken his time to pull her into his trap. And now that the shit had hit the fan, he'd shown his true colors. His inhibitions were stripped away. Rachel could be in great danger. But if I went to the cops and she was okay, she would get into so much trouble by her dad and her entire community. She'd hate me for sure.

"Hey, are you all right?" I glanced over to see a tall, slender man with a goatee reaching out to steady me when I stumbled again.

Too bad the man didn't show up when I was being attacked. "I'm okay." Seeing that he wasn't convinced, I said, "No, really, I'm fine."

"You need a ride? I'd be happy to drop you off at the hospital."

The thought of trying to explain everything to Dad and the authorities, without ultimately getting Rachel in trouble, gave me an even worse headache.

"Seriously, man. I can drive myself." I pulled myself together and walked as normally as possible to my car. When I got in, the man was still watching me. I waved at him, smiling. The cut on my lip began bleeding again with the action.

Sniffing in the pain in my ribcage, I started the engine and lightly touched the gas pedal. As carefully as I could, I pulled onto the roadway. Glancing back, I saw the man getting into his pickup truck. I said a silent thank you to the universe.

I was still conflicted about whether I should go straight to the authorities, but I did have a plan.

And that was to tell Sam.

CHAPTER 17

ᘇᕈᗈ Rachel ᕉᖶᕉ

The scenery flashed by in a blur. All I could see was the image of Justin lying crumpled on the ground. His face was bloody and swollen and his one eye was already bruised. I sniffed at the sight, wiping away the tear that fell from my eye.

"Don't go getting all Mother Teresa on us, Jewel. That boy deserved it," Avery said. He reached over and patted my leg. I recoiled from his touch, sliding further away and pressing against the door.

"I want to go home," I said flatly.

"Don't be a party pooper. We're going to hang out at the bridge for a little while—right, Avery?" Sadie said.

"Of course, darling." He reached down and pulled up a bottle of bourbon whisky from between his legs and added, "Just look what I have for the occasion."

Sadie and Charlotte whooped in the backseat and Jasper said, "Nice."

I just turned away and continued staring out the window. I felt sick inside, and my head throbbed. The two mixed drinks I'd had at the bar were still affecting me. Every few seconds, I'd close my eyes and try to clear my head.

I was ashamed of where I was and what I was doing. Poor Justin had been beaten because of me. He'd stood up to Avery for my benefit—and I couldn't do anything to help him. For all I knew, he was still lying there in the parking lot.

Seeming to read my mind, Charlotte said, "He's probably fine, Jewel. It wasn't that bad. I've seen fights at school that were way worse."

"Then I'm glad I don't go to your school," I muttered.

"Aw, come on. I didn't hit him that hard," Avery coaxed. "And besides, I was just protecting you."

"Protecting me?" I faced Avery with narrowed eyes.

"Yes, ma'am. The last thing you need is that kid running back to your parents and telling them that you've been sneaking out, partying for months."

"Justin would never do that, and you had no good reason to hit him like that," I spat.

"He would have given you away for sure," Avery said with surety.

"You beating him up is worse." I exhaled loudly. "What do you think is going to happen when he shows up at his house beaten to a pulp? I can tell you. His sister and his brother will force him to tell them what happened and that's when my cover is blown."

Avery laughed. "Don't worry about that. He'll be too afraid to tell anyone the truth."

We'll see about that, I thought to myself.

It was difficult to listen to Sadie and Charlotte chirping happily away after what had just happened. I'd accepted that they were party girls, and even enjoyed that side of their personalities. But for them to watch cold-heartedly as someone was attacked, and show no sympathy at all, was incorrigible. They obviously had no conscious at all. I rubbed my head tiredly. Why was I hanging out with these people?

Then I remembered my long day at the birdhouse factory, followed by another hour helping Mother with the wash when I got home. I was nearly an adult and I had absolutely no say about how I lived my life. That's why I resorted to picking such bad friends. And they got me booze—the one thing that made me forget about Sarah.

I'd had another dream about her the night before. This time, when Noah and Elijah Schwartz lifted the metal, only Naomi was there. She was crying and Noah picked her up. I looked around for Sarah, calling her name. The dream changed and I was back in our old bedroom that Sarah and I shared. The wind was howling and the walls were shaking. The window exploded into a million shards of glass and I covered my eyes. And then I heard her voice. It was as soft as the cooing of a dove, and I strained to listen.

"I don't want to die . . . I want to marry Micah and have children . . . I don't want to die . . . "

I dared to open my eyes. Her face was rotted and torn. Blood oozed from the cuts.

"Please don't let me die, Rachel."

I'd woken in my bed, soaked with sweat and unable to breathe properly for several minutes. My heart had pounded so hard in my chest that I thought it would burst out of my ribcage. Even now, my heart began racing just thinking about it.

That's what happened when I slept without alcohol to numb my senses.

Avery turned onto the narrow, gravel road that led to the old stone bridge. Forest encroached on both sides of the roadway here, and moonlight shone through the newly leafed out branches eerily. I shivered, both hating and loving the place.

After a few moments, we finally reached the bridge. Instead of driving over it, Avery turned onto an even narrower dirt road that wound its way through the brush until it bowed back under the bridge. It was only a dry creek bed now. On another occasion, Sadie told me that when the dam was built some years earlier, the creek had been emptied and sealed off. Since the new highway had gone in, the old road wasn't used any longer, and the entire area was overgrown with bushes and vines.

I gazed at the stone structure as Avery parked, shutting off the engine. This was the place we usually hung out. Beneath

the curved archways was a fire pit, surrounded by several wood-
en stumps and a large, long log that served as a bench. At this
hour, the moon was almost directly overhead, but its rays still
glowed through the ornate openings in the stonework.

I didn't argue anymore with Avery. When he got out of
the car, I simply followed him. Sadie, Charlotte, and Jasper
were ahead of us and their ruckus shouts echoed through the
quiet of the night. I dragged behind, thinking about Justin.
What would he do? I couldn't imagine that he could hide what
happened to him from his family. Surely he'd have a serious
black eye and bruising on his face in the morning. I felt guilty
for worrying about my own butt. I couldn't help it. If Father
found out what I'd been doing, there was no telling how he'd
react. I would obviously be punished severely and temporarily shunned from the family and community, but there were
even worse things that could happen. Father might insist that I
live in one of those special boarding homes for troubled Amish
teens. I'd heard stories about how horrible they were. And there
was absolutely no chance of escape. The places were completely
locked down, like prisons.

I remembered that Levi had been sent away to one of those
homes after he'd tried to force himself on Rose. He had managed to escape. It was whispered that he'd hit the attendant on
the head with a two by four, rendering him unconscious.

The others walked beneath the bridge, but I paused for a
moment to look up at it. Each time I came here, I was just as
fascinated as the first time I'd seen the bridge. The stonework
was exquisite. My gaze followed the curve of the bridge that
was made by the purposeful laying of differing sizes of stone.
Someone had labored long and hard to create such a structure.
And now, here it was, alone and forgotten in the woods—with
only the local teenagers for company.

"Come on," Sadie shouted to me.

Reluctantly, I entered the cool, damp air under the bridge.
I was sure that during the summertime there were all kinds of

snakes, insects, and rodents taking refuge in this place, but for now, it was still vacant of any noticeable critters.

Jasper was lighting some dry kindling and Charlotte and Sadie were already seated on the log. I took the nearest stump and sat down. I still felt a little dizzy and was grateful for the seat.

"Here you go, Jewel. You first," Avery said.

I looked up at his face, wondering how I had ever thought he was even mildly attractive. Now, I only saw the evil leer that he wore when he was punching Justin. I blinked, trying to erase the vision. I took the bottle from his hand, and since Avery had already removed the cap, I brought it to my lips. The liquid smelled sharp and my eyes immediately watered at the fumes. I knew it was potent stuff and I was happy for it. Taking a swig, I swallowed. I couldn't help making a face as the amber colored liquid burned its way down my throat.

I coughed, but took another drink. This time it didn't hurt quite so much.

"Hey, don't drink it all," Sadie protested.

"There's enough for everyone, darling," Avery said.

His voice sounded far away even though he stood right beside me. The alcohol was working quickly.

I took one more sip as Avery smiled at me. Then I handed the bottle to Sadie. I didn't bother to watch her and Charlotte drink. I stared at the newly born flames wicking into the air, the warmth from the fire puffing up around me.

The heat on my skin made me think about Micah. He was probably sound asleep in his bed. I blushed at the thought, hoping if anyone noticed, they'd think the redness of my cheeks was from the fire. I'd come closer to kissing Micah than I had any other boy. If we hadn't been interrupted, I'm sure we *would* have kissed. Then what? Would he have actually asked me to court him—even though our families hated each other? The thought of doing something that would make Father so angry, and yet he really couldn't punish me for it, was very appealing indeed. But did I really have any feelings for Micah, besides a forgotten crush?

I couldn't answer that question. It felt very nice to be with Micah, calm and soothing. He understood me and he was one of my people. It would be easy being with Micah on many levels. But then there was Justin, poor, chivalrous Justin. He'd proven his worthiness tonight, but as much as I enjoyed sneaking off into the English world, was I ready to officially become one of them? I didn't know the answer yet. There were times, especially when the girls took me to the mall and we shopped for clothes and then ate lunch at the food court, that I was certain the English world was the place for me. Then on nights like this, when I witnessed brutality that I'd never encountered within the Amish community, I became appalled at the thought of being one of them.

For Noah, it was different. He never wanted to be English, never longed to wear nice clothes, drive a car or stay out all night with friends. He was Amish through and through. He'd only become English to be with Rose and their child. He loved her enough to leave behind everything he'd ever known.

Not me, though. If I left, it wouldn't be for a man. It would be for me.

The bottle was back in my hands and I drank without thought. Two, maybe three sips I took, before I handed it off to Jasper. He sat down, bumping into Charlotte on the log. Soon, the bottle was passed again and Jasper was kissing Charlotte. I watched in perverted interest as his hands ran up and down her sides and his mouth moved on hers.

The crackle of the fire and the wet kissing sounds echoed in my head. The breeze gusted and the fire's smoke drifted at me. I coughed and moved my stump away from the smoke and closer to Avery. He had his arm around Sadie and her mouth was on his neck. But he wasn't paying attention to her. He was looking at me.

Jasper and Charlotte got up, giggling. They grasped hands

and ran back to the vehicle together. I guessed what they were going to do. Heat flamed my cheeks once more.

I was swimming in my head again. My mind was thick—so heavy. The world was becoming blurry and I reveled in it, knowing that when I finally laid my head upon my pillow, I wouldn't dream. I wouldn't see Sarah.

"Jewel . . . come here . . . " Avery was whispering, and yet the words boomed in my head. I looked up and Sadie was slumped over the log. She looked uncomfortable, but she was still giggling and rubbing her face.

Avery stared at me. His mouth was moving—he was talking. But I couldn't hear him anymore. The world was fuzzy and my head felt empty. I tried desperately to get a grip on my mind, to shake it awake. But it eluded me.

When Avery's hand touched my face, my mind screamed to "go away," but I didn't say a word. I couldn't control my voice. It was as if I couldn't talk at all.

His lips touched mine and inside, I cried. What have I done?

CHAPTER 18

······ Justin ······

When I walked into the kitchen, I was surprised to see Sam and Noah sitting at the table, both with a bowl of cereal in front of them. For all the more important things on my mind, I made a mental note that Sam had managed to corrupt Noah—and how I'd have to make fun of Noah for it later.

"What the hell happened to you?" Sam said, rushing at me as if he was a crazed mother. Noah wasn't too far behind him.

Sam touched my face and I flinched away. "Shh, don't wake Rose." That was the last thing I needed.

"Who did this to you?" Sam growled.

I looked between Sam's furious, vein popping face and Noah's worried frown, and wished they'd been with me an hour earlier.

"This guy, Avery, and his friend, Jasper." I sat down and took the ice pack that Noah handed me. It stung when I pressed it to the side of my face, but I held it there anyway.

"Why, Justin . . . just spit it out," Sam demanded. He was leaning back against the counter, his arms folded in front of him.

I had already figured out that Sam, Noah, and Rose all knew how to keep a secret, and I had faith that Rachel's was safe with them. But I still worried about how Noah would react when he learned that his Amish little sister was hanging out in bars. I glanced his way, wishing that he was upstairs, asleep with Rose.

Noah understood my hesitation. "You can trust me. I'm here to help you, in any way I can."

I raised my finger between the both of them. "Do you promise not to tell Dad or insist on going to the police or something stupid like that if I do tell you?"

Sam answered immediately, "Of course—you know that, bro."

Noah was a little slower to respond. "I won't tell your dad, and I'll let you and Sam decide about the authorities, but I can't keep a secret from Rose. She'll get it out of me."

I smiled and my face hurt all over again. "Rose is okay." Noah breathed out in relief.

"So tell us what happened." Sam took the seat across the table from me.

By the time I'd finished explaining everything to them, from the first night I'd seen Rachel at Dewey's, to me driving her to her house for potatoes, to our latest encounter, Sam was vigorously rubbing his face. Noah was staring at the wall in wide-eyed shock.

"If I didn't know you to be an honest person, and if your face wasn't battered, I wouldn't believe you, Justin," Noah said carefully.

"Of course he's telling the truth." Sam slapped Noah on the back. "Sorry, bro. Sisters are sneaky little beings. It's not the end of the world." He faced me again. "Do you have any idea where this guy might be right now?"

I nodded apprehensively. "As they were walking away, I heard Avery mention something about taking the party to a bridge." I paused and looked questioningly at Sam. "Do you know what he was talking about?"

Sam smirked and grabbed his car keys off the table. "Sure do."

"Where are you going?" I asked, following him to the door and grabbing his shoulder to stop him.

"No one touches my little brother. This Avery dude is about to realize the huge mistake he made," Sam said calmly.

"Then I'm coming too," I told him.

Sam nodded in understanding. "All right then." He looked over at Noah. "What about you?"

"Yes, I'm in. You may need help."

I was surprised to see the look of determination on Noah's face.

"This isn't going to be pretty," Sam pressed.

Noah swallowed. "I know. I remember the incident in the city alleyway when we got lost last year."

"What incident?" I asked with sudden curiosity.

"Oh, this will be much worse," Sam confirmed.

"As long as we're back before Rose wakes up, we're good." Noah lifted his brown jacket from the hook and turned to me. "This isn't just retribution for what was done to you. My sister is out there and I have to bring her home."

I felt more respect for Noah than I ever had. Although I wondered how beneficial a person raised as a pacifist would prove to be.

Sam looked between Noah and me. "Let's do this."

$$\bullet \bullet \bullet \bullet \; \bullet \; \bullet \bullet \bullet \bullet$$

The drive down to the bridge from the main road put me in mind of one of those creepy B movies, where a group of rowdy teenagers were hacked up in the woods by a serial killer with a chainsaw.

"Why would anyone party in a place like this?" I asked Sam.

"Oh, it's really cool, actually. Wait until you see the old bridge," Sam said excitedly.

The fact that the closer we got to the possible confrontation, the happier Sam became, was somewhat disconcerting.

"I take it that you've been here before?" Noah asked. He looked about as apprehensive as I was feeling.

"Yeah, a couple of times, but it's been a while." Sam hit the brake, slowing the green dually even more. Then he turned off the headlights. Luckily, there was enough moonlight to see.

Sam pulled off the gravel road a little ways and parked. Tall grass brushed against the sides of the truck with the stiff breeze.

He looked over. "We go on foot from here."

The ominous feeling that I'd been carrying around since we'd left the house turned into a rock in my gut. Maybe this was a mistake. As much as I wanted to make sure that Rachel was all right, I was also irritated with her that she would hang out with such psychopaths in the first place.

Sam went first, followed by Noah, and I brought up the rear. My stomach was still sore from the punches, and the side of my face throbbed despite the ice pack. I hadn't even checked my appearance in a mirror yet, and could only imagine how awful I looked. I didn't see Dad every day, so there was a possibility that my face would heal before he even had the chance to find out.

"I don't understand why Rachel would come to a place like this with strangers," Noah whispered.

Sam stopped and looked over his shoulder, lifting his finger at Noah. "Don't go getting all emotional about Rachel. We'll appraise the situation first and then act."

"What exactly is your plan?" Noah asked, his whisper coming out harsher this time.

Sam sighed. "I hope your sister isn't in a compromising situation." I rolled my eyes at his choice of words and groaned when he went on to say, "We're going to teach those douchebags a lesson and then we'll get Rachel out of there."

"That's it—that's your plan?" Noah shook his head in agitation.

"You just have to go with flow in this type of situation." Recognizing a possible mutiny when he glanced between Noah and me, he added, "Just be ready for anything."

"Justin is in no shape to fight anyone," Noah said stiffly.

"Agreed. It'll be you and me, bro." Sam was finished with the conversation and began walking again.

We stayed in the tall grass and weeds beside the road and moved slowly. Sam stopped several times, raising his hand for us to follow suit. My heart pounded in my chest and I could only take quick, shallow breaths. Sure, I liked the part of the plan where Avery and Jasper were going to be taught a lesson, but I began worrying that people like them might have a gun. And then what would we do?

As we turned the bend, the stone bridge came into view. It rose threateningly above the bushes and a thick, wooded tree line swallowed up the land beyond it. The silver car that had nearly run over my head earlier was parked not too far ahead, and I could just make out the yellow-orange light of a campfire beneath the first archway of the bridge. We found them after all.

I was deliberating whether I should be relieved or worried at the discovery, when Sam *shushed* us. He bent down and went into full burglar mode. Noah and I followed suit, but I thought Sam was enjoying this ambush way too much.

I could almost feel the anxiety rising off of Noah. He was completely out of his element. This might be my first time too, but I'd watched enough action movies and played enough video games to be somewhat prepared for what was about to happen. Noah was totally clueless.

I reached out and touched Noah's shoulder, reassuring him. He smiled back and then bent down, mimicking Sam.

It seemed to take forever to approach the bridge. We moved stealthily, passing by the car that was rhythmically shaking. The windows were fogged up and Noah shook his head in disgust as we skirted the vehicle.

I held my breath the rest of the way until our hands touched the cold, smooth stones of the bridge. I'm not really a praying sort of person, but when I realized there was a couple in the car, I silently begged God that Rachel wasn't one of them.

Relief flooded through me when I spotted her sitting on a stump beside the fire. But it was short lived. One of the girls looked to be passed out on the log and Avery was kneeling beside Rachel, who was slumped over, staring at the fire. She swayed, and I guessed that she was drunk out of her mind. Avery's lips had just touched Rachel's when both Noah and I bounded out from behind the bridge's wall. I only caught a glimpse of Sam's *what the hell* look before we were all out in the open.

"Let go of her!" Noah roared. He ran at Avery and knocked into him, sending both of them sprawling on the ground. They were dangerously close to the flames.

I was only a few steps behind, and went directly to Rachel. I grasped her hands and pulled her away from the melee. She looked up at me with a startled, glazed over expression. But she didn't fight me. She simply pressed her face against my chest and started crying.

Even though Noah had the element of surprise, Avery was a seriously tough dude. The two rolled around in the dirt, punching and kneeing each other. Avery managed to roll on top of Noah, and when he did, he pushed down on Noah's arm in an attempt to burn him in the fire.

Sam had been standing idly by, allowing Noah to have the glory of the attack, until it became apparent what Avery was trying to do. Sam shouted, "That's enough!"

Sam lunged at Avery, pulling him off of Noah. Noah immediately rebounded and jumped on Avery once again. Now it was Sam holding Avery, while Noah pummeled him.

As the wetness of Rachel's tears began to penetrate my shirt, I was mesmerized, watching the formally Amish man beat the crap out of Avery. I honestly didn't think that Noah had it in him. I was sorely mistaken.

Avery's face was washed in blood and he slumped over in Sam's arms. He barely had a chance to get a word out. But now, he was mumbling, begging for mercy.

"What the hell's going on here?" Jasper said, zipping up his pants. Charlotte was standing wide-eyed behind him. Her shirt was on inside out.

Sam shoved Avery to the ground and rushed at Jasper. Sam's solid punch hit Jasper in the face, and then a second jabbed him in the stomach. Sam followed up with a knee into Jasper's jaw when the man doubled over. Then Sam hit him again . . . and again.

"Stop it, Stop it!" Charlotte screamed.

Rachel still wept against me, not even daring to look. The other girl roused and slid over to the other side of the log to watch the scene in confused horror.

Noah was still kicking Avery, and Sam placed a punch so solidly on Jasper's face that I heard the crack of his nose and saw a spurt of blood fly through the air. I began to disengage Rachel, fearing that if I didn't stop my brother and my brother-in-law, someone might get seriously injured—or even killed.

But Rachel clung to me, and at the moment that my worry became palpable, both Sam and Noah let up. Sam dropped back and Jasper fell to his knees. Charlotte threw her arms around him.

Noah loomed over Avery, who was clutching his stomach. I was pretty sure that the man looked worse than me.

"Don't you ever come around my sister again—even if she seeks you out, you had better make yourself very scarce." Noah kneeled down close to Avery's face. "Because if I catch you *near* her, or even hear anything at all about you being near her, I will kill you. Do you understand?"

Avery spit a wad of blood at Noah. "Not if I kill you first."

"What the hell, is this the *Mechanic?*" Sam growled. He bent down beside Noah and said, "That goes for me, too, only this kid—" he pointed at me "—is my little brother. And if you ever do anything that so much as hurts his feelings, it will be me coming after you. And unless you've got bodyguards or eyes in the back of your head, I don't think you'll be on the winning side." Sam looked around at the carnage. The girls were sobbing, and Jasper's hand was splayed over his bleeding nose. "We're even, as far as I'm concerned. We won't go to the cops or take Justin to the hospital, so I think you two assholes can man-up and do the same." He looked between the girls. "Whichever one of you dingbats is more sober can drive these losers home." When no one moved, he jumped to his feet and faked out the girl behind the log with a rush. She jumped up and went to Avery's side, helping him to his feet.

Jasper could walk a little better than Avery, and pushed Charlotte away when she crowded him with assistance. She went to Avery and took one of his sides, while the other girl grasped the opposite. I watched them hobble away, wondering what it would be like when I saw the girls in school the next day.

When the car's engine revved up, Rachel finally stepped back. Her face was a wet mess and her hair was tangled. The scent of alcohol wafted off of her. "I'm so sorry," she said.

"What is wrong with you, Rachel? How could you do this to Mother, Father, to yourself?" Noah verbally attacked her.

Rachel began crying again and I held my hand up at Noah. "That's enough. This isn't the time."

Sam backed me up. "He's right—not a good time."

Rachel ran a few feet away and vomited. The sound of her throwing up was enough to make me feel nauseous. Why anyone drank, I had no idea.

Noah rushed to Rachel's side. He pulled her hair out of her face and held it back. He patted her on the back, saying, "It's all right, you'll be fine. We're going to take you home. You'll feel better in the morning."

She wasn't going to feel better in the morning—she was going to feel worse. And who knew what kind of fallout there would actually be. Could we all manage to keep the goings on of the entire night a secret? I doubted it.

But what I was really wondering was whether Rachel had finally learned her lesson.

CHAPTER 19

Rose

I heard Sarah Ann's babbling coming through the baby monitor and I rolled over, yawning. After an extra-long stretch, I finally opened my eyes. I was just about to kiss Noah's sleeping face when I pulled back. There was a bruise on his left cheek and a cut above his right eye. Weirder still was the leaf clinging to his hair.

Since Sarah Ann wasn't crying yet, I ignored the monitor and stared at Noah's face, thinking. I was certain he didn't have those marks on his face the evening before. But then, I did go to sleep early, too exhausted from the work at the dress shop to keep my eyes open. Something must have happened later in the night.

I reached over and gently shook Noah's shoulder. His eyes opened and adjusted to the dim, morning light spraying through the windows.

"Hello, sweetheart," he said, grasping me around the waist and pulling me against him.

The touch of his warm mouth on mine caused an ignition of a thousand sparks in my belly. I opened my mouth, partially forgetting about his bruise and the leaf. I rubbed my hand up and down his bare back. He was trying to remove my night shirt, when he shifted position and groaned.

I jumped back. "What the heck happened to you?"

Noah pushed the hair out of his face and asked sheepishly, "What?"

I frowned at him and plucked the leaf from his hair, showing it to him. "There usually aren't leaves in our bed—and your face has a bruise and a cut on it."

Noah sat up against the pillows. "Nothing gets by you." He took my hand and kissed it. "Your brother got into some trouble last night."

"Which brother—what kind of trouble?"

Noah took a measured breath. "It was Justin. It's a long story, but basically, he was at a bar last week and—"

"A bar—is he crazy?"

I was about to leap from the bed to hunt Justin down, when Noah captured my wrist. "Please calm down and let me explain."

I relaxed back into the pillows while a million thoughts penetrated my mind. Justin didn't go to bars. There must be so much more to the story.

"He was forced to go out with a couple of friends from school on our date night. Sam made him leave the house—he didn't know that the two boys were going to take Justin to a bar." My face scrunched as I pictured Sam and what I was going to do when I got my hands on him. But I remained silent and nodded for him to continue.

"He ran into my sister there and—"

I couldn't stop myself from interrupting. "Rachel—at a bar!" I shrieked.

Sarah Ann's chatter was becoming more incessant and I wished that Noah would talk faster. Any moment our baby was going to start crying. I motioned Noah with my hands to hurry up.

"You're the one who keeps interrupting me," Noah pointed out.

"Sorry—go on," I urged.

"Long story short, Rachel has been sneaking out for months and hanging out with a bad crowd." He took a shaky breath. "She's been drinking, too. Justin went back to the bar last night to talk to her, ask her how she was handling the work at the birdhouse factory, when two guys insisted that she leave with them. Your brother tried to stop them and they beat him up pretty badly."

He stopped, waiting for my response.

"They . . . hurt . . . him?" I said slowly.

Noah nodded. "Not terribly . . . I mean, he has a black eye and some bruises. He doesn't need a doctor or anything."

The thought of anyone hitting Justin chilled the blood running through my veins. Red light blurred my sight for a moment. I had to take a deep breath and focus on looking back at Noah.

"Go on," I whispered.

"When he showed up last night looking as if he'd been run over by a car, Sam nearly went ballistic. Justin told us the story. As it turned out, Sam knew the place where they were—a bridge at the edge of town, parallel to the highway. There's a dry creek bed and people party there all the time."

"And you and Sam visited the place to teach those guys a lesson?" I half asked and half stated. I was still furious, but knowing how Sam probably reacted, I was feeling better by the second.

"Yeah, but also to get Rachel . . . out of there." Noah's eyes were tearing up. His voice cracked.

I hugged him as he buried his face against my neck. "You should have seen her. She was drunk, and this man was kissing her. If we hadn't shown up when we did, I can only imagine what would have happened to her."

I leaned back and wiped his tears away with my fingers. "Is she all right?"

He nodded.

"Did Sam give those guys payback?"

His eyes searched mine and then he began crying harder. I was baffled by his emotional state, but then realized that he must have tried to help Sam, and that's how he ended up with the bruised and cut face. But then it occurred to me that maybe Sam had been injured—or worse.

"Is Sam okay?" I breathed.

Noah nodded and sucked in a wet gulp. "He's fine, Rose. We're all fine." He swallowed. "It's the other men—what we did to them—what I did to one of them."

"You beat someone up?" I asked, trying to restrain the excitement in my voice. I didn't want to freak Noah out with my display of happiness that those two jerks got what was coming to them—and that Noah had taken a part in it. I was like Sam. I kind of craved violence.

"He was taking advantage of my sister. He'd gotten her drunk purposefully—to . . . rape . . . her," Noah stuttered the words out.

I pulled him against me harder and murmured, "You did the right thing. Don't ever question yourself."

"But I lost control. I damaged him badly. It's not my way, not my way," he muttered into my hair.

"Maybe it wasn't your way, but things have changed. You're not the same person you grew up as. You're the type of person who protects his family any way he can now. I'm proud of you."

As I rocked Noah in my arms, I wondered about Rachel. I'd always known the girl was troubled, but even I was surprised at the extent of her issues.

Maybe a little visit with my sister-in-law was finally in order.

CHAPTER 20

⚜ Rachel ⚜

My head throbbed and the inside of my mouth was dry and swollen. When I hadn't come down the stairs at the usual time that morning, Mother had come up to see if I was all right. She had felt my head and fussed over me for a moment, before insisting that I stay home from work.

That's when Father walked in. He looked at me with no sympathy. I assumed that he'd spoken to Tonya moments earlier and learned of my ill words with her. *"You will not be coddled, Rachel. Get up and go to work. And with a better attitude today,"* he'd ordered me. Mother tried to argue with him about it, but he'd turned away and left the house without eating breakfast.

I tried to focus on my task and pushed another board over the blade. It split neatly apart and I stacked each piece in the proper pile.

My underarms were sticky with sweat and I paused to wipe away the moisture from my forehead. There were no fans, and even with the large sliding doors wide open, the air barely stirred. It was an unusually warm day for early spring, and I inwardly wondered how we would all survive the prickling heat of summer when it arrived.

As I cut the boards, I tried not to let my mind wander, but I couldn't help it. The room, filled with tables, machines, and a dozen girls, faded away to be replaced with moonlight and a stone bridge. The flames flicked impatiently in front of me and the sound of tree frogs whistled through the air.

I tried hard to remember everything, but there were large gaps in my memory that worried me. I recalled Justin being there, hugging me. Noah was there, too, and he was rolling around on the ground, fighting with Avery. I'd been afraid for him, but also shocked that he'd appeared out of nowhere. I'd sat beside Justin in the truck, my head on his shoulder, crying the entire way home. The words Noah had said hurt me, but he'd been right. That's probably why they had hurt so much. He didn't speak to me again, nor I to him. The drive home was still fuzzy.

But the part that I was straining so desperately to reveal was whether I'd let Avery kiss me—or something even worse. Try as I may, I wasn't sure. I thought I had felt his lips on mine. I had the sickening feeling that he *had* kissed me. I'd been out of my mind and could have let him do almost anything.

And then there was the blood and crunching sounds of fists and boots hitting flesh that continued to boom in my head. And I had caused all of it.

"She isn't ready for her break yet. The girls go out together at noon," I heard Ingrid say.

I looked up, curious as to who she was talking to. My heart sped up when I saw Rose facing off with Ingrid, her hands on her hips and her chin jutting forward.

The two girls already knew each other from when Rose temporarily became Amish. And searching my memories, I was pretty sure that Ingrid was one of the girls who had opposed Rose's presence within the community.

"Oh, come on. It really doesn't matter if she takes a break now or in a half hour, does it?" Rose implored with a determined voice.

"Actually, it does," Ingrid said, not backing down.

I watched nervously over my shoulder as Rose and Ingrid stared at each other. Abruptly, Rose leaned forward and whispered something into Ingrid's ear. Ingrid listened and then tilted her head. After an agonizing moment, she nodded and called me over. "Rachel—you can take your break now!"

I touched the switch to shut off the table saw and untied my apron. As I reached Rose, I noticed that Ingrid was talking to a couple of the other girls. Curiosity needled me, but I fell in line with Rose and walked through the open doorway silently.

The outside air was still warm, but the light breeze made me feel instantly better. We were heading toward the picnic table beneath the sycamore tree, and I risked a sidelong glance at Rose, and the plastic bag she carried.

Rose eyed me. "How are you feeling?"

Her tone was neutral, maybe even a little bit sympathetic. I swallowed the knot that formed in my throat. She already knew everything.

"Like I've been dragged by a runaway horse through a parking lot," I replied honestly.

We sat down across from each other and Rose began pulling things out of the bag. "I figured you would. Here's a ginger ale . . . crackers . . . and gum." She pushed the items toward me and shrugged. "I've only had a hangover once—the ginger ale really helped."

My gaze met my sister-in-law's and I sniffed. Rose pulled a tissue out of her purse and handed it to me.

"You'll feel better by tonight," Rose promised.

I blew my nose and looked out at the plowed cropland on the other side of the white board fence. The smell of crushed up earth was strong in the air and if I squinted, I could just make out Mr. Fischer in the distance with his team of Belgian horses working the rows. It was such a familiar smell and sight that I felt a little better.

When I turned back to Rose, I marveled for a moment at her beauty. I'd always thought she was the prettiest girl I'd ever met. With her large, sky-blue eyes and pouty lips, she could have been a model. But it was her sheer force of personality that made her something special. She seemed to always get what she wanted, and that was a trait I admired.

"How did you get Ingrid to let me take my break early?"

Rose smiled wickedly. "Well, I remembered Ingrid—especially the time that she snuck out behind the barn with Abner Yoder during a volley ball game. I simply reminded her of the incident, and the fact that Bishop Lambright probably wouldn't be too pleased to hear about it, especially since she's now courting his own nephew, John Lambright."

I grinned back. "You actually threatened her?"

"Not at all. I told Ingrid that Martha Lambright is coming to the dress shop today, and mentioned to her how much Martha enjoys a good gossip. And that perhaps Ingrid herself might come up in the conversation."

"Thank you," I said, feeling my eyes moisten. I wiped them with the sleeve of my dress.

"We're sisters now. I'm here for you." Rose smiled reassuringly, and then opened the box of crackers. She handed me a few. I was glad she wasn't pushing me into a conversation that I wasn't ready to have yet.

"Is Noah angry with me?" I asked reluctantly.

Rose thought for a moment before answering. "Noah loves you. Nothing is going to change that. But I won't lie. He's pretty upset about everything.

"Is he going to tell Father and Mother?" My heart began pounding. I held my breath.

"Of course not. He wouldn't do that to you. He's worried that you're in over your head—that you're going to do something that you will *really* regret."

"It was just that one time," I lied.

"That's not what Justin said," Rose countered.

I looked away. I'd been lying and sneaking around for so long, it just came naturally. But I should have anticipated that Rose wouldn't let me get away with it, especially since her brother had been beaten up because of me.

Justin's swollen and bruised face popped into my mind. When I glanced back at Rose, I saw him in her face.

"I'm so sorry about Justin. I had no idea that Avery and Jasper would do such a thing." I took a shuddering breath. "Justin was just trying to help. He realized what horrible people they were, even though I didn't."

"Justin is pretty perceptive. He's also very loyal to the people he cares about." Rose said the last part carefully.

I glanced up questioningly. Could it be possible that Justin had feelings for me—even after the previous night?

Testing the waters, I said, "He must hate me, too."

"No one hates you," Rose said firmly. "Look, I'm not here to judge. I know firsthand how difficult it is to be Amish, and then with Sarah's death and all, it's been a really rough time for you." She captured my gaze. "If you need to talk or need help in any way, call me."

"I will." I nodded.

I ate some more crackers and sipped some of the ginger ale. I burped a moment later, making me feel better. Rose asked me a few questions about the factory, and I could tell by her frowning expression that she felt extremely sorry for me.

"Maybe your dad will cool down and change his mind about all this," Rose said, as she motioned to the white metal sided building.

"I doubt it. I'll be bringing in a good amount of money to the household, and with Jacob and Noah gone, it certainly helps out."

"Oh, don't get me started," Rose said rolling her eyes.

Rose understood our ways well enough not to question them out loud, but her feelings showed easily. It was moments like these that I was sure she didn't regret going back to being English one bit.

After break time was up, I walked Rose back to her truck. As Rose clutched the truck's door handle, she turned and said, "Are you really okay?"

"I'm better now," I said truthfully.

The *clip-clop, clip-clop* got our attention and we both looked up. Driving the buggy was none other than Micah Schwartz. My insides tingled at the sight of him.

"Hmm, I wonder what he's doing here," Rose commented, still watching his approach.

"Ingrid mentioned this morning that the Schwartzes were building a new storage shed behind the factory." I shrugged. "I guess he's here to work."

Rose studied my face for several long seconds, making me silently squirm. Could she possibly know about me and Micah?

"He's a really nice guy. It's unfortunate that his father is such a jerk," she said.

"I have to be going," I said restlessly.

Rose reached out and touched my arm, stopping me. "You're too secretive—and some things don't need to be kept secret."

My lips pressed tightly together. As nice as Rose was being, I wasn't going to talk to her about Micah. I wasn't sure what was going on myself. But the intensity in her gaze made me fear that she wasn't going to let me off the hook easily. So I changed the subject.

"Is Martha really going to the dress shop today?"

Rose chuckled at my strategy, but it worked and she went with the flow.

"Yeah. Actually, I'm running a little late for the meeting. Miranda's babysitting Sarah Ann at the shop while Suzanna and Summer pick up more cloth."

"I wish I was working for you, instead of here." The words were out of my mouth before I could stop them.

Rose's face brightened. "Maybe you can."

"Father will never allow it. He's the one who voted against the shop," I reminded her.

"Never say never." Rose gave me a quick hug and got into the truck.

As she backed up, her hand shot out the window. I waved back. But my heart was so jittery that it was difficult to make it a steady motion.

Without even looking, I knew Micah was patiently waiting behind me.

For a moment, I was afraid to face him, worried that he'd see right through me, and know what I did the night before.

"How are you today, Rachel?"

Hearing his voice calmed my nerves instantly and I wondered why. When I finally turned, Micah was smiling broadly. He was holding a single, yellow tulip in his hands.

He held it out, waiting for me to take it.

I shifted on my feet. If I took the flower, it would mean something, and I just wasn't ready.

"I have to get back to work," I said, hurrying by him.

I turned the corner and entered the building just as the bell rang and the other girls began preparing for their break.

I tried to convince myself that the dejected look on Micah's face didn't matter to me at all. But then why did my heart feel as if it was breaking?

CHAPTER 21

Rose

$\mathscr{S}$unshine streamed through the thinning clouds by the time I pulled up to the shop. I parked on the far side of the hitching rail and leaned back for a moment. Rachel was a tough little cookie, no doubt about it. But I wondered if she really was in over her head. The degree of intoxication that the guys had found her in was startling. It was almost as if she'd been purposely getting as drunk as possible. But why? Was it because of Sarah's death? Or maybe it simply had to do with the difficulties she faced being Amish. Whatever it was, I had the gnawing feeling that she wasn't reformed just yet. The entire situation upset Noah greatly, and that's what bothered me the most.

I stared out the window at the wooden-sided building. We had all pooled our resources and bought paint for the outside walls. Noah and Matthew had already painted the front of the shop a happy blue color. Combined with the white trim, the place was beginning to look more like a dress shop and less like a bakery. The sign was hung with dangling chains that allowed it to gently stir with the breeze, and the silver metal roofing caused a glistening glare that could be seen from the roadway. The two maple trees that bookended the building were just now leafing out. Through the crack in my truck's window, I could hear their branches brushing against the siding.

I smiled. I couldn't think of a more perfect location for the business. But would it be a success? That question would be left unanswered for a little while longer. If everything went smoothly, we'd be open for business a week from today, and then we'd know whether the community would really support us. A rush of worried butterflies batted around in my stomach at the thought. There were still so many obstacles to overcome.

The door jingled as I opened it. Standing together at the counter were Miranda and Martha Lambright. The breath caught nervously in my throat when I saw the bishop's wife. She didn't drive her own buggy, opting for a driver to bring her. Since there were no cars in the parking area, either, I assumed that she was planning to stay for a while.

Martha was holding Sarah Ann in her one arm as she sifted through the material laid out on the counter with her other hand.

"Hello, Rose," she said when she saw me. She smiled and I noted that Miranda looked relaxed.

I breathed a little easier and replied, "Hey there. So what do you think?" I motioned around the room with my hands.

"I'm so impressed with how much work you've done thus far. It looks completely different than when it was a bakery." Martha held up a strip of material. "And I love the fabric you've picked out."

"I can't take credit for that. It was Suzanna and Ella that chose the fabric. Miranda, Summer, and I have been in charge of cleaning and organizing."

Sarah Ann responded to my voice by kicking her legs and stretching her arms out for me. Martha squeezed the baby and then brought her over. *"Seiss boppli,"* Martha said.

My Amish translation wasn't the greatest, but I'd learned quite a few words during my time with them. She had told me Sarah Ann was a sweet baby.

"Thank you," I said.

Martha rubbed her hands together and glanced around the room. I caught Miranda's raised brow.

"You girls have done a good job. When will you begin making the dresses?" Martha asked in a business-like manner.

I looked to Miranda for the answer.

"Suzanna, Ella, and I have been sewing in the evenings at home. We have a small rack's worth already, but the real work begins this week. We're hoping to have a variety of colors and sizes available on opening day."

I watched Martha's head bob up and down in satisfaction. I was suddenly very curious about her level of interest. It seemed more than just a check-up-on-us kind of visit from a temporary silent partner. Sarah Ann wound her fingers into my hair as I waited for Martha to say what was on her mind.

She turned to Miranda. "You will fit the girls and women and then make alterations to the already made dresses?"

"Yes, Ma'am." Miranda looked a little intimidated, but she managed to go on to say, "We discussed the best way to make our shop unique and truly efficient for both the customers and for us. We decided that if we had a steady supply of dresses for our patrons to choose from, they would be more likely to buy one. And the fitting process can be quick and relatively easy."

I glanced back at Martha for her reaction. She wore a satisfied smile that surprised me.

"Very good idea." She nodded approvingly. "You're right. What our women need is a little more convenience in their lives—and this does the trick nicely."

"To be honest, I'm surprised that you supported the idea in the first place," I said, reaching into the cooler section of the diaper bag to pull out a bottle of milk. I went to the sink behind the counter and filled up a bowl with hot tap water, and then I set the bottle into the container to be warmed.

Martha was waiting for my full attention, and Miranda was shuffling the fabric around, listening.

"I've never had the blessing of my own child, but I've helped raise more than a dozen nieces and nephews. So I've had it relatively easy, but I've always felt for my sisters and their hardships. Raising a large family, cleaning the house, doing the laundry, and even helping with the family business leaves very little time for sewing. But still, they manage to get it all done. They've had to trade any peaceful time to call their own in order to accomplish their roles as mother and wife." Martha took a deep breath and eyed me. I could have sworn I saw a tear in her eye. "Most of the women have been up to the challenge, but there have been a few who have found it too difficult and given up hope."

I knew my eyes were wide and Miranda's hands had stalled over the fabric. I think we were both holding our breath.

"My youngest sister, Mary, was a beautiful young woman with five active young'uns. But it became too much for her to bear. My other sisters and I had no idea of the turmoil she was going through—depression and such." Martha took a shuddering breath. "She couldn't swim, you see. I was the one who found her. I'd stopped by to bring her family a couple of berry pies I'd made. The babies were in their cribs crying and the toddlers were scampering around the house unattended. Through the window, I saw the oldest, a five-year-old boy, sitting on the bank by the pond. I rushed out to him, terrified that he might fall into the water. I asked Jory where his Momma was." Martha paused to make eye contact with me. "He told me she had walked into the water . . . and never came back out."

"She drowned herself?" I asked with incredulity.

Martha nodded. "I searched the water and saw her bonnet bobbing near the reeds. Her hair was floating up from the brown water."

Martha brought her apron to her face and wiped around her eyes. She had spoken with little emotion, but the feelings were still there, pulsating throughout the room in a wave of sorrow.

I handed Sarah Ann to Miranda and went to Martha, embracing her in my arms. Martha accepted my hug for a moment, and then pulled back. "Despite what the men think, it is a good thing what you girls are doing. Some women need the help more than others, and this shop will give them one less thing to fret over when there's little time to sew."

I took a deep, measured breath. "Honestly, I had no idea how important this business might be to some of your people."

"Oh, it goes beyond our community." Martha gazed at me hopefully. "I believe that women in other Amish communities will travel the distance to shop here, too. Do you have any papers with the information about the shop to hand out?"

"Why, yes." I walked around the counter and pulled a folder out from one of the drawers. I returned to Martha and handed it to her. "I had these flyers printed the other day."

Martha flipped through a few of them. "Perfect."

"You're welcome to take some if you want. Summer and I were going to stick them in mailboxes next week, but it certainly won't hurt to begin passing them out sooner."

"Would you go a step further perhaps, and drive me out to the Hickory Ridge settlement today? I can introduce you to some of the women there and we'll give them these flyers."

Martha's sudden anxiety to deliver the news about the dress shop to this other community was very obvious. She was the one who was now holding her breath.

"I don't know this Hickory Ridge settlement," I said flatly, glancing at Miranda.

"It's a rustic community, about fifteen miles to the east," Miranda told me. "They don't even have indoor plumbing and their buggies are open."

"Are you kidding me?" I looked at Martha.

"The women there endure more hardship than we do," Martha confirmed.

The images of poor women filling up basins of hot water from the stovetop and fumbling their way in a dark yard to the outhouse pummeled my vision. I didn't have to be asked twice.

"If Miranda will watch Sarah Ann, we'll drive out there right now," I said.

"Of course I will, happily," Miranda offered.

"Thank you, Rose," Martha replied.

"No need to thank me. I'm more than glad to help." I picked up my purse off the table. "Besides, this is a win for everyone, I think."

I followed Martha out of the dress shop with apprehension about visiting this new community. And I'd always thought the Meadowview Amish had it bad. I could only imagine what horrors were awaiting us.

CHAPTER 22

❧ Rachel ❧

I looked at Ingrid with my jaw dropped. Since my cutting machine had quit working, the blonde girl had put me on clean up duty. I was in the middle of pulling the trash bag out of the container when Ingrid had asked me to do another errand.

"Why are you looking at me as if I have two heads?" Ingrid thrust the pitcher and plastic cups into my hands.

I didn't question her further and hurried out of the building. The clouds were all but gone and the bright sunlight made me squint. But I wasn't about to complain. I despised wintertime and was relieved that it was finally over.

The grass had turned green almost overnight and it squished beneath my feet as I made my way around the corner of the factory. Glancing up, I immediately spotted Micah on a ladder. His back was to me, and I admired his great balance as he stretched out from the ladder and banged a nail into a board. Paul was stacking a few long boards from beside the wagon and I went to him first.

"Thank you," he said, taking the cup full of water.

As I approached Micah, my mind was wary, but my body was excitely anticipating the encounter. I swallowed down the nervousness and tried to forget that I had rejected his offering of the flower just a short time earlier.

"Are you thirsty?" I called up.

Micah jumped a little and then glanced at me. He began climbing down.

When he was on the ground, I handed him a cup of water. He managed to keep his eyes on me while he drank.

He handed the empty cup back, and I was beginning to turn away when he said, "You look tired."

For some strange reason, the fact that he'd noticed and even cared enough to mention it, touched me. Especially after I'd refused his gift.

"I had a rough night," I said, not wanting to elaborate. I thought I sounded mysterious, and secretly enjoyed it.

"Do you want to talk about it?"

I glanced around. Paul had moved around the far end of the new construction, and although I could hear him hammering, I couldn't see him anymore.

"This isn't a good place to talk." His gaze was steady and waiting. I thought up a half-truth. "I've been having bad dreams lately—mostly about Sarah. They keep me awake at night."

Micah's lips tightened with concern and I had to look away. The flow of emotion I'd felt when I'd ignored him earlier swelled inside of me again. He was too sweet of a boy to play games with. I was ashamed of myself for even hoping that I could have something with Micah. I wasn't good enough for him.

"You need to be well rested to work with the saws. Have you tried chamomile tea before bedtime?" Micah said thoughtfully.

I almost laughed. I'd found something much better for getting me to sleep, but of course I couldn't tell *him* that.

"No, I haven't. But Mother has some of the herb in the pantry. I'll give it a try tonight." I smiled at him. "Thank you."

Again, I shifted my weight, about to leave, when he rushed on to ask, "Will you be at the ball game tonight?"

I thought of the baseball game that the local boys were having at the schoolhouse that evening and was conflicted. I had been planning on feigning illness so that I could attempt to contact Sadie. I needed to find out how Avery and Jasper were faring, and to see if she and Charlotte were angry with me. Along with everything else, my English friends had been swirling around in my mind all day. I might not even be able to call them friends any longer, and I wasn't really sure how I felt about that. The girls had always been kind enough to me, and I'd enjoyed my escapes into their world, but Avery was something else altogether. I'd never forget the way he'd repeatedly punched Justin or came on to me while I was drunk. He was an evil man. I'd never enjoyed the youth events the way Sarah had. She got along with everyone and always had girls to team up with on the nets or to sit with beside the ball games. I usually sat alone. I looked up at Micah's expectant eyes and it occurred to me that if I did go, I had something to look forward to. And that was meeting up with him—and maybe even a kiss if we snuck off somewhere.

I didn't want to hurt Micah. For me, it was about exploring the possibilities, but I knew for him, it was much more. If I were English, it wouldn't be such a big deal if I flirted with Micah, but in my world, it was serious business.

Still, how would I ever know my true feelings for Micah if I didn't experiment a little? I wasn't like the other girls who knew who they wanted to marry when they were twelve. I wasn't sure about anything these days.

Who would it hurt if I did go to the ball game? No one, I reckoned. Before I could change my mind, I said, "I'll be there." Then I left him in a hurry.

As I walked away, I couldn't keep the smile off my face. For the first time in a long while, I experienced the warm jolt of anticipation.

CHAPTER 23

Rose

*I*t was a beautiful day. The sun was shining and the bright green leaves on the trees seemed to be growing before my very eyes. I rolled the truck's window down on my side a little further, enjoying the warm wind blowing around inside the cab.

Martha sat next to me. She was looking out the window, seemingly lost in thought. Her story and her openness surprised me. I'd always thought of Martha Lambright as the steadfast, follow-the-rules Amish woman, but now I knew differently. She had her own personal reasons for inciting change in the community.

The thought of Martha finding her dead sister floating in a pond made me shiver. The Amish certainly had more drama in their lives than outsiders assumed. I'd lived as one of them for several months and I was married to a previously Amish man. I was still being shocked by one thing or another on a regular basis. I guess it just proved that no one was immune to bad things happening to them.

Feeling uncomfortable with the silence in the truck, I said, "Are we almost there?"

Martha came out of her trance. "Oh, yes. Turn left at the next intersection." I made the turn and Martha went on to say, "The property here on the right is my parent's farm. They don't farm it anymore, as they're both in their seventies. My brother-in-law and two of my brothers are running it now. One of my sisters lives in the white house on the hill over there." She pointed it out, "We'll stop there first."

"You were raised in *this* community?" I asked.

"Yes, I was. I know the rustic life very well." Martha smiled fondly. "I met Abram at a mutual cousin's wedding. When we were eventually married ourselves, I couldn't believe how much easier the Meadowview Amish women had it. Living in a house that had running water and a bathroom was such a luxury for me. And the idea of a real refrigerator, powered by gas, instead of an icehouse, was a convenience I had only dreamed of."

I thought about Martha's upbringing, and how difficult it must have been for her as we drove by the never ending fields of churned, dark brown earth. Martha gestured for me to turn onto a gravel driveway that led to a farmhouse. There was a cluster of white barns below the house and even from this distance, I could see the movement of several children playing in the barnyard.

"Why don't all the Amish live the same way?" I asked.

"Even among our people, there are many acceptable ways to live. The rustic Amish believe that the use of any kind of modern convenience or comforts separates them from God. Whereas the Meadowview community believes that some improvements are necessary to our survival. We've adapted more than our cousins, and our reward has been larger numbers of our young people remaining Amish."

I smiled to myself. Martha was lucky to have married Abram all those years ago. Otherwise, her life probably would have been much different.

Then I remembered the Amish boys at Katie and Jacob's wedding—the ones that Suzanna and Miranda were hanging out with. They had been smoking and drinking. Something tickled at my memories. Weren't they from the Hickory Ridge community?

"Is this group of Amish different in other ways?" Seeing Martha's brow raised questioningly, I added, "I mean as far as the rules are concerned? I'd heard that their Ordnung is more lenient than ours."

I wondered why I'd said, *ours,* when I certainly wasn't Amish any longer. We passed two young boys carrying buckets from one barn to another. They slowed to wave at us as we drove by. Three toddler age girls were digging in the flower beds, while a girl who wasn't much older looked on. When I parked the truck and turned off the engine, all the girls ran up to us.

"Yes, they are much looser than we are with the young'uns. They've traded amenities for more freedom. Whether it is God's will or not, is left up for debate." Martha gripped the door handle, but paused. "This is my sister, Miriam's home. I fear that she's having a tough time of it here lately. She gave birth just a few weeks ago and she's overwhelmed."

"How many kids does she have?"

"Seven now. But Miriam's only twenty-eight, and having the children all so close in ages has added to the burden." Martha ignored the little hands knocking on the side of the truck and looked seriously at me. "I warn you, she's out of sorts. Don't take it personally if she acts . . . unfriendly in any way."

I got out of the car slowly, and took a moment to study the house as Martha greeted her many nieces and nephews. The house was small for such a large family, and it didn't have the same overly manicured look that the Amish homes in the Meadowview community had. The paint on this house was peeling and last year's flower beds hadn't been cleaned out. Two black dogs were playing tug of war over a piece of garbage from a knocked over trash can, ignoring our arrival completely. And an assortment of toys littered the ground. Martha was definitely right about her sister being in over her head.

Martha introduced me to all the little ones in a flurry of names that I couldn't possibly remember. Martha handed each child a peppermint from her pocket and speaking in German to them, sent the children away. The little boys returned to their work in the barnyard and the girls began digging again. The older girl openly stared at us as we walked up the porch steps. In most societies, small children wouldn't be left unattended without an adult, but I'd already learned that the Amish were pretty laid back when it came to supervising their children. It was the teenagers they worried about.

Martha went through the front door without knocking and I followed her in. The kitchen was overly warm from the woodstove in the corner, making me feel instantly sleepy. I wondered why anyone would have the stove going on such a nice spring day.

Before I could comment to Martha about it, she silenced me with a finger to her mouth. We crept up to the bassinette by the stove and looked down at the sleeping baby. It was extremely small, even for a newborn. Sarah Ann had been seven pounds at birth, and this baby, who was supposed to be a few weeks old, appeared barely that weight now. But he was sleeping soundly, wearing an old fashioned nightgown and a blue knitted cap.

"His name is John, same as his grandfather. He was born early and has struggled with some health issues," Martha whispered.

Martha left me beside the crib and began clearing the dirty dishes from the table. I glanced around at the messy kitchen and the dirty floor and felt a bit overwhelmed myself. I joined Martha in the cleanup, picking up a handful of plates with half-eaten food on them.

Martha quietly directed me to dump the debris into the hog bucket and wipe off the plates with a towel. The sink had the kind of pump handle you'd expect to find in a barn. I went to lift the handle, but Martha stopped me.

"You must fill a metal pail with water first, then set the pail on the stove to be heated." Martha continued to whisper.

"Seriously?" Now I understood why the stove was cranked up.

"It's quite tedious, I agree," was all Martha said on the matter.

I did as I was instructed, wondering where Miriam was hiding. A few moments later, we had the kitchen straightened up, and I was washing the dishes in the lukewarm water. Martha was sweeping the floor when a toddler burst through the doorway, sobbing hysterically. Several of the other children followed her in, and the girl who had been staring at us, chattered away to Martha in German.

"*Aarem boppli!*" Martha said, dropping the broom and picking up the child who looked to be about two years old. Her cap was nearly falling off and her dress was too big for her. She was barefoot and that's where her injury was.

From the gist of the conversation between the older girl and Martha, I gathered that the baby girl had accidently dug into her foot with a shovel. I grabbed the bucket that still was halfway full and brought it to Martha.

"Good thinking, Rose," Martha said as she lowered the child into the bucket. Instead of causing the girl to shriek louder, the water had the opposite effect. With tears making pathways on her dirty face, she began giggling. But it was too late. The baby had woken from the commotion and began to cry loudly.

That's when Miriam finally arrived. She appeared from the darkened hallway with her tangled brown hair pulled back in a ponytail, and not wearing a cap. Her brown eyes were bloodshot as if she'd just woken from a nap. I was amazed at how young she looked.

Miriam seemed to hardly notice me at all. She ordered the other children out of the house loudly in German and then picked up the crying baby. Although her movements with the baby were gentle, her lack of affection toward the baby was evident.

"Momma, Momma," cried the injured child. Miriam made her way over to where Martha was washing the girl's foot.

Miriam glanced at the cut on the foot. It wasn't very deep and Miriam shrugged it off. She told Martha that a bandage would suffice, and then she went to the rocking chair beside the stove and sat down. In a swift motion, she lifted the flap of her dress and placed the baby against her breast. The baby immediately latched onto the creamy colored skin and began sucking away. Miriam repositioned the flap of fabric to cover herself up again and then turned hard eyes on me.

"Who are you?"

Martha paused from doctoring the toddler and introduced me. "This is Rose. She's the English girl that married Noah Miller."

I was surprised when Miriam made a snort of acknowledgment that she knew who I was. I guessed that gossip of that kind of juicy nature traveled from community to community.

"Hello," I said, approaching the woman with my hand extended.

She touched my hand with a limp handshake. "You were a smart girl to get your lover to go English, instead of the other way around."

"Miriam," Martha chastised. "We were all heartsick to lose both Noah and Rose from our community. It's not a thing to celebrate."

"I disagree with you, dear sister. If a girl isn't born and raised among us, how could she ever accept such burdens?" Miriam said the words in a straightforward manner that I wasn't used to hearing from the Amish. Suzanna was the only other Amish girl I knew who sometimes spoke her mind. Even Rachel kept her secrets.

I noticed that Miriam's accent was heavier than Martha's, telling me that she rarely spoke English. If it weren't for the bags beneath her eyes and the frowning expression, she'd be an attractive woman. I saw the resemblance between Martha and Miriam, but where Martha had laugh wrinkles at the corners of her eyes, Miriam had none.

"That is beside the point. Noah Miller is the one who left his people, not Rose," Martha said. She took a large bandage from a basket on the wall and fastened it to the child's foot. "You might want to have the girl's foot looked at by a doctor. She may need a tetanus shot."

Miriam waved her hand in dismissal. "Ach, she's had some of her shots, and Isaac will not allow money to be spent where it is not needed." She looked back at me. "I still do not understand why you brought this English girl to my house."

Martha sighed heavily and for the first time I felt truly sorry for her. She wanted to help her sister, but the woman was stubborn and difficult. Most sisters would have quit bothering. But the Amish were very loyal to their own. Maybe it was a special kinship that they felt with others who had chosen to live their way, or maybe they were just gluttons for punishment.

"Rose, go ahead and give Miriam the flyer." She turned to Miriam. "That will explain everything."

I handed Miriam the flyer and stood back, watching her flip it open and read. Martha kissed the small girl on the check and sent her out to play with the other children, while Miriam continued to scan the paper she held.

"Your husband approved of this?" Miriam asked with a disbelieving tone.

"The matter was brought before Abram and the ministers. There were two in favor and two against. Abram was one of those opposed to the idea, but he asked me to cast the deciding vote, knowing full well which way I'd go."

"That man has always spoiled you. Taking you to live in that cushy place and not minding that you didn't bear him any children. *Tsk, tsk,* and now this?" Miriam complained.

Cushy place? I realized that Miriam had it worse off than Martha did, but no Amish woman had it easy. I could vouch for that firsthand.

"This is a good thing, Miriam. There are times during planting and harvesting when it's almost impossible to sew a dress or make clothes for the children. Your life will be a little easier," Martha said, sitting down beside her sister. I continued to stand, leaning back against the table.

"Isaac won't allow me to purchase a dress," Miriam said.

"You don't know that for sure. The men seem to be coming around in our community," Martha offered.

"You can ask him yourself," Miriam's chin jutted toward the door just as a man, I assumed to be Isaac, came in.

Martha stood and greeted the man, *"Hoe gaat het, Isaac."*

Isaac was a heavy-set man with a full brown beard. His voice boomed as he exchanged pleasantries with Martha. After a moment, he turned his attention to me. He rattled off in German as he glanced my way.

Miriam responded in English. "She's married to Noah Miller—Amos's son."

Isaac's eyebrow lifted at the scandal. He nodded and said curtly, "Hello."

Before I could say a word, Miriam spoke up once again. "Here, give him this."

Since she'd motioned to me, I took the flyer and passed it to Isaac.

"What is this?" Isaac asked, as his eyes skimmed the paper.

"Rose and some of the other girls in the Meadowview community have opened a dress shop. Martha is supporting the idea and invited me to consider having a dress made," Miriam said.

I watched Isaac's face turn from passive to hostile in the blink of an eye.

"This is not our way," he said simply, dropping the flyer onto the table. He dipped his hat to Martha and said her name and then did the same to me. He was out the door again a moment later.

"You see what I am up against. Ach, it's no use," Miriam said weakly.

Martha crossed the room and took her sister's hand and

KAREN ANN HOPKINS

held it. "It's the little things that make the most difference in our lives. Have faith that after a time, the men will begin accepting the shop. I've prayed about it, and I believe we have the Lord's blessing."

"I hope you're right, good sister. For I'm at my wits end." Miriam looked at me and added, "Good luck with your shop, Rose—you're going to need it. Most Amish men think like my husband."

When we were back in the truck, pulling out onto the roadway, I exhaled. "That didn't go very smoothly," I told Martha.

"Every sprout of an idea begins with a seed before it takes root. If God wills it, Isaac will see the light," Martha said.

"And what if he doesn't?" I asked.

Martha turned to me with sadness in her brown eyes. "Then I'll lose another sister," she said plainly.

CHAPTER 24

🌿 Rachel 🌿

"Why did you come along if you're going to wear that sour face?" Peter asked with a grimace.

I glanced at my little brother and noticed for the first time that he was as tall as I was. When did that happen? He had the same straight nose and wide-spaced dark eyes that Noah possessed, but his spirit was less rebellious, putting me in mind of my oldest brother, Jacob. Everything was by the book with him, and Peter seemed to have the same temperament. I was bothered that he'd spoken to me with such authority.

"What does it matter to you whether I smile or not?" I snapped.

"For one, you're not much fun to be around, and for another, you'll never be asked to court with such a face." Peter wasn't looking at me, instead focusing on unbuckling Juniper's strappings.

"Do you think I care about that?" I leaned in close and hissed, "I'm not like all the other little hens searching for their rooster around here. I'm perfectly content by myself, thank you very much."

"Jah, right," Peter scoffed. "I think it's just an act."

I was too angry to respond. Once Juniper was completely unhitched, he led the horse away to the hitching rail, and I stood rooted in place. I wondered if everyone thought the same of me. I spread my mouth into a smile and it felt strange, so

I let it go. I'd always been serious, even as a child. I favored Noah in that way. The rest of the Miller children were outgoing and friendly, even little Naomi was always singing tidings to everyone. Noah could at least fake it. I just avoided contact with other people as much as possible. *So what was I doing here,* I asked myself for the twelfth time.

I looked around in wonder at all the activity. The evening air was cool and dew was already forming on the thick, green grass. The sun had set behind the low hills to the west a few moments ago, and with the loss of the sun came the buttery light of dusk. The periodic sound of a bat hitting a ball rang through the air, along with the cheers of the spectators.

I walked slowly between the parked buggies until I reached the last one. I stopped and peeked around it at the ball game. It looked as if most of the community's youth were present. About two dozen girls lined the one side of the field, alternating from standing and sitting positions in small groups. Their dresses were similar to a rainbow from this distance. Shades of blue, maroon, and green fluttered in the breeze, while the boys playing the game wore dark pants, white shirts and black suspenders. I noted that a few adults watched from the discreet distance of the hilltop that the school was situated on. A whinny of a horse called out from somewhere behind me. I sighed. I'd been looking for Micah, and he was nowhere to be seen.

Again, I asked myself the same question: *what was I doing here?*

I smoothed down my hunter green dress and rolled my eyes at my silliness. Even if Micah did show up, he wouldn't pay attention to me. Peter was right. I did frown all the time. And who wanted an angry woman? And then there were all the things that I did that no one even knew about. Micah would never want me if the truth came to light.

"You'd think they'd all be too tired to run around the bases like that."

I nearly jumped out of my skin and whirled around.

Micah was grinning at me, but he quickly lost the amused look and added, "Don't you agree?"

"You snuck up on me," I accused, feeling the spreading heat on my cheeks.

"No. I walked up the same as I usually do. You were just very distracted with your spying," Micah said with feigned seriousness.

I stared at him for a moment, daring him to break contact first. But I was the one to look away. I chuckled.

"You caught me. I *was* spying." I motioned for Micah to join me and he stepped up to my side. "Do you see Harriet standing at the far end?"

"In the dark blue?" Micah asked.

I nodded. "She wants to catch Ben's eye—that's why she's standing so close to the batters."

"How would you know that? I thought you didn't gossip with the girls," Micah said.

"I don't. But it's impossible not to overhear the other girls talking at the factory from time to time."

Micah joined in and said, "Seth is sweet on a girl named Claudia."

"Where are they?" I scanned the field, not seeing them.

Micah thumbed back toward the hitching shed. "They're behind the shed."

"Alone?" I whispered. Claudia was a prim and proper favorite of the bishop's. What would he think, and do, if he knew of her sinful behavior?

Micah nodded with a smirk. "I guess spring is in the air," he said lightly.

The sky darkened another notch, making me feel reckless.

"I wish we were somewhere else," I breathed.

I glanced up and saw Micah's head tilted thoughtfully. When he spoke, it was in a whisper. "Aren't you feeling sick?"

"No, what makes you . . . "

He interrupted. "You know, if you were sick, you'd need someone to drive you home, right?"

There was a twinkle in his eyes, and his excitement pulled me in. "Yes, I suppose. But if I were truly ill, I'd simply go to Peter and ask him to drive me home. Or better yet, I'd drive myself home and tell one of the other boys to let Peter know."

"What if you couldn't find Peter?" Micah smiled knowingly. "I saw Peter heading down to the creek with several other boys a few moments ago. If you did go looking for him, you wouldn't find him." Micah raised a brow. "Then what would you do?"

"I'd have to drive Juniper home myself." I scrunched up my face. "But that would be just me, not the both of us," I pointed out.

"I could hide in the buggy. My driver dropped me off earlier and I was going to hitch a ride home with someone anyway. I'll just walk through the fields, or maybe I can stop by Justin's later to see if he'll give me a lift."

I looked at Micah with new eyes. I never imagined him to be so devious. The knowledge sent a quiet thrill through me. The idea that Micah considered Justin a close enough English friend to ask such a favor, was intriguing, too.

"It's a good plan," I said. "You stay here and I'll get Juniper hitched up."

Micah graced me with a wicked smile and a tingling sensation spread out in my belly. When I felt the heat fanning my cheeks, I left him to get the horse.

Thankfully, the roadway was fairly deserted as Juniper trotted over the pavement. When I passed the old widow, Mrs. Burkholder, I was forced to stop and chat for a moment. I politely answered her questions about how my family was doing and then said goodbye, snapping the reins across Juniper's back.

The horse shot forward. I reveled in the *swoosh* of cool, nighttime air that blew in through the open buggy windows.

"That was close," I called over my shoulder to Micah. He was curled up in a ball on the floorboard of the buggy.

Micah laughed. "Leave it to Widow Burkholder to swoop in for some gossip."

"What would you have done if she'd somehow spotted you?" I asked in a loud enough voice to be heard over the pounding hooves.

"I wasn't worried. She's not spry enough to stand up and crane her body to look inside the buggy. Besides, no one will suspect that you're carrying a hidden passenger. It's way too scandalous."

It definitely was a scandal and my heart raged at the thought of it. It was less nerve wracking to sneak out late at night and meet up with my English friends, than to sneak an Amish boy home with me. Especially an Amish boy like Micah, who my parents would rather not have me involved with in the first place.

Our newly built farmhouse came into view and Juniper automatically picked up speed when he realized that he was close to home. We slowed only for the turn and then struck back into a trot all the way to the barnyard.

When I pulled Juniper to a stop in front of the stable, Micah peeked up from the back seat. "Now, you're sure no one is home?"

I smiled. So he was afraid after all. Actually, that was a good thing. It told me that he had a rebel heart, but a bit of sense, too.

"Father and Mother took the smaller children to the Wittmers' farm for dinner this evening. Father enjoys talking to Clarence, and they usually stay late. With all the gossip swirling around about the dress shop, I'm sure they'll be even later than usual."

I climbed out of the buggy and was immediately greeted by Betsy. She wriggled all over and pushed her nose into my hand. I stroked her face, and then joined Micah as he began unhitching Juniper.

My heart fluttered and my breaths were short. I didn't like the feeling at all, and had really only experienced it with one other boy before—and that was Justin. My mind went back to the night before and everything that had happened. As my hand worked to undo the straps on Juniper's harness, I remembered Justin's bruised and bloodied face. I also vaguely recalled pressing my own wet face into his shirt and how he'd held and comforted me. He had smelled nice, too—a piney-musky scent.

But here I was, sneaking around with Micah, and thoroughly enjoying it.

"I'll take that," Micah said as he grasped the collar from my arms. "The quicker we get your horse put out, the quicker we can go for a walk."

"A walk?" I followed him into the tack room.

Micah hung the collar neatly up on the racks with the others and turned to me.

"Before Noah broke up with Constance, Peter took me back to your pond to fish. If you're up to it, I'd like to see if the fish are active?"

"Sure, we can do that," I said quietly, wondering.

Maybe Micah wasn't really interested in me in *that* way, after all. We brushed Juniper off together in silence and then let the horse go into the pasture. Darkness was nearly complete, but the full moon gave off a bright glow that illuminated the fields around us so that we could see clearly. Micah hung Juniper's halter and lead rope on the post, and we began walking up the narrow dirt lane that meandered through the grass to the pond.

"I'm glad the girls won the vote to have the dress shop. I think it's a good thing for the community," Micah said.

"Really?" I toyed with the ends of my bonnet strings. "Most of the men are against it. What makes you different?"

"It just make sense, is all. I see how hard my Ma works. She never has any spare time. At least Da gets to go hunting and to the livestock sales. I can't really remember when the last time was that Ma did something for herself." He shrugged. "Maybe having the option to buy a dress or clothes for the children, instead of make them, will give her a little bit of free time."

"Why can't the others see it the way you do?"

"It's hard for them to change. They're fearful that one thing will lead to another, and before long we'll have television sets and computers in our homes."

Micah had said it seriously, but I glanced his way to see a grin on his face. We both broke into laughter. It felt good to laugh again.

When we calmed down, I straightened up. "I don't think it will make a huge difference in our community at all. But it gives me hope that small changes can take place—that we're not stuck in the exact same way forever."

"You want to stay Amish, don't you?" Micah said with the wide eyes of sudden clarity.

"There are times when I can't imagine remaining Amish. But I don't want to be English, either," I replied stubbornly.

There was a moment of silence, with only the sound of the tree frogs and the crickets chirping around us, before Micah finally said, "There aren't many other alternatives, are there? I mean, I suppose we can join the Mennonites." His voice rose excitedly. "And then I could drive a big black pickup truck."

We'd just reached the crest of the hill, and the pond spread out below us in the shape of a kidney bean. The moonlight shimmered off the water and a few Mallard ducks drifted along the surface beside the reeds. I stopped Micah with my hand on his arm, and he looked back at me with an open face.

I let go of his arm, and still feeling the tingling sensation in my fingers at touching him, I said, "You said *we*—why did you say that?"

For an instant, Micah looked doubtful, but the expression passed and he smiled warmly. "I thought that we might some-day be together, doing the same things, sharing the same life."

KAREN ANN HOPKINS

Fear gripped me. It pricked my insides until I felt as if I was going to throw up. I could admit that I cared for Micah, and maybe even had a crush on the handsome Amish boy. But there were things still holding me back. And I didn't want to hurt Micah. He deserved better than a confused, sinful girlfriend.

I couldn't let the opportunity to confront him pass by, though. It wasn't my nature to sit back and let things happen. I needed some control over my life.

"Are you still in love with my sister?" I asked bluntly.

Micah walked a few steps away and then came back. Our eyes met. "A part of me will always love Sarah. She was the first girl who ever caught my eye. And for a while there, I thought that she was going to be my wife. It's difficult to completely get over someone who you cared for so much." His gaze became fiercer. "What I'm beginning to feel for you is real, too. I love your independent spirit and the way you speak your mind. Your need to be alone is something I admire. I'm not a big joiner, either. I think something special could develop between us—if you'd just give me a chance."

I looked at Micah closely. He was several inches taller than me, and his untidy brown hair was a little too long. I knew the light spattering of freckles over his nose would multiply with the hot sun of summertime, and his green eyes reminded me of lush grass. I wanted nothing more at that moment than to simply kiss him—but a kiss wasn't simple to our people. It meant a commitment to court, and eventually marry. In a heartbeat, I saw our entire lives rolled out before us. We'd have a white farmhouse and eight children. Micah would be a farmer and I'd be a housewife. He'd love me with all of his heart, and be a good husband and father. But was that the life I wanted? All the other girls seemed to easily make up their minds by the time they were sixteen, but I wasn't like them.

I wanted to test fate. If I was truly meant to be with Micah, then nothing I would say would prevent that from happening.

"I have feelings for you Micah—but I also care for another."

Seeing Micah's face drop, crushed me. I wanted to take the words back and tell him that I wanted only him. But it was too late. Micah opened his mouth to speak, but then closed it again.

When he finally did respond, he wasn't angry, just sad sounding. "Do you mind me asking who it is?"

"Can you keep a secret, Micah Schwartz?" I said, holding his gaze.

"You can always trust me. I would never betray you or purposely cause you harm."

I believed him.

"It's Justin."

CHAPTER 25

.... Justin ....

The knocking at the door startled me. I set down the book I was reading, and leaned over the back of the couch to peer out the window. "Hmm," I muttered to myself when I didn't see a car in the driveway. The knocking sounded again. This time Hope started barking.

"All right, girl. I've got this." I patted Hope's furry black and white head. The dog escorted me to the door anyway.

I opened the door a little ways and was surprised to see Micah standing on the porch. He was wearing a black knit hat and a black coat. His pants were dark blue and his boots were also black. His bright green eyes seemed to shine amidst all the dark clothing.

"Hey, dude, what's up?" I asked, but suspecting already that it probably had something to do with Rachel.

"I hate to ask this of you—are you busy right now?" Micah said, as he peeked around me to look into the foyer.

"No busier than usual. Do you need something?" It was beginning to feel a little awkward. I barely knew the kid.

"Yes, I need a ride home. I'll pay you for the service, I promise." Micah insisted.

I picked up on a sort of desperateness to Micah's demeanor that I couldn't quite put my finger on. It intrigued me, and then I was also just a nice guy.

"Sure, no problem. You don't have to pay me, either. I was

in need of some fresh air." I winked at Micah. "I'll get my keys. You can go get into the car if you want."

"Thank you, Justin."

Never a dull moment around here, I mused, as I watched Micah walk away.

Once we were on the road, Micah said, "If you don't mind me asking, what happened to your face?"

I smiled gingerly and the action still made my face hurt. I'd almost forgotten that I looked as if I'd been run over by a semi.

"Some guys beat me up last night." I looked sideways at Micah.

"Why would they do that?"

"Because of a girl, of course," I said dryly.

"Turn here," Micah told me, almost too late.

I hit the brakes and made the turn with squealing tires.

"Sorry about that," Micah said. He was quiet for a moment, and then asked, "Did you fight them back?"

I chuckled and a pain shot through my stomach. I swallowed the discomfort. "I never really had a chance. The one guy was holding me while the other was doing the punching. But don't worry, they got their dues."

"Revenge?" Micah asked stoically.

I was impressed. I didn't think an Amish kid would know anything about the word.

I nodded. "Yep, my brother, Sam, and Noah confronted the guys and basically told them never to bother me and—" I stopped myself. Micah might be intelligent enough to figure out the other person I was talking about was Rachel, if I mentioned her name directly. I couldn't let her secret life slip. I had to be more careful. "And then they took them out for me."

"Took them out?" Micah questioned with raptly staring eyes.

There was a buggy ahead of us and I slowed down when I caught up to it. The horse's hooves were striking the pavement rhythmically. The sound vibrated loudly into the car through the open windows. I checked all the mirrors and carefully pulled around, passing the buggy. I noticed Micah turning his head away from the buggy, and I wondered if he was concerned about being caught for some perceived wrongdoing.

I shrugged. "You know, took them out—beat 'em up the same way they did me."

Micah seemed distracted. "Your world is very violent."

It was true, but it still bugged me that he said *your* world. It reminded me of how Rachel also thought that she lived in a separate universe from the one I lived in. I tried to brush off the offended feeling.

"Yeah, well, I'm sixteen and that's the first time I've ever been struck by someone. Even my parents never spanked me," I pointed out.

"That amazes me," Micah said. He motioned for me to make another turn. "Mulberry Road, to the left."

"What amazes you?" I suspected what he meant, but with the Amish, you never really knew.

"That your father has never punished you. I'm the least rebellious of all my brothers, and I've had my bottom whipped several times in just the last year," Micah said with a level tone, and not a resentful one.

"I've been punished hundreds of times. But Dad has never physically touched me. Usually, I get my game privileges or my phone taken away for a few days." I smiled. "Now, I do remember Mom spanking Sam when he was about nine years old. He had put glue in Rose's hair while she slept, and cutting her hair off was the only way to get it out. Mom wasn't pleased."

"You must miss her very much," Micah said softly.

I glanced his way. There was only pity in his eyes and I realized he wasn't mocking me. It struck me odd that I had only hung out with Micah a couple of times, and I'd had more conversation with him than I'd had with Mason and Gavin put together in the entire school year. I was starting to get what Rose saw in some of the Amish people.

"Of course I do. Everything changed when she died. Honestly, we never would have moved to Meadowview if she was still alive," I said cautiously. I wasn't sure about getting too deep into my personal life with Micah.

"Here it is," Micah said. He pointed to a farmhouse sitting prettily on a hillside.

I pulled onto the winding driveway and followed it up to the barns.

"You can let me off here. My folks go to sleep early and the car's engine will wake them," Micah instructed.

Micah began to open up his billfold and I stopped him. "No man, really. I don't mind giving you a lift from time to time."

Micah settled back into the seat as if he was staying awhile. He cleared his throat and I instantly became worried.

"I know this is none of my business. But I care about her and I don't want to see her get hurt." He looked at me with pleading eyes, and a nervous knot formed in my gut. "She's had a lot to deal with this past year and she's a bit unstable. She might not behave rationally—and it seems that I may be the only person aware of her situation."

"Who?" I drew the word out to illustrate my feigned confusion.

Micah took a breath and then shot the words out. "Rachel Miller. Are your intentions serious about her? If they are, I won't interfere. I believe a person should make up their own mind about who they spend the rest of their life with. But if you're just . . . playing with her affections . . . I have to ask you to stop. It just isn't right."

Micah continued to stare at me, but he sat back once again. I marveled at his declaration and his set-in-stone face. He was serious. My level of respect for Micah Schwartz climbed even higher, but I was still wondering what had even brought the subject up in the first place. Perhaps Rachel was sharing more information with Micah than I first thought. But still, I had to be careful how I proceeded.

"You've got it all wrong, Micah. I have no interest in Rachel in that way," I lied. "She's my brother-in-law's sister. I see her occasionally, but that's about it."

Micah looked doubtfully at me. "Then why did she tell me that she has feelings for you?"

That took me aback. I looked out the window into the darkened barnyard. There was a calico cat daintily walking on the top fence rail and I watched as it paused, swishing its tail. An instant later, it jumped into the shadows, chasing something. The moonlight lit up the field full of cows beyond the barns, but the barnyard itself was dark and eerie looking.

Could it be possible that Rachel *actually* had feelings for me? I seriously doubted it. The only real emotion I'd seen from her was when I held her in my arms the previous night, but that was because she was drunk out of her mind and her English friends were being busted apart. Even when I'd seen her at her sister's funeral, she lacked emotion. She was tough and I admired her for that. She was intelligent and that intrigued me. She was beautiful and that attracted me. But for crying out loud, she was Amish. I could only imagine the rampage Amos Miller would go on if his daughter ever hooked up with an English guy—and a Cameron to boot. Just contemplating it was insane. But I couldn't completely get her out of my mind, either.

And then, I wondered how much Micah really knew about Rachel. I decided the best course of action was to deflect suspicion. "Maybe she got the wrong idea. I was just being genuinely nice to her when I was helping rebuild her family's farm."

Micah continued to look at me, making me squirm in my seat. I wished that he would simply get out of the car and leave me alone with the accusation. It was weird to be so calmly discussing a girl with a guy who I knew was madly in love with her. It was all wrong.

"You're a good person, Justin. I can see that. You need to make up your mind about Rachel, so she can move on with her life." He sighed heavily. "It's taken me a long time to get over Sarah enough to move forward myself. I'll be honest with you. I care for Rachel and only want her happiness. Please talk to her."

He stepped out of the car. "Thanks again for the ride," he said, and then he was jogging through the shadows toward the house.

• • • • ● • • • •

I quietly opened the door and stepped into the dark house. Hearing voices coming from the family room, I stealthily walked into the room without being noticed. Rose and Noah were on the couch, pressed into each other's sides with a bowl of popcorn between them. Sam had his arm around Summer on the loveseat. They were watching a classic horror movie, and I'd entered the room at the same moment that the little demon/ghost girl was streaking down the hallway about to decapitate a young woman huddling in a corner.

I picked that moment to shriek, "Watch out!"

All four of them jumped, the popcorn went flying, and Hope began barking. I leaned up against the wall, laughing too hard to speak when Rose rounded on me.

"You idiot, you're going to wake the baby!" She crossed the room and pushed her finger into my face. "And if she wakes up, you'll be the one rocking her for the next two hours to get her back to sleep."

I sobered at the thought. Sam threw a pillow at me and said, "Nice one." Noah shook his head, and Summer still clutched her chest.

I was about to leave the room, when Rose flicked the lights on. "Whoa, you're not going anywhere."

Sam grinned and used the remote to turn off the TV.

I reluctantly sat down in the recliner and folded my hands over my stomach. Rose began picking up the popcorn, but Summer stopped her. "I'll do that. You go on and have your talk."

There wasn't really much for Summer to pick up anyway. Hope was already chowing down.

"Where were you?" Rose asked with the narrowed eyes of a very suspicious person. "We were just getting ready to pull in when we saw you pull out. And there was someone in the car with you."

"Don't you have anything better to do than spy on me?"

"You've got to be kidding—you're the one who got beat up at a bar last night over an Amish girl. We should have a full team of security guards on you." Rose growled the words out.

"She has a point," Sam chuckled.

"You stay out of this," Rose told Sam before she confronted me again. "You are my responsibility, Justin. Until you're eighteen, I've agreed to take care of you so you don't have to live with an always absent father and a new stepmother. You owe me a straight answer here."

I glanced at Noah. His expression looked neutral, and there was a small gash above his eye. Sam's face was completely clear of any marks. If Rose knew how over-the-top hit man they went on those two guys, she'd be grilling them right now, instead of me.

But seeing the desperate worry on Rose's face, and thinking that she looked a lot like a younger version of Mom, I caved.

"It was no big deal. Micah Schwartz showed up on the doorstep, wanting a ride home. I obliged him. That was it," I said evenly.

"Do you swear on Mom's grave that you're telling the truth?" Rose said.

"Is that necessary?" Sam interrupted.

"Yes it is. Shut up, Sam," Rose hissed.

"I solemnly swear on Mom's grave that I'm telling the truth," I said without hesitation.

Rose was satisfied, and she sat back down beside Noah.

She looked at Noah. "I don't get it. Why is Micah Schwartz suddenly showing up to ask Justin to drive him around?"

"I don't know," Noah said.

"Maybe it's because he's after Rachel, and he thinks Justin is, too." Summer paused from her cleaning to offer her suggestion.

"My sister, Rachel?" Noah asked. "What does Micah Schwartz have to do with her?"

Summer shrugged. "Suzanna thinks Micah is sweet on her. It's a little sick if you ask me. He was courting Sarah first."

Noah's face was showing alarm and Rose put her arm around him. Sam interjected his two cents. "He's taking a huge step down going for the little sister. Sarah was a nice girl, but Rachel's nothing but trouble."

"Sam—shut up," Rose shouted. She realized her mistake when the beginnings of Sarah Ann's full blown squalling fit came through the baby monitor. She looked around for someone else to blame, but then closed her mouth and left the room.

"Sorry, bro. I didn't mean be rude. It's just an observation," Sam said sheepishly.

"No, you're right about my sisters. Most people wouldn't say it out loud, but Sarah was sweet and kind, and Rachel . . . well, Rachel . . . has always been a troubled girl. Even when she was a child, she was difficult. I'd try to make her laugh with a joke or by walking on my hands, or something like that, and she wouldn't even crack a smile. She'd just sit there, probably thinking that I was the one with the problems. It used to worry Mother, but Sarah would always say that Rachel was the most special of all the Miller kids—that she was the truly honest one." Noah sounded tired. "But after what I witnessed last night, I think she's completely out of control." He looked back and forth between me and Sam. "Something really bad might happen to her if we don't intervene."

"Whoa, wait a minute. What are you thinking?" I sprang back to life, leaning forward in the chair.

"I'm going to tell Father about where we found Rachel last night . . . and what she was doing," Noah said with rising determination.

"That's a bad idea," I said.

"Yeah, you might want to think about that a while longer," Summer offered. "That will get her *so* punished."

"She needs to be disciplined! She snuck out of the house and got drunk . . . with men," Noah said harshly. He turned to Sam, "What would you do if it was Rose in the same predicament?"

Sam's mouth became a thin line. He took a slow breath and exhaled. He hesitated, obviously uncomfortable with being put into the hot seat. "If it were me, I'd tell Dad."

I buried my head in my hands. "You're going to destroy her if you do it," I warned Noah.

"And I won't let you, Noah," Rose said, stepping back into the room with a groggy looking Sarah Ann in her arms. "Give her a little time to work things out on her own. If she's still a mess in a week or two, then talk to your dad."

Noah gave up immediately, reluctantly nodding. Rose faced me. "You need to talk to Rachel. Micah is the best thing that could happen to that girl. And the only thing holding her back, might just be you."

"When can I talk to her? Amish girls are about as unavailable as the president to a guy like me," I pointed out. "I just got lucky at Dewey's Bar—and that bouncer will never let me in there again."

"You'll get your chance tomorrow morning," Rose said.

"Aww, man, tomorrow's the beginning of Easter break at school. I don't have to get up early," I whined, hating the sound of my own voice.

"That's perfect. I told Noah's mom that I'd drive Rachel to the birdhouse factory tomorrow." She turned to Noah.

"I guess your mom needs her help in the morning with the laundry."

"How does this put me in contact with Rachel?" I asked, dreading the answer.

"Because you're going to be the one picking her up," Rose told me.

"Amos Miller already threatened my life if he caught me with his daughter. I'm not stupid," I said.

"Father's crew is working with mine on a house in town tomorrow. He'll leave the house long before you pick Rachel up," Noah assured me.

"Do you really want me to talk to your sister?" I asked Noah.

Noah ran his hand through his dark hair and then stood up. He held his hands out to Sarah Ann and she lurched toward him. He took her from Rose and kissed her cheek.

Finally, Noah answered me. "I only hope you can help. I don't want to lose another sister."

Rose said goodnight to Summer before she left the room with Noah. Summer was sitting beside Sam and without any shyness, she gave him a kiss on the lips.

"You're not going already, are you?" Sam snaked his arms around her, trying to hold her in close.

"Momma let me borrow the van only because I promised her I'd be home before eleven o'clock. If I don't make it back in time, she'll never let me borrow it again," Summer said as she wiggled away from Sam.

"Why does she need her van at this hour?" Sam pouted.

"She does her grocery shopping at night when no one else is in the store. She likes it that way."

"That's crazy," Sam said, but he got up anyway and walked with Summer to the door.

"I'm not denying it. She is crazy." Summer stopped beside me and patted my head the same way I'd pat Hope. "Good luck tomorrow."

"Thanks," I muttered.

I couldn't see them, but I could hear Summer and Sam making out in the open doorway. I ignored them, wondering what everyone thought I could say to Rachel that would make any difference in her life.

And what about my life? I wasn't even sure if I wanted to push her into Micah's arms, or try to keep her for myself.

CHAPTER 26

❧ Rachel ❧

I quietly closed the door behind me and took the porch steps two at a time. The grass was already damp, and I hated the foot tracks that I left behind me as I raced toward the barn with Betsy on my heels. I wasn't taking any chances this time. When I reached the door, I pushed the dog through the opening.

"Hush, Betsy. Be a good girl. I'll be back soon to let you out," I promised the dog.

Once the door was secure, I sprinted across the shadowed side of the house. When I reached the road, I only slowed enough to catch my breath. I guessed that it was nearly eleven-thirty and I worried that I would be late. Father and Mother had arrived home at ten o'clock with the children, and by the time everyone had chatted for a while, cleaned up and said their prayers, it was almost eleven before they were in their beds. I had waited until the moment when I'd heard Father's snoring to tiptoe down the stairs and across the kitchen floor. It had been my scariest escape yet and my heart still pounded furiously in my chest.

I didn't bother with the safety of the ditch and bushes. After a moment, I slowed to a jog, my lungs nearly bursting with the effort. I crossed onto Martin Road, and kept jogging until I saw the headlights parked in the pull-off beside the woods. I waved, making sure they saw me. I began walking, breathing heavily. My lungs stung and my heart still beat erratically. I wondered if it was worth all the trouble, but then dismissed the thought. Yes, it was definitely worth it.

The tinted windows kept me from seeing inside the small black car as I approached. Just as I reached the driver's side door, the window came slowly down.

"I don't know why I even answered your call. You don't deserve my generosity." Sadie spit out a piece of gum. It nearly hit my foot.

"Thank you so much. I'll owe you one," I said, not sure if I sounded contrite enough. I looked across the seat at Charlotte. She was scowling at me. "How are Avery and Jasper? Are they all right?"

"Jasper has a broken nose, and he doesn't even have insurance, so it's going to heal all crooked." Charlotte snarled the words out.

"Avery's pretty messed up, too, but nothing is broken," Sadie said.

"I'm so sorry about that. I had no idea anyone would come looking for me." I was telling the truth.

Sadie stared hard into my eyes, and then sighed. "I know. You were just as freaked out as we were. And to tell you the truth, they deserved it. That kid, Justin, shouldn't have been beaten like that. If it had been my little brother, my older brother would have done the same thing."

I nodded. Feeling a little more at ease with Sadie, at least. Charlotte still glared at me.

"I'm glad you understand," I said, reaching for the door handle on the backseat passenger's side.

"Wait." Sadie hesitated, glancing at Charlotte. "I think we need to cool it for a while." Sadie met my gaze squarely again. "It's nothing personal. We just don't want to stir up any more trouble."

My face must have shown my disappointment. She added, "It's not forever. Just give it some time for things to settle down."

I smiled tightly and turned away. Sadie called out to me, "Wait!"

I looked over my shoulder. Sadie was holding out a brown paper bag. I couldn't tell its contents, but I had a suspicion about what was in it.

"Here, you take the rest. You probably need it more than we do," Sadie said, holding the bag out the open window even further.

My heart hammered in my chest. I thought of Justin and pictured his disapproving face. It caused the breath to catch in my throat to think of how shocked Micah would be. But most of all, Sarah was on my mind. She would be so sad.

The bag continued to be wagged back and forth, while a battle raged inside of me. I knew it was wrong—that it would only destroy me. But I was weak. And so very depressed.

I hesitated on the balls of my feet. My head hurt with thoughts of the people I cared for and the cold, hard realities of my life. Tomorrow, I'd rise at five o'clock to start the laundry for Mother, and then I'd climb into Rose's truck and head to the factory. My day would be full of boards to cut. The other girls would ignore me while they gossiped behind my back. And all the while, there would be the pain of knowing that when I returned home, my sweet sister, Sarah, wouldn't be there. She would never be there again.

And even though I had true feelings for Micah—feelings that could actually grow into love—I would forever think of my dead sister every time I looked into his eyes. I'd be cursed with wondering whether he was thinking about Sarah when he looked at me.

Then there was Justin. Kind, brilliant, and brave, Justin. What was I going to do about him?

My vision blurred for an instant, and the need to erase all the badgering thoughts became too much. I returned to the car and took the bag from Sadie.

"Thanks," I muttered.

I began walking on the road and didn't even glance back when I heard the car's engine spring to life. Its headlights danced across the pavement while Sadie pulled forward and then did a U-turn. I listened to the motor as it became fainter, until once again, I was surrounded by the quiet of the countryside. Pushing my legs ever faster, I reached the corner of our farm quickly. I followed the fence line until I almost reached the barnyard. I paused and glanced at the dark farmhouse, imagining my parents and younger siblings fast asleep. In the distance, a pack of coyotes yapped at the moonlight.

When I reached the clump of bushes beside the buggy shed, I put the bag beneath my arm and clenched. I needed both of my hands free to push aside the spiky branches. A moment later, I was hidden beneath the newly leafed out foliage. I took a deep breath, thankful that the nighttime air was unseasonably warm.

The bag sat heavily in my hands and I stared at it. I'd already recognized the shape and feel of the prize it held. In my mind, I both thanked and cursed Sadie. She was the best, and worst of friends.

The desire became too much. I pulled the bottle from the bag and removed the cap. Not even reading the label, I brought it to my lips and drank deeply. The burning, nasty taste scorched my tongue and then set my throat on fire. I ignored the painful sensation, taking another swig. It worked quickly. Very soon, my vision blurred—and my mind became deliciously numb. There was no birdhouse factory, nor a frowning father. No, Justin, Micah—and no Sarah.

The world was peaceful once again.

CHAPTER 27

Rose

$\mathscr{S}$arah Ann rolled in her playpen, alternating between mouthing a pink felt dolly and blowing bubbles. My heart swelled with a love like no other. My baby had a head full of her father's thick, dark hair, but at four months old, her eyes favored my blue ones. She had Sam's naughty laugh and Sarah's patient manner. She truly was a combination of both her Amish and English roots. What I really wanted to do was go over to her and pick her warm heaviness up for a cuddle.

"Focus, Rose. You're going to sew your finger to the cloth if you don't," Suzanna warned.

I looked up and the room came back into focus. Summer sat on the counter. The sunlight coming through the window caught the highlights in her hair. I frowned for a moment, envying her. Not because of her hair. She had the task of putting the different buttons, needles, and thread spools into the sale boxes.

"Rose Miller," Suzanna said my name again.

"What?" I snapped.

For once, Suzanna's blond hair was pulled neatly up beneath her white cap. She wore a light maroon colored dress that almost looked pink. I had to begrudgingly give her credit. She looked the part of a dress-making business woman.

Ella continued to peddle her own sewing machine, threading the blue cloth she pushed through, and trying to ignore the sewing lesson that I was having to endure. But the amused grin on her face said plainly that she was failing.

The occasional thud and scrape in the backroom reminded me that Miranda was there, putting away the newest supplies. I was much more suited to that job, too.

"You're the one who wanted to be involved with the actual dressmaking. And now you're not even trying. You'll never get any better at this rate," Suzanna snorted.

I sighed. She was right. I *had* begged to do some of the sewing. But Suzanna was ruining everything with her compulsively perfectionist ways.

"Maybe I would do better if you'd actually let me sew. You keep making me redo my threads," I argued.

Suzanna made an attempt to take a calming breath, but her voice was still harsh when she spoke. "Your seams are crooked. No Amish woman is going to buy a garment that is less than what she can make herself."

"So, I'm a little out of practice." I shrugged.

"You seem to have forgotten everything Ruth taught you," Suzanna shot back. She was working on her own light green dress, and I noticed that even though we began at the same time, hers was nearly halfway finished.

"If you'd just let me continue on, it will come back to me. All this stopping and rethreading is breaking up my rhythm," I replied.

Suzanna and I stared at each other. We were both strong-willed individuals, and we usually enjoyed each other's company more so because of it. But here lately, we were doing nothing except butting heads.

Unexpectedly, Ella spoke up. "It might help Rose to sew the entire dress, just for practice. That's how I learned," Ella suggested.

I looked smugly at Suzanna, who shot a threatening glare at Ella.

"We don't have the luxury of Rose wasting time on a dress

that can't be sold. Our grand opening is next week, if you've forgotten," Suzanna said with slow emphasis.

"Then put me in the storeroom and let Miranda finish the dumb dress," I said hotly.

Suzanna frowned at me as if I were a child—and a stupid one at that. "Miranda was on the machine all day yesterday. And besides, the storeroom has to be organized just right. Since you're not a seamstress, you wouldn't set it up properly.

I saw Ella's eyes widen considerably. She looked down at her own work, probably wishing she were somewhere else.

The sudden urge to really chew Suzanna out was dampened when I thought of Miriam and her depressing life. Most Amish women didn't have the right to say much about anything, but they seemed perfectly content. Then there were those like Miriam, who really struggled with their circumstances. Suzanna would go insane if all she had to look forward to were babies and housework. This dress shop was her outlet—and it *was* her idea. With an effort, I swallowed my pride. After all, I got involved in the business for Suzanna and Miranda's sakes. And after the visit with Martha's sister, and knowing that her other sister had committed suicide because of depression, I was painfully aware of how important the dress shop was to my friends, and the entire community.

I also had to admit that Suzanna probably did know better than me in this instance. But I anticipated a time coming along when it would be Ella, and not me, facing off with Suzanna over business decisions.

"You're right. Can you show me again how I get the seam straighter and neater?" I said with a level voice.

Summer smiled with relief and Ella glanced admiringly at me. Their responses made me feel instantly better. But it was Suzanna's soft voice as she once again began to explain to me how to improve my seams that really lifted my spirits.

The jingle of the bell lifted all of our heads. It was Rebecca Miller, my mother-in-law, and Ruth.

"Hello," Suzanna called out, leaving me alone at my pedal driven sewing machine. She spoke to Rebecca and Ruth in German for a moment, before she walked with a beaming face into the backroom. From the gist I was able to get from the conversation, we'd just made our first sale of a bolt of fabric to Rebecca.

"Sorry to come in before you're officially open, but I need the fabric today and don't really have time to ask the driver to take me all the way into town," Rebecca spoke to all of us. She then met my gaze and smiled, "I couldn't pass up a chance to see my adorable granddaughter, either. May I?" Rebecca motioned to Sarah Ann who was still happily playing with her toy.

"Of course," I said, watching as Rebecca crossed the room and gathered Sarah Ann up in her arms.

"Are you sewing a dress for sale, Rose?" Ruth had snuck up behind me when I'd been paying attention to Rebecca. She leaned in to scrutinize my work up close.

I suddenly felt ashamed of my messy stitching.

"I'm trying . . . Suzanna and Ella have been helping me." My cheeks became hot. "I don't think anyone will actually buy anything I make, though."

Ruth straightened back up and met my gaze. I could tell she was thinking hard. When she finally spoke again, I breathed, not realizing that I'd been holding my breath.

"I'm very busy with prepping the garden right now, but I could use another casual dress. Since James voted in favor of this business, I don't think he'll mind if I order one myself," Ruth said with a raised brow.

"You'll be our first customer," Ella gushed.

"Not surprising. The other women in the community are waiting to see how it goes over." Ruth rolled her eyes and frowned. "Basically, everyone's wants to see which families support the shop, and which ones don't."

"Have you heard any news about where the Yoders and the

Schrocks stand?" Miranda asked quietly, but with anticipation showing clearly on her pale face.

Ruth shrugged. "I haven't heard from any of the Yoders, but the Schrocks oppose the idea wholeheartedly." Seeing all our faces drop, Ruth added, "Charity King told me the other day that she and her sisters will frequent the store, and so did Mary Ester Wittmer."

I quickly thought of the families Ruth had mentioned. The Schrocks were a large clan, but there were even more Yoders. If the Yoders went with us, the Schrocks wouldn't matter at all. The King sisters could mean a lot of business, too. And they were highly respected within the community. Mary Ester was in her sixties and somewhat of a rebel herself, so I wasn't surprised that she'd show support.

"That's better than I thought," I mused out loud.

"There's one condition on my dress," Ruth said pointedly. "I want you to be the one to sew it, Rose."

I returned Ruth's challenging stare, with my own look of disbelief—and fear. I couldn't possibly make a dress for the elderly Amish woman. Never in a million years would it turn out suitable enough for her high standards.

I was about to politely decline when Ella spoke up, "Ruth, do you mind if I help Rose a little with the dress—she's still learning, you know."

Ruth wagged her finger at Ella. "I know she's still learning—I'm the one who taught her how to sew in the first place." She snorted and then looked resolved. "You may help Rose, but she'll be doing most of the work or I'll not be buying it."

Ella looked at me expectantly. I forced myself to nod in agreement to Ruth's terms. "If you can have the dress ready by Saturday, I'll wear it at the next church service. It will serve as a little bit of advertising for you girls," Ruth said simply.

Suzanna, who had been standing close to Rebecca, but listening raptly to our negotiations with Ruth, offered, "We'll deliver the dress to you by Saturday, Ruth. You have my word."

KAREN ANN HOPKINS

"Here, I'll show you how to take the measurements," Ella told me as she squeezed my shoulder.

I worked with Ella, pulling the measuring tape around Ruth's torso and down the length of her arms. Holding the notebook, I wrote down the numbers Ella recited, paying close attention to exactly what parts of Ruth's body she was measuring.

There was excited chatter around us as Rebecca spoke with Suzanna and Miranda, oohing and ahhing about how cute the shop looked. Summer joined us at Ruth's side and told the woman that she'd personally drive the dress over herself, using my truck, of course. I couldn't stop the smile from creeping onto my face. It was turning out to be a good day after all.

The bell rang again, only this time, to my surprise, it was Martha and Miriam who came through the door. Martha was smiling broadly, and Miriam, who'd been quite messy the last time I'd seen her, was all cleaned up. Her hair was pulled snuggly up under her cap and she wore a hunter green dress and apron that were wrinkle-free.

"My, what a gathering we have here," Martha said. She proceeded to say hello and introduce her sister to everyone before she came over to me. Reaching her hand back, she grasped Miriam's and tugged her sister forward.

I looked between Martha and Miriam expectantly.

"Go on," Martha urged Miriam.

Miriam finally met my curious gaze. "I'm sorry for my rudeness the other day. It was uncalled for and I am ashamed. But something wonderful did come from your visit. After my husband finished his chores and came in that evening, he told me that he'd reconsidered the idea of having dresses made for me and the girls. He reckoned that if I had more time to focus on the garden and canning this year, we'd save enough money on our grocery bill to pay for dresses." A tear slipped out of Miriam's eye, and I had to fight not to follow suit when I felt my own eyes begin to moisten. "You see, Isaac is a good husband. But like the other men, he's afraid of change and possibly being ridiculed by other families for his choices. He told me he was sorry for such feelings and said that if it was being allowed in the Meadowview community, he'd go along with it in our own family as well." As an afterthought, she added, "As long as it's not officially banned in Hickory Ridge."

"That's wonderful news." I sniffed in the tears that threatened to fall. "Suzanna and Miranda will take the orders for you." I pointed at the girls, who had obviously overheard the entire conversation. They were already waiting close by with pen, paper, and a measuring tape.

Ruth stepped up beside me and said, "Change is on the wind."

Yes, it was.

CHAPTER 28

❧ Rachel ❧

I thudded my head against the glass. The pain to the outside of my skull wasn't nearly as bad as the throbbing on the inside. I rubbed my burning eyes and looked out the window at the scenery. The farms passed by in the gloomy cloudiness of impending rain. The air smelled heavy with wetness.

"So . . . you went out again last night," Justin made the statement with apparent disapproval in his voice.

I was so very tired, and in no mood for a lecture. "No. I didn't," I snapped.

Justin snorted a laugh. "You're partying alone now?"

I whipped my head around and faced him. "How dare you talk to me that way—you don't know anything!"

"That's right, I don't have any idea what's going on with you. Why not tell me, and then maybe I can help you," Justin implored. He only held my gaze for an instant before he was facing forward again, watching the road.

The intensity of his words affected me. I leaned back against the seat and sighed. Why did I always push people away? Maybe it was just easier to suffer in silence, alone. I glanced at Justin's profile, noting the bruising on his cheek. The swelling had gone down considerably, but the purple and red mark appeared darker today. It was a reminder that he had taken a beating for me.

My heart opened up a bit. Perhaps I should give him a chance.

"Even before Sarah died, I had difficulties getting along with people. I wasn't mean or anything like that. I just didn't really care to spend time in the company of others. I'm a loner, and in my world, that doesn't work out very well." I stared out the window again. Light rain was now falling. "The Amish are a social people, you see. The other teens think I'm odd and the adults believe I'm a rebel of sorts. I don't think I'm either. I'm just me."

Justin nodded, as if he understood, and then asked, "I noticed that about you from the start. The other Amish were always in small groups. Usually the boys with the boys and the girls with the girls. You were always alone . . . or with one of your siblings."

"I spent the most time with Sarah. She accepted me completely. And she never pushed me to be the prim and proper Amish girl that I wasn't. I loved her so much for it, but I never showed it. I was a terrible sister to her—envying all the attention she got from everyone else—especially from Micah." I didn't plan to say so much. I shut my mouth, taking a quivering breath.

I met Justin's gaze for an instant, and knew from the quick look that he understood. I was suddenly free. Tears trickled out my eyes and I didn't even bother to wipe them away. For the first time, I'd spoken my true feelings about Sarah to someone. Justin probably hated me now.

Justin reached over and took my hand in his. He squeezed it. Softly, he said, "Don't blame yourself. Every single one of us has moments of anger toward our siblings. Sam drives me crazy with his lofty attitude. And to be honest, Rose is a little self-centered. But I still love them—the same way you loved Sarah."

"But that's just it. I never loved her before she died. I was resentful that she was everyone's favorite and that she could do no wrong in anyone's eyes. Then when Micah began showing her favor, it completely undid me. I wished horrible things on my sister. And look what happened to her. It's my fault she's dead!" My voice had risen sharply by the final words.

There was silence in the car for a moment while Justin turned up the road to the birdhouse factory. He continued to hold my hand when he parked, making the butterflies in my belly multiply. He finally looked back at me.

"Before Mom died, I was angry with her. Some stupid part of my thirteen-year-old brain thought she had a choice or something—that if she really wanted to, she would have beaten the cancer, and lived." He swallowed, and glanced away. "When she was gone, my anger turned to guilt. I hated myself for blaming her. She had suffered horribly in those last days. I would do anything to go back in time—to give her a hug and tell her that I loved her."

I let out a breath, and gripped his hand tightly. Our sorrowful souls reached out, touching one another.

"What did you do to . . . deal with your feelings?" I stuttered, too full of emotion to speak easily.

"I'm still dealing with them. It's a daily struggle sometimes to even get out of bed. When Mom died, it was as if a part of me went with her. Rose has Noah and Sarah Ann to keep her mind off of it. Sam is just very resilient." He met my gaze and seemed to realize that I needed something more substantial to help me with my own depression. He shrugged. "I guess I've escaped reality by immersing myself in video gaming and reading."

I couldn't stop laughing. The rain pounded the car and I was glad for the noise to lessen the barking sound I'd made. I was also grateful that the heavy streaks of water running down the windows obstructed anyone's view to the inside of the car.

"I can't play video games . . . but perhaps Mother will allow me to pick up a few books from the library," I said, contemplating the idea as I said it.

"That would be a lot better than drowning your sorrows with alcohol." Justin grinned.

204

"I have to go . . . but thank you for . . . everything," I said.
"I'm available if you want to talk again. You know where
I live." Justin squeezed my hand once more and then let go.
Having my hand back made me feel empty inside all over again.

Gripping the door handle, I pushed it open and jumped out
into the deluge. Raising my head to the sky, I let the cold water wash away my headache, and my sins. I had felt filthy with
imaginary grime ever since I'd woken that morning. The talk
with Justin had been enlightening in a way. But I couldn't quite
compare my situation to his. He had been upset with his mother,
but he hadn't wished her dead. At one point, I had wished Sarah
to be somewhere else—which was as good as putting her into
the grave. I really was a bad person. And for the first time ever, I
worried about a higher punishment than Father's.

I splashed through puddles until I was finally under the
cover of the building. I hung my jacket on a peg and dropped
my lunch cooler onto the shelf. As I walked to my station,
shaking the water from my dress, tiredness pushed at me once
again.

By the time I'd stumbled into my bed the night before, it
had been nearing two o'clock in the morning. That meant I'd
barely gotten three hours of sleep. And then there was some
explaining to do when Mother asked me why I was still wearing yesterday's clothes when she'd peeked into my bedroom.
Luckily for me, my mother was a very trusting soul. She dismissed the entire thing after I'd given her a lame excuse about
how I'd fallen asleep reading the Bible.

It wasn't as easy to explain to Father why Betsy was still
shut up in the barn. In that instant, I'd simply denied knowing
anything about it, letting blame fall on my younger brothers.
It was a cruel thing to do, but Father wasn't so angry that he
was going to whip anyone. He merely explained very loudly to
the boys that the dog needs to be outside to alert the family of
anything amiss on the farm and not locked away in the darkness of the barn.

I glanced at my finger tips and buried them into the folds of my navy dress. They were dirty from digging into the soft dirt in order to bury the empty bottle of whiskey beneath the bushes. I worried a little bit that the bottle would be discovered, but figured if it ever was unearthed, it would probably be long after I was already an adult, living somewhere else. At least that's what I prayed for, anyway.

I pushed the board over the blade, and as it split in two, there was a whistling sound and a spray of wood dust. My goggles protected my eyes from any debris that might shoot up into my face, but they were always itchy and sweaty, and I hated them.

My mind drifted to about an hour ago when I'd passed by Micah on the way to the restroom. He and Paul had most of the tin roof already up on the structure, and were able to work under cover even though it was still raining hard. He'd tried to stop me to talk, but I'd completely ignored his attempt, refusing to look him in the eye. Part of me was embarrassed by my diminished state, and the other just didn't want to deal with the sweet Amish boy. He *was* too good for me. And the sooner he realized it, the better off he'd be. Even though it constricted my heart to think about Micah courting another girl, it was probably for the best. He'd never have any peace or happiness with me.

I was beginning to think it was inevitable that I'd become English someday. My people would see me for what I truly was and they'd shun me. I'd have no choice but to leave. I wondered if I could even count Justin as a friend if such a thing happened. We'd definitely had a special moment in the car that morning, bonded in a way, but he was an honorable person. If the Amish wouldn't have me, he might not, either.

The sound of the other cutting machines echoed in my head, and my stomach growled from emptiness. It was only eleven o'clock. I yawned. My head was still fuzzy. I loved the way the alcohol allowed me to sleep nightmare-free, but I hated the sickness in the morning. Could Justin be onto something? Would reading books have the same effect on me, without the hangover? It was definitely worth a try. I'd ask Mother about hiring a driver to take us to the library on my next day off from work.

A sharp discomfort in my hand was quickly followed by wetness. I looked down in horror. There was a puddle of blood beneath that saw blade that still twirled on high speed. Dizziness spun my head around and around. I could hardly breathe.

My pinkie finger was lying beside the piece of wood. It had been cut cleanly off at its base.

I backed away from the machine, clutching my ruined hand with my other one. Blood flowed down my arm, bubbling up through the fingers of my good hand with angry gushes.

My finger has been cut off. My finger is off. It's off.

I cried out and someone's arms were around me. It was Ingrid.

"Oh, no, Rachel." Her eyes were wide with terror, but her voice was cool calmness. Her composed manner cleared my thoughts, and I finally took a shaky breath.

"Let me see," Ingrid ordered, prying my hands apart. Her eyes widened even more when she saw only four digits on my right one. She called out to the nearest girl who was instantly by my side, holding me upright. It was Elayne—one of the girls who never spoke to me. But now, she wouldn't stop talking. She murmured soothing words of encouragement as Ingrid sprang to the machine and turned off the switch.

Without hesitation, Ingrid picked up my finger and dropped it into her apron. I watched her run to the nearest lunch box cooler and toss the sandwich and milk bottle out.

She then set my finger into the ice. Ingrid spoke to another girl while she did this, instructing her to call a driver, any driver, to come quickly.

Another girl appeared with a white towel. She wrapped it around my hand to stop the bleeding. In less than twenty seconds from the time that Ingrid had looked at my hand, she had returned and was hugging me.

"It will be all right, Rachel. We'll get you to the hospital. It will be fine," she told me.

My legs trembled, and then buckled. The room spun around me as I slipped to the floor in Ingrid's strong grip. She stayed with me, though, not letting go. But as we went down, she dropped the cooler and my finger came out with some of the ice.

Seeing my finger on the floor was just too much. I cried out for the second time, and then the world went black around me.

CHAPTER 29

······ Justin ······

I cut off the engine, flung the door open and ran through the doorway. There was a crowd gathered at the far end of the building and that's the direction I went. I squeezed past the girls until I finally saw her.

Rachel was sitting on the floor between a sturdy looking blonde girl and Micah. Her head was resting on Micah's shoulder and her eyes were closed. The blonde girl was holding a blood-stained towel to Rachel's hand. My stomach rolled for an instant and I swallowed down the hot bile in my throat. *Get a grip,* I told myself.

Micah looked up at me. "Thank you, Justin, for coming so quickly. One of the drivers was too far away and we couldn't reach the others," he said breathlessly.

When he said my name, Rachel's eyes popped open. Her gaze met mine and I could see pain there. I immediately knelt down in front of her.

"Is the finger . . . in . . . one piece?" I stuttered.

The blonde girl answered me. "Yes. I have it on ice." She handed me the cooler. I didn't open the lid.

"Good thinking. I called Dad on the way over here and he said that fingers can be reconnected if kept cold," I said, motioning for the girl to move aside.

"Micah, let's get her up. Time is of the essence here," I told him.

Rachel was groggy in my arms as we lifted her.

"So stupid . . . it's all my fault," she mumbled between wet lips.

"Nonsense. It's just an accident," I told her.

I had the car parked right next to the doorway and one of the Amish girls took the cooler from me and put it in the front seat while another opened up the door to the backseat.

"No. I did this," Rachel gave me a desperate look as I guided her into the seat beside Micah. The rain was hitting my back with the force of a thousand tiny smacks. I was already thoroughly drenched.

I lifted her legs and carefully shoved them inside. Before I shut the door, I said, "Not now, Rachel. You can blame yourself later, after we get you to the hospital."

As I shut the door, she stared blankly ahead. I figured it was a combination of shock and being Amish that made her more contrite about chopping her finger off than most people would be.

Before I jumped into the driver seat, I turned to the strong looking girl and asked, "Aren't there any adults here?"

"I'm eighteen," she replied. "My parents went into town to shop for supplies for my older sister's wedding."

I shook my head in disgust, but didn't say anything. I didn't know who I was more upset with—the owner of the factory or Rachel's own father for forcing her to work in such a place.

After I turned onto the roadway, I glanced into the rearview mirror. Rachel's head was once again resting on Micah's shoulder. His face was pale, but he held the bloody towel to her hand with solid determination.

Micah caught my gaze and I looked away. I didn't want to feel jealous that he was comforting Rachel, but I did.

"Is it true that the doctors can put her finger back on?" Micah asked.

Rachel's eyes were closed and I assumed that she was too out of it to be listening very hard. I pressed the gas pedal a little harder. A horse and buggy could be around every corner on this road. When I finally made it to the main road, I could open it up a bit.

"My dad's waiting with the surgeon. There's a real possibility, but it depends on how clean the cut was and a bunch of other factors." I paused and looked in the rearview mirror again. Micah was rubbing Rachel's arm affectionately. "Were you there when it happened?"

"No. My brother and I were working on the addition. One of the girls called out to us. Paul took his horse and buggy down to the English neighbor to see if he would drive Rachel into town. I didn't wait for his return to call you."

"You're lucky. This is the first day off for Easter break—normally I'd be in school." I decided not to mention to him that I'd already chauffeured Rachel once that morning. There wasn't any reason to complicate matters worse.

"This is the second time you've come to my aid." Micah paused, and then added, "Well, this time you came for Rachel."

My heart thudded in my chest and my skin tingled with worry. The only other time I'd ever experienced such anxiousness was during the last few days of Mom's life. I didn't like caring so much for a person—especially not someone who I had no business caring for in the first place.

The inside of the car was quiet for the rest of the trip, except for Rachel's random moaning. I was lost in thought, wondering how I played into this whole drama.

When I glanced into the mirror and saw Rachel's brown eyes staring back at me, I knew one thing for certain. I was definitely invested.

●●●● ● ●●●●

"Where is the finger?" Dad asked me as a nurse helped Rachel into the wheelchair.

"Here." I handed the cooler to him. He passed it off to another nurse who jogged back into the building ahead of us.

"Rachel, hang in there. You're a lucky girl. We have an excellent orthopedic surgeon here today to operate on your hand," Dad told Rachel as a nurse wheeled her through the automated doors.

Micah and I hung back, allowing Dad and several nurses to take Rachel away. Once the group had disappeared into a hallway where red doors closed solidly behind them, I finally relaxed a little. I didn't always respect Dad's parenting abilities, but I had complete faith in him as a doctor. Rachel was in good hands.

Micah snorted out an angry laugh and I turned to him.

"That was your father, correct?" Micah asked.

"Yeah," I responded tentatively.

"He said Rachel was lucky—why would he say something like that? What could be more unlucky than cutting your own finger off by accident?"

He had a point. "He only meant that she was lucky to have an experienced surgeon here to do the surgery. Perhaps if she came in tonight or tomorrow, someone else would be doing the surgery who wasn't as competent." The tortured look on Micah's face made me uncomfortable. "Here, why don't we go sit in the waiting room," I suggested, motioning Micah into the large room to the left of the entrance.

Micah went in without argument and sat down on the first available seat he came to. He buried his face in his hands.

"Look, dude, she'll be all right," I said.

"Her finger will never work right." Micah groaned. "She won't be able to do her drawings . . . she'll be miserable."

I leaned back in the chair. Rachel was already depressed. This would put her over the edge.

"We'll just have to wait and see," I said quietly.

The minutes ticked by while Micah and I sat silently beside each other in the brightly lit room. I thought about Rachel's troubled spirit and her self-destructive ways. Even though I didn't really know her back then, I was convinced that she had issues before her sister was even killed in the storm. Rachel was the type of person who was very hard on herself. She buried her own emotions, rarely opening up to anyone. But she had let me in a little bit.

Rose came into the waiting room, alongside Amos and Rebecca. When she saw me, she rushed over and dropped onto her knees before me.

"Ingrid called me at the shop and told me what happened to Rachel." She looked up at Rachel's parents and added, "I drove straight over to the Millers and picked up Rebecca and Amos."

She hesitated, and Amos blurted out, "How bad is it?"

I met the fearful gaze of the red-bearded man, thinking how different his demeanor was now from when I'd faced him in his barn.

"She cut her entire pinkie finger off on the table saw," I said bluntly.

Rebecca gasped. Rose stood up and put her arms around her mother-in-law. Amos's eyes were wide with shock.

Micah surged from his chair, and a feeling of dread washed over me.

"If you hadn't forced Rachel to work at the factory, this wouldn't have happened in the first place. She was exhausted from doing both the house chores and the job." Micah's voice rose even higher and I noticed a few others seated in the room were staring. "You expected too much from her, and now look what happened."

I didn't need to see Rose's hard-eyed pleading look in my direction to know what to do. I placed my hand on Micah's shoulder and tugged at him. "Hey, come on. We'll wait out in my car."

He shrugged my hand off. "No. I'm staying here to see Rachel when she's out of surgery."

"And what makes you think that you deserve a place

waiting along with her own family, boy?" Amos growled in a low, threatening voice.

The air tingled with silence for a moment. The few other people in the room continued to gawk at the strange scene of the two Amish men arguing. Rebecca was dabbing her eyes with a tissue and Rose wore a grim expression on her face.

"Because I care about her," Micah finally said.

The tension in the room seemed to leave with his words. Amos sighed heavily and tugged on his beard. I sat back down, realizing that Amos' response was something of a surrender. Where that left me, I had no idea.

When Dad walked in, I remained seated while the others crowded around him. I was still close enough to hear the conversation.

"Amos, I'm sorry to see you under this circumstance, but I do have good news for you." Dad took a breath and continued. "Dr. Venito is replanting the digit as we speak. He's very optimistic that the surgery will be successful. The cut was clean, and since the kids had the presence of mind to keep the finger on ice, it was in the best possible condition for reattachment when it arrived."

"Will she be able to use the finger?" Rebecca asked.

Dad nodded vigorously. "Yes, I believe she'll have mobility with it. First, Dr. Venito will set the finger in place—he'll stabilize the bone with wire or a plate and screws. Once it's connected, he'll repair the tendons, nerves, and blood vessels the best he can. A bulky dressing will be applied to protect it. She may need some cosmetic reconstructive surgery later on— possibly even a skin graft. It will be a long process."

"That's amazing that they can put it back on like that," Rose said to no one in particular.

"Yes, it is. I am in debt to you, David. Once again, you've come to the aid of one of my children,"

Amos said reaching out to shake Dad's hand.

"Dr. Venito is the one you should thank after the surgery.

I merely made a call to have the best person possible working on your daughter." Dad released Amos's hand and went on to say, "There's a chance that she'll have a reaction to the medication. And even if everything goes as smoothly as we hope, she'll still have reduced nerve function and movement. She may deal with pain and stiffness for quite a long time."

A heavyset, no-nonsense sort of nurse walked in and asked Amos and Rebecca to join her in the admission office. When the Amish couple was gone, Dad motioned for me and Rose to join him in the hallway. Micah remained seated, staring blankly at the wall.

There was a constant stream of doctors, nurses and patients moving about in the hallway, so Dad pulled us into a corner and leaned in close.

"What happened to your face?" Dad asked sharply.

I'd already planned my answer in my head a thousand times. I only hoped Rose went along with it.

"I fell off Lady," I said simply.

Dad's eyes became saucer size. "What! Why on earth were you riding your sister's horse?"

Rose came immediately to the rescue. "I've been teaching him to ride, Dad. What's wrong with that?"

Dad looked between us with suspicion in his eyes, but he let it go.

"You better be more careful next time. That horse isn't for beginners," Dad said, staring hard at Rose, before facing me again. "What's going on with this girl?" He asked pointedly, shifting his gaze back and forth from me and Rose.

"Uh, what do you mean?" Rose was the first to speak. She glanced at me with the *this isn't good* look.

"The first thing the nurses did was run some simple blood work. She had a .06 percent blood alcohol content. This isn't enough to declare her legally drunk, but it's high enough to impair her abilities—especially with cutting machinery," Dad said with a deep frown etched on his face.

Rose and I glanced at each other. I had promised Rachel that I wouldn't say a word about her partying and I wasn't going to break that promise. But I wasn't going to stop Rose from spilling the beans, either.

I nodded softly, giving Rose permission to tell Dad everything.

"Rachel is a bit of a party girl," Rose said lamely.

Dad rolled his neck in agitation and I heard several cracks. Then he sighed. When he finally looked back at us, he was scowling.

"I guess it doesn't really surprise me that an Amish kid is sneaking out and drinking, but the fact that she's only sixteen and working with heavy power equipment at work is another thing all together. The Amish get away with bypassing all sorts of laws because of the general religious freedom act, but this may just be illegal, even for them."

"What are you going to do?" Rose asked uneasily.

Dad ran his hand through his dark brown hair. I noticed that the peppering of gray at the temples was spreading. Middle age and Dad's stressful job were getting to him, it seemed.

"I don't know yet. That's why I didn't say anything to Amos and Rebecca about the alcohol in the girl's system. I want to talk to some people and see what might be the best way to handle the situation. You two can help by gathering as much information as you can."

"What kind of information?" I asked hesitantly.

"How many other underage kids work in this birdhouse factory for starters? One of the nurses mentioned that she's aware of Amish girls working at the butcher shop, too. Anything you can find out that applies to kids working with dangerous equipment, I want to know about," Dad said, leveling a hard look at each of us.

Rose nodded slightly, but I didn't.

"Dr. Cameron, I need you to sign these release forms," a perky nurse interrupted.

"Sure thing." Dad glanced back at us as he walked away. "I'll stop by the house this evening to discuss this in more detail."

Rose grabbed my arm and pulled me through the automated front doors and out into the dull sunlight of the cloudy day. The rain had stopped and the air was cool, but not uncomfortable.

"This is terrible," Rose said, placing her hands on her hips.

"How do you figure?" I took a few more steps away from the hospital entrance.

Rose followed me. "Don't you see? Dad's always had issues with the Amish culture. Now he might have the opportunity to get the law involved."

"Maybe it's not such a bad idea," I suggested, lifting my face to a sunbeam shining through the clouds. I closed my eyes and breathed a silent prayer for Rachel's surgery to go well.

"Are you kidding me? This could cause all kinds of problems for the community," Rose said loudly.

I faced her. "Rachel shouldn't have been working in that place. Micah is right. Maybe the Amish need to change some of their rules, on the grounds of safety alone."

Rose shook her head in agitation. "I know—I agree. But you can't compare their culture to ours. It works completely differently. The kids don't go to school after eighth grade; many of them beginning working on their farms fulltime or at one of the local Amish businesses. It's just the way they do things. Rachel's accident happened because she was drinking last night—not because she was sixteen."

"Yeah, I'm sure the alcohol and her overall state of mind contributed to her cutting her finger off, but don't you think that sixteen is a little too young to be working with woodcutting equipment?" I argued.

Rose didn't answer my question. She turned away and called over her shoulder, "It's more complicated than that, Justin."

She had no idea just how complicated it really was.

CHAPTER 30

❧ Rachel ❧

I was afraid to open my eyes. I could hear Father and Mother quietly talking in German, and the pings of the monitor that was attached by a cord to my arm. There was a dull pressure of the needle sticking into the vein in my wrist, but my injured hand was completely numb. There was only the heaviness of bandages to feel.

I knew that the doctor had sewn my finger back on. It was kind of similar to the way I would sew a sleeve onto a dress. I remembered the bloody stump and wondered what my finger looked like now. Thinking about it made it difficult to breathe evenly.

Ingrid had warned me many times about focusing on the job and being careful. But my mind had been where it always was—in the clouds. Now I had a ruined hand to show for it. And then there were so many thoughts rattling around in my head about Micah and Justin. They'd both been there in my time of need, confusing the matter even more about my feelings for each of them.

I could sense someone standing beside the bed and I squeezed my eyes tightly closed. When the hand touched mine, I knew it was Mother.

"Sweet, Rachel. I know you're awake. You used to make the same expression when you were a small girl, when you feigned sleep, not wanting to get out of bed."

Mother's voice was soft and coaxing, and I opened my eyes.

My eyes skipped over her to look at Father who was standing beside her. He frowned and his red hair was sticking messily out from beneath his hat. He must have left the house in a hurry.

"Are you in pain?" Mother asked.

"A little," I said. My mouth was dry and it was more difficult to speak than I'd imagined it would be. "Did they really put it back on?"

"Yes, the doctor told us the surgery was successful. He believes you'll have some use of the finger after it heals," Mother said.

I glanced at Father, wondering about his silence. Usually he was the one talking, and not Mother.

He caught my gaze, and stepped forward. An amazing thing happened. Father bent his head and began to cry.

The only other time I'd seen him cry was when he'd learned that Sarah was dead. I watched in morbid fascination as his face became red and wet. Were the tears for me?

Mother sat down on the lone chair in the room and Father inched even closer. After a moment, he cleared his throat and wiped his face with his handkerchief. When he looked at me, his eyes were bloodshot.

"I'm so sorry. I sent you away to work at the factory for the wrong reasons. And now, our Lord is punishing me," Father said.

Even though I already knew why he'd insisted that I take the job, I still wanted to hear it from his own mouth. His regret made me feel little better—even though I'd just had my finger stitched back on.

"Does that mean I don't have to go back?"

Father barked out a short laugh. "No, child. You will be staying at home with your Mother for the foreseeable future."

Deciding to take advantage of his generous mood, I became brave and took a chance. "It was very nice of Justin to drive me to the hospital, and for Micah to come along, too. Are they still here? I'd like to thank them."

Father's expression darkened, but he nodded in understanding. "Yes, they were both in the waiting room, the last time I checked. It is right for you to express your gratitude. But really, Rachel—we're going to have to sit down and have a long talk about these two boys once you're home."

Father's voice was loud, but not surly. His mood could change in a heartbeat, so I said a silent thank you to God for Father's calm demeanor and smiled up at him.

"I'll get them," Father said, motioning for Mother to join him.

"Give me a moment alone with Rachel, Amos. I'll meet you in the waiting room," Mother said as she stood up.

Father sighed heavily and left the room.

I looked warily at Mother. Sometimes she was more frightening than Father.

"Are you aware that Micah has feelings for you?" she asked kindly.

I took a breath and stared at the ceiling. So the cat was out of the bag.

"Rachel?" Mother's voice was more insistent.

"What do you want me to say? I can't control how he feels," I said stubbornly.

"Do you care about him?" Mother pressed.

"Does it matter? Father will never allow it. He'll forbid it, the same as he did when Micah asked to court Sarah." I met her gaze with narrowed eyes. I really didn't want to discuss this right now. A throbbing pain was developing beneath the bandages and my head was beginning to pound.

Rebecca's face tightened in response to my words. "That is not true. Your father only wants what is best for you, as I do. He realized long ago what a mistake he made by not giving his blessing to Sarah and Micah—and he has regretted it ever since." She paused, tilting her head in thought. "Our relationship with the Schwartzes is on good terms. That's not the issue anymore."

"Then what is?" I used my elbow to sit up straighter, daring Mother to speak her mind with a hard stare.

"He's a kind boy—a special boy in so many ways. I know he'd do everything in his power to make you happy . . . but I fear you're going to hurt him."

Her words hung in the air. Even my own mother thought I was terrible person, and she didn't even know about my sneaking out at night.

"That's why I asked about your feelings for him. Courting is serious business and shouldn't be taken lightly. Micah has already been through so much pain with Sarah's passing. The feud between our families is finally over." She smiled sadly. "I'm sure you don't want to do something that will cause more hurtful feelings to spring up."

"You don't think that I can be a good wife for Micah— that he'd be happy with me?" A tear fell from my eye onto my cheek. I sniffed, trying desperately to push down the overwhelming sense of anxiety that coursed through me.

"Of course you could make him happy—and be a wonderful wife. That's not what I meant." Mother touched my forehead, tucking loose strands of hair behind my ear. "You've always been a bit of an actor, playing games with people, testing their emotions. This is something that you must not do with the Schwartz boy. There's too much at stake. If you truly want to be with him, I'll support you wholeheartedly, as will your Father. But if you don't, leave the boy alone. As far as Rose's brother goes, I certainly hope there's nothing going on there. That is one relationship that you know we will not support. It would be a terrible mistake on your part—something that you'd regret later."

Mother was not one to speak her mind very often. She left most important decisions to Father. The fact that she was speaking so plainly was the same as a slap in the face. My mother did know me well.

Before I had the opportunity to respond, Micah walked in,

followed by Justin. The two stood at a discreet distance away, close to the open door.

I glanced back at Mother. "I understand."

She seemed satisfied with my answer and leaned down to peck my forehead with a light kiss. When she was gone, I looked back at Micah and Justin and said, "Come in."

Micah came right up to the bed. His face was flushed. "How are you feeling? Does it hurt at all?"

I smiled a little at his brashness. I noticed Justin was still hanging back, looking uncomfortable. When my gaze met his, I saw concern in his eyes.

"It's beginning to throb, but not too much," I said.

"My dad said your finger will probably work normally once it's fully healed," Justin offered.

I glanced between the two young men in front of me. They were both handsome and kind. Micah was sweeter and shared my way of life. But Justin's witty charm couldn't be ignored, either. The anxiety I'd felt the night before when I thought about Micah and Justin returned. My stomach churned with indecision.

To chase away the conflict, I said, "One good thing to come out of all of this is that I won't be working at the birdhouse factory any longer."

"I'm glad your father changed his mind," Micah said.

"You probably had a lot to do with that," Justin said to Micah. I watched Micah blush and then I gazed at Justin who went on to say, "Micah, here, gave your dad quite the earful on your behalf."

"I only stated the obvious. Mr. Miller just needed a little coaxing." Micah grinned.

"Thank you, Micah. It means a lot to me that you'd speak up for me." I glanced nervously at the clock, knowing that Father and Mother would return soon. I needed to talk to Justin alone.

I thought quickly. "Micah would you mind getting me a cola. I think I saw a machine down the hall."

Micah at first looked thrilled at my request, then his face clouded as he glanced at Justin.

"I think it will settle down my stomach," I added.

"I'll be right back," Micah said, tapping the air with his finger. He hurried from the room without a backward glance.

When he disappeared around the corner, Justin moved forward and leaned down. He put his hand over my wrist, just above the bandages. A bubbling thrill raced through me at his touch. I was momentarily taken aback, unable to say a thing.

Justin's mouth lifted in a lopsided smile and some of his dark hair fell across his eye. He tossed his head a little to shake the strands back. "Are you really all right? That's quite the ordeal to go through."

I swallowed and stared up at him. His hand still rested on my wrist, and the bubbles of excitement were replaced by the sweet feeling of warm honey.

Somehow, I found my voice. "It was awful—my finger was lying there on the table beside the saw." I closed my eyes to erase the picture in my mind. When I opened them back up, Justin was patiently waiting. "I'm so glad the doctor reattached it. Maybe it's even worth it. Now I don't have to work at that awful place any longer."

"I don't know about that, but the color is back in your face and your eyes are clear. I'm just glad you're okay," Justin said in a mature voice. He leaned in even closer and I could smell the woodsy cologne on his skin. The scent tickled my nose invitingly. I had the strongest desire to kiss him. But I could see that wasn't his intention. "I know you were drinking last night . . . and so does Dad."

Anger heated my cheeks. "How could you betray me? I trusted you!"

"Shhh—I didn't say a word. He discovered the alcohol from your bloodwork. I didn't tell him anything."

Shame washed over me. "He must think very poorly of me," I muttered.

"It's worse than that. He might go to the authorities. He thinks you were too young to be working in a factory in the first place," Justin said in a fervent whisper.

"Why would he do that?" I could hardly breathe.

"My dad's all about the cause, and he's always had an issue with the way your people live," Justin said.

My free hand closed over Justin's, tugging at the IV that was attached to it. "If he really does this, it could destroy the entire community. You must stop him."

"I'll do what I can, but once he has a mission, it's difficult to change his mind." He must have seen the explosion of fear I was experiencing plainly on my face. He took a deep breath. "We need to meet again—to talk alone. Any ideas how to make that happen?"

I answered quickly. "Yes, I have something to talk to you about, too. Tomorrow at midnight, meet me in the stable behind my house." Justin nodded, but that wasn't enough. "Please don't get caught. It will ruin my life if you are."

Justin pulled away just as Micah reentered the room.

But it was too late. Micah had seen me holding Justin's hand.

CHAPTER 31

Rose

I stared threateningly at the three men sitting at the kitchen table. Dad's views didn't surprise me in the least, and frankly, neither did Sam's. They had both been against the Amish culture from the get-go, but Noah's attitude was baffling.

"So you're okay with Dad going to the district attorney about this?" I asked my husband.

Noah leaned back and sighed. "It's not an easy decision—trust me. Rachel had no business working with those saws. Father was just trying to make a statement about his control over his family. And look what happened to Rachel—on top of everything else she's been going through."

"Why can't you just go talk to Amos, Dad? I bet Bishop Lambright and the other ministers will change their Ordnung voluntarily if they know it will save a lot of grief with the authorities," I pleaded.

The idea of the outside world interfering with the community sent a chill down my spine. That's what made the Amish so unique—they got away with doing things that no one else could. I'd had my own issues with the lifestyle when I first moved into the neighborhood, but after living among them and learning their ways more intimately, I started to understand their motives. The Amish just wanted to keep their traditions. Granted, some of them sucked and needed to be changed, but bringing the outside world in seemed like a complete disaster to me.

"It's not so simple, Rose. There are other things that should be addressed as well, and this is our opportunity to force some changes to take place," Dad said firmly.

"They won't be Amish anymore if you have your way." My tone matched Dad's resolve.

Dad shook his head. "You're making too much of this. You, of all people, should know how backward their ways are. Just look at all the trouble you had to go through to open a little dress shop in the community. It's downright absurd."

Before I could respond, Sam said, "You're a snob, Dad."

"Why do you say that?" Dad faced Sam.

"Rose is right. You're turning this into an opportunity to promote your own agenda." Sam spread out his hands questioningly. "What harm would it do to at least talk to Mr. Miller before you get the authorities involved?"

For once, Sam and I were on the same team. I said a silent "hooray," wanting to throw my arms around my older brother. But I controlled myself and looked at Dad instead.

The silence was interrupted by Noah's voice. "Maybe it is a good idea to talk to Father first," Noah suggested.

Dad was soundly outnumbered.

"Fine. I'll speak to Amos in the next day or two. But it wouldn't hurt for you to ask around the community and see what others think about the issue," Dad said.

Relief instantly washed over me, but I wasn't ready to celebrate just yet.

Everything hinged on how Amos reacted to discussing the matter with Dad. Amos Miller was a temperamental man—I could only imagine what he would do.

Late afternoon sun streamed through the shop's windows, making me feel sleepy. And it didn't help that I'd been up most of the night with Sarah Ann. She began teething something terrible that week and nothing seemed to soothe her.

Miranda was patiently rocking my fussy baby in her arms while I tried to work on Ruth's dress. I glanced up at Ella. Her face was scrunched in concentration as she looked over my stitches.

"This is much better. Very good." Ella nodded appreciatively.

I blew out a sigh of relief. "But do you think it will be good enough for Ruth?"

"She'll love it," Ella said with a reassuring smile.

Ella returned to her sewing machine and was about to begin stitching her own project when I said, "Ella?"

Ella looked up. She was a very pretty girl, with large hazel eyes, a small nose and pouty lips. But now that she was actually behaving nicely, she was really beautiful. It still amazed me that a girl I had counted as an enemy not so long ago, I now considered a friend.

"Yes?"

"How long did you work at the butcher shop?" I asked.

"For about six months." She puckered her lips in distaste. "Why do you ask?"

"It occurred to me that if Rachel hadn't been working at the factory, she wouldn't have cut her finger off." I hesitated and met Ella's curious gaze. "I mean, sixteen seems kind of young to be working with saws, don't you think?"

Ella relaxed in her seat, taking a breath, before she spoke. "Yes, I agree. But several girls have cut their hands at the butcher shop, too. It's definitely more dangerous for the younger girls—they don't pay attention."

"Sandra Graber chopped her finger off when she was cutting watermelon for her family's dinner. And Lottie Troyer broke her arm when she fell off the ladder painting a room in her house," Miranda said.

I watched Miranda gently lay a sleeping Sarah Ann down in the playpen. She came over and pulled up a chair beside me.

"What's your point, exactly?" I asked, intrigued by Miranda's comments.

"Home can be a dangerous place for some women," Miranda said with a shrug.

I was about to ask her for more details about Sandra's finger when the bell jingled. I sat up a little straighter under Bishop Lambright's scrutiny. He glanced between Ella and Miranda, but looked pointedly at me when he said, "I was on my way home from a meeting with Merle Fischer about your sister-in-law. How is she doing?"

My mouth was suddenly dry. The tall Amish man instilled automatic fear at the sight of him. Judging by the wide-eyed worried faces that Ella and Miranda wore, I was willing to bet, he had the same effect on them as well.

"She's home resting now. The surgeon said the operation to reattach her finger was a success. There will be some scarring and loss of mobility, but she'll be able to use it again," I told the bishop.

"Nasty business all around, if you ask me." The bishop wandered over to the play pen and I stood up, afraid that his commanding voice would wake her. I shouldn't have worried, though. When he spoke, it wasn't much louder than a whisper.

"Is this your little girl?" he asked me.

"Yes it is," I said cautiously.

The bishop tilted his head as he looked at my baby. When he turned back to me, he said, "She's a beauty."

Inside, I beamed. "Yes, she is," I agreed.

Bishop Lambright looked around the shop and I glanced at the other girls. Ella shrugged, but Miranda was watching every move the man made.

"Seems as if you've managed to get everything in order here. When is the official opening?" the bishop asked.

"Monday," I replied. "We're going to have cupcakes and punch. Are you stopping by?"

"No, no. I'll be busy, I'm sure. But the Missus will probably attend," he said simply.

Sensing his agreeable mood, I pressed him further, "If you don't mind me asking, do you think girls Rachel's age should be working with cutting machinery or knives in general?"

The bishop's mouth spread into a thin line. There was a moment of stillness while he considered his answer.

"That's exactly what I was speaking with Merle about today. I don't have daughters of my own, so I never really thought much on it before. I'm beginning to wonder if these teenagers have the sharpness of mind at that age to do their jobs safely." The bishop shook his head. "Ach, girls are so flighty nowadays."

What he said bugged me a little bit, while at the same time gave me some hope that Dad wouldn't have to go all Kung Fu on the elders, after all.

"So you're thinking about changing the girls' age for certain jobs?" I rushed the words out and then realized my mistake when Bishop Lambright's bushy white brow lifted.

"Not that it is any of your concern, but I'll call a meeting on the subject next month," the bishop said. He tipped his hat and nodded to us as a group. When he was going out the door, he passed Suzanna and Summer coming in.

It took a few minutes for me to recount everything that the bishop had said to Suzanna. She was at first terrified to see him in the shop. But after I explained to her that he seemed to be reluctantly supporting the business now, she visibly relaxed.

Before I could join Suzanna and the other girls sorting the new material that Suzanna deposited on the counter, Summer jerked my arm.

I noticed at that point that Summer was wearing a skirt and dress shirt. Granted, the skirt was denim, but combined with the heels and sparkling barrette in her hair, she was quite well dressed.

"What's the occasion?" I asked.

Summer's brow arched. "Thank you for noticing that I'm all gussied up—Suzanna didn't until we were already on our way back from town." She spread her hands out dramatically. "So, how do I look?"

"Beautiful, of course," I said.

Her voice dropped to a whisper and I wasn't exactly sure why.

"Sam's taking me out to Antoinette's tonight." She leaned in closer. "Don't tell Suzanna. I don't want to listen to her riding me all day tomorrow about it. You know how she gets."

My grin turned to a smile. I nodded. "So Sam is finally stepping up?"

Summer's eyes twinkled. "He's been a lot more supportive here, lately. I don't rightly know what's gotten into him. But I'm not complaining, that's for sure."

"You go on then. Have a good time," I told her.

"He just texted me; he's pulling in right now." Summer turned away, taking a step, and then she stopped and rushed back. She threw her arms around me in a bone-crushing hug. "I'm just so happy!"

When the door closed and the jingling stopped, I sighed in contentment. It seemed as if everything was finally right with the world.

CHAPTER 32

❧ Rachel ❧

My feet were soaked from the heavy dew on the grass by the time I reached the sliding door to the stable. The opening was just wide enough for me to squeeze through. Before I stepped into the inky darkness, I looked back over my shoulder. A sliver of moon hung high above the farm like a thin slice of vanilla cream pie. The moonlight cast long shadows off the house and trees. I continued to hold my breath, listening for the sound of a door opening or any voices in the night. After a moment, I breathed again, satisfied that I had once again escaped unnoticed.

Was Justin already waiting for me in the dark barn, or was he still making his way across the field? I strained my eyes, searching for his shape in the distance. I swallowed. Maybe he wasn't even coming. My heart was beating rapidly from doubt and anticipation.

As I slipped through the doorway, I chastised myself for being a fool. Why was I inviting more trouble into my life? I already knew the answer, but I wouldn't admit it to myself.

Cool, alfalfa scented air wrapped around me as I stepped further into the darkness. I was barely able to make out the walls and the stall doors.

"Justin?" I whispered loudly.

I heard Betsy's heavy panting in the corner before Justin spoke. The sound of his voice sent a tremor through me.

"I'm here. Just getting to know your dog." He flashed his

cell phone in front of him for an instant, and his face became fully illuminated. He was smiling.

The light went out as quickly as it had come on, and he made his way slowly toward me. Now that I'd been in the dark for a couple minutes, I could see better and it seemed that Justin could, too. When he reached me, he took my good hand and squeezed it. The warmth of his hand felt strange and nice at the same time.

He let go. "How does your finger feel? I hope this isn't too much for you to come out here like this—you probably should be resting."

His concern made my heart swell.

"Oh, I've been lying around all day long. I needed to get up and stretch." I held out my bandaged hand. "It's surprising, really. Besides some throbbing and itchiness, I can't feel much of anything."

"Dad said it would take a while to heal. When you begin physical therapy, it will probably hurt some," Justin said.

I nodded. I'd heard it all before. The surgeon and the nurse who released me had said the same thing.

"Your father stopped by today. He explained some things to me as well," I said.

"Did he talk to your dad?" Justin's voice was hesitant and I wondered why.

"No. Father wasn't home. He spoke some to Mother, telling her the same things he explained to me. Maybe he's changed his mind about going to the authorities."

"Perhaps," Justin said absently.

It was awkward standing in the middle of the barn aisle. I motioned for Justin to join me on a bale of straw pushed up against the wall. He sat down next to me, not too close, but near enough that his arm and knee brushed softly up against my side. We sat quietly for a moment. I savored the tranquility of the barn.

Justin broke the blissful stillness. "What did you want to talk to me about?"

All day long, I'd been rehearsing in my mind what I'd say to Justin. Now that he was right next to me though, I faltered, wondering if I'd made a mistake asking him to come.

"I . . . um . . . need your help with something." I took a breath and swallowed. It was difficult to say the words out loud. "You're the only one I trust with this—" I met his curious gaze "—secret."

"I'm here. Just tell me what I can do for you." Justin's blue eyes glimmered in the darkness and I couldn't really make out the bruises I knew were still on his face. I was mesmerized by his intense stare. I began to sway forward and stopped myself. Facing forward I took a long breath.

"I think I have a problem . . . with the drinking. I *was* affected by the alcohol when I had the accident."

"Where did you get the liquor?" Justin's head was tilted as he tried to understand.

"Sadie gave it to me. I met up with her the other night. Charlotte's still upset with me about what happened, but Sadie thinks that Avery and Jasper got what was coming to them. She's sorry about what they did to you."

"First off, you have to stop hanging around with those girls. They're bad news—and they'll bring you down with them," Justin said forcefully.

Since Justin usually was so laid back about things, his tone startled me.

"Yes, you're right, I know. It's just so hard. My days are tedious and boring. At night, all I do is have nightmares about Sarah . . . only she's dead . . . and bloody . . . "

"Shh." Justin put his arm around me.

He pressed my head against his chest and rubbed my shoulder. The act was familiar and friendly. I still wasn't sure if he even wanted me in a romantic way.

"Of course you're having bad dreams about your sister. It was horrible what you experienced when the house came down. You're finally opening up and that's the first step to healing." His voice was velvety soft.

"What's the second step?" I mumbled into his shirt.

"A good therapist." Justin chuckled.

I pulled back. "This isn't funny."

"I know. I'm just trying to lighten the mood." He pulled me back into his side and I let him. "But I'm being honest about you talking to a professional. My Dad can help with that, you know."

"Maybe . . . " I said, pausing. "But my parents would have to know everything, and I'm not ready for that yet."

"They wouldn't need to know *everything*. Whatever you tell a phycologist is confidential. All you have to tell your parents is that you're messed up because of Sarah's death," he insisted.

"You think this person can help stop my need for the alcohol? I can't sleep without it—it makes my mind wonderfully numb, completely blank sometimes," I admitted.

"Sure. My dad's fiancé is a psychologist. I'm sure you'd like her."

My spirit felt lighter and I sat up straighter. "I'm so tired of being like this." I met his gaze. "I will do it."

I expected Justin to be happy with my proclamation, but he was frowning, looking perplexed. My breath caught in my throat.

"Why aren't you talking to Micah about this?" Justin said flatly.

The uncomfortable feeling of guilt washed over me. "Why would I speak to him about such a thing?" I snapped.

"Micah made it very clear that he's really into you. The only question I have, is how do you feel about him?" Justin's eyes dared me to look away.

Just hearing Micah's name doused the warm flames that were springing to life inside of me. Micah's bright green eyes, freckled face, and sun-kissed brown hair sprang to mind. I didn't want to hurt him, like Mother thought I was going to do. But he'd somehow wiggled his way into my heart, in spite of all of my attempts to run him off.

I couldn't lie to Justin, and I couldn't tell him the truth, either. I didn't want to lose him.

Micah's face disappeared in my mind, and I saw only Justin before me. I reached up and lightly touched his bruised face. He sighed and the sound made me braver.

When my mouth touched Justin's, his lips immediately parted. Justin was bold, slipping his tongue into my mouth without hesitation. A million butterflies exploded in my belly, and I all but forgot about my hand. Justin's hot breath fanned my face and I savored it, pressing my cheek against his.

"You're not alone, Rachel. I'm here for you," Justin whispered into my ear.

His mouth was on mine again, and I realized that Justin's kisses numbed my mind, but in a much better way than the liquor ever had. I clung to him, feeling safe for the first time in forever.

And from the way Justin's hand tangled in my hair and his lips moved urgently over mine, I finally had my answer about whether or not he had feelings for me.

CHAPTER 33

••••••• Justin •••••••

The light was on in the living room. With light steps, I walked over and peeked in. Rose was sitting in the recliner. Her eyes were closed and Sarah Ann was asleep on her chest. The baby wore one of those thick, blanket-type sleepers and her face was turned away from me. All I could really see of her was the dark, fuzzy hair on her head. I smiled at the kid's cuteness and turned to duck out of the room when Rose whispered, "Hey, wait a minute."

After the night I'd had, I wasn't sure if I even wanted to talk to Rose. She was very perceptive and would probably read me like an open book given the chance.

"I'm tired. What do you want?" I yawned for effect.

Her mouth twitched and her eyes were bright and wide awake. With sudden clarity, I realized that she'd been waiting up for me.

"You just arrived home . . . but you didn't drive your car . . . and you weren't dropped off by anyone else. You know what that means?" She looked pointedly at me.

I grinned in defiance.

"You snuck across the field to see Rachel." Rose took a deep breath after she said it. She was working hard to keep her composure. Of course, having a baby sleeping on top of her probably helped my cause, too.

"So, what of it—you're the one who wanted me to talk to her?" I challenged.

"Yes, the other morning when you drove her to the birdhouse factory, not sneaking around in the middle of the night." She made a low groaning, sighing sort of sound. "Why are you doing this? I thought you were smarter than that." Rose's tone lost some of its zing, almost as if she was giving up.

I sat down on the couch and rubbed my face vigorously with my hands before resting them on my knees.

"Is it really that bad?" I asked, meeting her gaze. "Look at you and Noah—you're deliriously happy."

Rose pressed her lips tightly together and glanced away. When she looked back, she seemed calm enough.

"I wouldn't change my life for anything. Noah and Sarah Ann are my world—the two things that matter most to me." I sensed the *but* coming, and waited when she hesitated. "But we had no choice. As unbelievable as it is for some people to comprehend, we fell in love instantly. Even for all the troubles we endured, we kept coming together. We were born for each other."

"And that makes your situation acceptable, and mine and Rachel's not?" For the first time ever, I'd admitted out loud that there was something going on between me and the Amish girl. I felt a rush of satisfaction saying it. I also had to admit that it sounded insane coming out of my mouth.

"We didn't have a choice—it was just meant to be. You have a choice with Rachel. What's brought the two of you together isn't a crazy, profound love—it's her torment over losing her sister and your well-hidden sadness over Mom's death."

"Oh, so you're a shrink now?" I snorted.

"Sam and I cried and carried on when Mom died—you didn't. You kept it all inside. But I know it was killing you as much as it was us. You dealt with your emotions through video games and books. And now you've stumbled across another tortured soul, inside a pretty female body," Rose said.

I shook my head. "You don't think I can have real feelings for Rachel—or her for me?"

Rose's eyes wandered. It was difficult to get really angry with her. She was only trying to guide me, pretending to be Mom. And I couldn't find it in myself to argue about something that I was so unsure of myself. If Rachel hadn't been Amish, I'd probably already be madly in love with her. But she *was* Amish.

"Are you having sex with her?" Rose asked straightforwardly.

The question took me off guard, and the fact that it came from my sister made my stomach lurch.

"Of course not!"

Rose exhaled in obvious relief. "I don't think Dad could take another one of his kids having a teenage pregnancy." She said it lightheartedly, but I knew it was also a warning of sorts.

"Don't worry about that. I'm smarter than you and Noah put together," I said.

Rose rolled her eyes and then scooted her way into a standing position with Sarah Ann's limp body in her arms.

"If you're so smart, then I can trust that you won't do anything stupid. But I do worry about you, Justin. You're already in way over your head with that girl. She has issues that go way beyond her just being Amish. If you give her your heart, you'll regret it."

Rose stopped beside me and bent down to kiss my forehead. "You can always talk to me—about anything."

When I was alone in the room, I laid back on the couch and closed my eyes. The pulsating feelings returned to my body when I remembered Rachel's mouth moving against mine and her soft curves beneath my fingertips. When I bent my head and pulled my shirt to my nose, I could still smell the sweet, flowery scent of her. The desire to kiss and touch her again filled my mind.

Was this what falling in love was like?

Chapter 34

❧ Rachel ☙

I wiped the wooden table top vigorously with my good hand. The day was gloomy and wet outside the window, and because of it, the picnic dinner with the Schwartz family had been moved into the house at the last minute, only adding to my mental anguish. I would see Micah today for the first time since the hospital. Only a few days had gone by, but it seemed as if it was an eternity. Maybe it was the fact that I'd kissed Justin. I had expected it, but in a way, it was still a surprise. The way my body had reacted to him shocked me, too. Something had unfurled inside of me that had always been dormant. Now, all I thought about was Justin. I longed to see him again—and I dreamed about kissing and doing other things with him. I felt the heat on my cheeks and paused from my work to look around.

Mother was at the stovetop with her back to me. The scent of the spicy barbeque pork cooking was heavy in the air. I took a deep breath, savoring the smell, and my mouth watered. Naomi had the broom and was still sweeping the same spot she'd been working on a few moments earlier.

"Naomi, move on, girl—or you'll never get it done," I ordered the five year old.

"I'm going, I'm going . . . " the child mumbled.

I smiled. Naomi might look like Sarah, with her lighter hair and eye color, but she resembled me more in temperament, Heaven help her. I watched her bend down with the dust pan and pick up the debris. She trotted over to the waste can and dumped it in, and then returned to the sweeping. Little Naomi hadn't spoken very much right after the storm. And she had regularly awoken, screaming from nightmares in the days that followed, but unlike me, she did recover with time. She hardly seemed to remember the tornado taking the house down on top of her, and Sarah shielding Naomi with her own body. She never talked about Sarah dying, either. It was probably for the best. Still, I envied the little girl's young mind, so easily able to forget.

"Rachel, go change into a clean dress. They'll be here soon," Mother said, looking over her shoulder at me.

"I don't understand why Father invited the Schwartzes over for dinner in the first place." I took off my apron and hung it on the peg beside the pantry door.

"Your Father and Elijah have buried the hatchet, so to say, but there is still the task of forging a true friendship to work on. The Schwartzes are a large, influential family in the community. It is good for our families to have true healing," Mother said with a troubled gaze.

"Trying to fix me up with Micah has nothing to do with it, eh?" I said cuttingly. "I thought you warned me away from him."

Mother took a step back at my outburst. She used the towel in her hand to wipe her forehead. The kitchen was steamy from the large pot that the barbeque had been brewing in all morning.

"Your Father would rather see you courting Micah Schwartz than pining away over an English boy," Mother said forcefully.

"I'm pining away over no one. You are both way out of line for making such assumptions," I said bravely.

"Perhaps we are. But after everything that went on behind our backs with Noah, you can hardly blame us for being suspicious." Mother frowned. "If it's any consolation to you, I have told your father to leave it be and let things develop naturally with Micah if the Lord wills it. But you know, it's not his way to leave anything alone."

Mother turned back to her cooking, dismissing me entirely. I definitely picked up on the tone of resentment when she'd spoken of Father, and I was very curious about how that conversation had went. Mother hid her emotions well, but there were times when she became riled. On those rare occasions, she was a formidable woman indeed.

After dressing, I returned to the kitchen, wearing a light green dress that I thought complimented my brown eyes. I smoothed it down the front and looked around, determining what needed to be done next. The table was already set. Naomi was dressed in her Sunday clothes, and she had a piece of paper and a handful of crayons spread out in front of her on the children's table in the corner. Mother was wiping down the stovetop with a cloth.

When Mother saw me at the bottom of the stairs, she said, "I'm going to change my dress now. Everything is done here in the kitchen. The little boys are cleaning the mud off themselves in the basement." She paused and searched out the window. "It looks as if the rain has stopped. Why don't you go out behind the shed and pick some of those daffodils that are blooming and fill a vase."

I'd just cleaned up and I was irritated with the request, but I snatched my black jacket from the hook anyway. There was no use arguing with Mother when she wanted a flower bouquet on the table.

The breeze was cool, but not quite chilly. Here and there, the darker rain clouds were becoming more transparent, allowing some light to shine through. But I wasn't fooled by the lull in the weather. To the west, the clouds were still dark and ominous looking. I shivered and swallowed a lump in my throat. It was difficult not to be afraid of the low rumble in the distance. Every time a thunderstorm passed over, I cringed inside with fear. *I guess it will always be that way,* I told myself, as I walked through the wet grass to the shed.

I bent down to the yellow flowers and began snapping their stems. As I deposited them into the basket I carried on my elbow, a twinge of pain shot through my hand. I glanced down at the thick bandaging, having the sudden urge to open it up and see what my poor finger looked like beneath it all. Of course, I didn't do it. Dr. Venito had warned me about how important it was to leave the hand alone until I went in for my first checkup the following week. Still, it was a temptation to take a peek at its ugliness.

The wind picked up, bringing warmer air. I lifted my face into it and closed my eyes. Almost immediately, I could feel Justin's mouth pressed against mine. I licked my lips. The *clip-clops* of two buggies could be heard on the pavement in front of the house. I opened my eyes and watched the black horses pulling the buggies behind them. I only had to take a few steps to be hidden behind the shed. I groaned, assuming that Micah was driving the second buggy. Part of me wanted to see him, but the other part, probably the larger half, was tormented by his presence. I did like Micah—maybe even more than liked. But Mother was right. I shouldn't lead Micah on when I was so conflicted. And now, after what I'd done in the barn with Justin, it was even worse.

I resumed picking the flowers, trying to push away all the thoughts that were swirling around in my busy head. I listened to the muted sounds of greetings from the yard as I continued to gather flowers. When my basket was full, I straightened back up.

"How are you feeling?" Micah's voice sprang up from behind me.

I twirled around. I couldn't believe that he so thoroughly snuck up on me *again.*

Micah was wearing a blue shirt beneath his suspenders, and I noticed for the first time that he had a bit of stubble on his chin. He was old enough to grow a beard now. The realization made me shiver.

"I would feel better if you hadn't just given me such a scare," I admitted.

Micah smiled and glanced over his shoulder. "The adults and Constance went into the house. The kids all ran down to the pond."

"So we're alone," I said casually.

"As much as we can be, I guess," Micah said.

I motioned for Micah to step with me inside the thick bushes behind the shed. I didn't go as far in as I had when I drank the bottle of whiskey, but the leaves were much larger than they were then. As a matter of fact, they seemed to have exploded in a thick, green curtain with the rain shower that had just ended.

Micah was careful to scan the area one more time before he stepped into the shade with me. His eyes matched the color of the leaves around us, and I stared into them for a moment, too distracted to speak.

Micah wasted no time pulling something from his pocket. He handed it to me and I looked down at the wide, smooth strip of brown leather in my hand. Turning it over with my fingers, I read my name written across the one side in fancy cursive writing.

I glanced back up, my hand trembling.

"I gave the same kind of bookmark to Sarah a long time ago. She was touched by the gesture, but I found out later that she didn't really read much. So it wasn't the perfect gift for her." He swallowed, gathering courage to continue. "I wanted to give you a little something to cheer you up. I tried to come up with a different present, but after mulling over it for two days, I decided that you'd appreciate a bookmark the most."

I rubbed the smooth leather between my fingertips as I stared a Micah. His faced reddened at my scrutiny. I remembered the bookmark he'd given Sarah. It had been in the pocket

KAREN ANN HOPKINS

of her dress when she'd died. As far as I knew, Mother had put it somewhere for safe keeping—or maybe it was buried with Sarah. I didn't dare to ask.

I also remembered the intense jealousy that had come over me when I had found the bookmark beneath her pillow a few days before the storm. I'd been stripping the beds to wash the sheets when I'd stumbled upon the leather strip. I'd begrudged her the small gift from her suitor—the boy who I had a crush on.

My eyes watered and I stepped forward into Micah's open arms. His mouth met mine and soon we were kissing. My limbs were stiff as I leaned against him. He was careful not to jostle my bandaged hand when his arms went around me.

I had gone my entire sixteen years without kissing a boy, and here I was kissing the second one in a span of two days. I tried to completely focus on Micah, but I couldn't help comparing his kiss to Justin's. They were both soft and sweet, but Justin was a little more forceful, almost desperate feeling, while Micah kissed me with the patience of a person who thought he had forever to do it. Micah's tongue entered my mouth tentatively, waiting for mine to go into his first. I smiled as I kissed him, realizing that the Amish boy was a gentleman in everything he did.

When our tongues finally began twining together, Micah groaned into my mouth and the sound was music to my ears.

"Rachel!" My father's voice boomed out of nowhere.

Micah and I immediately jumped away from each other. I wiped my wet lips with the back of my hand and Micah tucked in his shirt, even though it still was.

Micah whispered, "I'll go around the other way and sneak back to the pond. He'll never know we were together." He winked and was gone.

Taking a measured breath, I walked around the side of the shed, meeting Father just as he was about to call out again.

His eyes narrowed when I appeared. He took a few more

244

steps to look behind the shed. When he turned back to me, the relief was evident on his face.

"Your mother is wondering where those flowers are." Father lifted his chin to the basket still around my arm.

"I'm on my way," I said. I hoped my voice didn't sound as flustered as I felt.

Father joined me on the walk to the house. "How is your hand?" he asked quietly.

"It's fine," I said.

Father's arm went around my shoulder and he pulled me closer. I felt as if I was a small child again. I dropped my head against his side. It was much nicer to get along with Father than to be at odds with him.

But even though the gesture lightened my mood, I couldn't help but notice that the dark rain clouds were almost upon us.

In a symbolic way, the sky opened up just as we reached the porch. A million rain drops pelted us as we ran the last few feet to get under cover. I looked over my shoulder at the watery world, and the breath caught in my throat. When would the rainy weather finally end?

And more importantly, who would I pick as my beau— Micah or Justin?

CHAPTER 35

······· Justin ·······

The images on the television screen flashed before my eyes as I thought back to the night before. I'd actually kissed an Amish girl in a barn. And now I couldn't get her out of my mind. A quiet heaviness came over me when I realized that there wasn't much hope of seeing Rachel again any time soon. She wasn't the same as a normal girl, who I could text and make plans to get together with later on. I could only guess when I'd see her next.

The thought frustrated me. I tossed the controller into my lap.

"Hey, turn the news on," Sam ordered when he burst into the room. He was out of breath and his face was wide with panic.

"Why?" I picked up the remote and switched the receiver over.

A moment later, we were both staring at the screen. Sam was kneeling beside me, poised on the balls of his feet. My mouth dropped open at what I was hearing and seeing.

"You were in the prison yard at the time of the breakout?" the petite blonde reporter asked the navy-blue uniformed security guard.

"Oh, yeah. I saw the whole thing go down right before my own eyes," the middle aged man said with a shake of his head.

"In your own words, what exactly happened?"

The man scratched his head nervously. "When the rain moved off to the east, Larry, our chief guard here, ordered a group of us to open up the yard. It was Cell Block D's turn. We went through protocol and got the inmates out." He took a breath. "That particular block is usually pretty well-behaved and nothing was out of the ordinary. And then BAM, there were screeching tires, and an instant later, the semi-truck plowed right through both barriers." At this point, the picture switched from the face of the guard to the mangled fences. There were dozens of police officers walking through the cut grass of the yard and the lights of even more cruisers and a swat van flashed in the background. The guard continued telling the story, and I leaned forward even more to hear what he was saying better. "The guards in the tower began firing at the truck. But man, everything happened so damn fast. Before I knew it, a group of five or six inmates ran toward the semi that was driving slowly through the yard. Two of the men were picked off by the tower guards, hitting the ground like bricks, but several of them made it to the back of the truck."

"And you saw the prisoners get into the trailer?" the reporter pressed.

"Yes, ma'am. I sure did. And then the truck made a U-turn, nearly on two wheels, and hauled ass out of here. The entire side of that truck was peppered. I would be amazed if anyone survived on the inside," the guard said.

The reporter turned back to the audience. "The tractor trailer was found twenty minutes later in the parking lot of an abandoned warehouse off Principal Road in the industrial park. Two inmates were found in the trailer, dead from multiple gunshot wounds, but two prisoners and the driver are still at large."

The words, *BREAKING NEWS, Lebanon Correctional Institution, Lebanon, Ohio,* streamed across the bottom of the screen, and above them were the arrest photos of two inmates. One man was a big dude. He had a square, fierce looking face and tattoos spreading out around his neck. But it was the picture of the other man that made my heart skip a beat.

Staring out from the television screen was a long, pale face. His hair was buzzed short, very different from the long, greasy locks he'd had that last time I'd seen him. But the single eye that stared out from the screen was still a black pool of craziness.

"Oh, shit," Sam muttered beside me.

"Levi Zook escaped prison today?" I turned to Sam. My voice rose to a much higher pitch than I intended.

"Sure looks that way," Sam said, rubbing his chin and continuing to watch the screen.

"How far away is Lebanon?" I asked.

Sam's gaze met mine. "I guess about two hours. The breakout happened several hours ago."

I could tell Sam's mind was now going in the same direction as mine. "Do you think he'd come to Meadowview?"

Sam snorted. "The crazy shit found his way to Aunt Debbie's house in the middle of Fairfield suburbia. Yeah, if he isn't bleeding in some ditch, he just might."

"Maybe we should call the local police," I suggested. My heart was racing uncomfortably.

"Call the police about what?" Noah stepped into the room. He was wearing a plain gray T-shirt and denim jeans. Dust and dirt from the work site still clung to him.

Sam bounded up. "Where's Rose and the baby?"

"Still at the shop—she told me she was staying late with the girls tonight to get everything ready for the grand opening." Noah's eyes became round with concern when he looked between me and Sam.

"It's probably nothing, but I don't think they should be over there alone." Sam ran his fingers through his mop of blond hair and added, "Levi Zook escaped prison today."

"What!" Noah reached into his pocket and pulled out his cell phone. As he dialed, he said, "Are you sure?"

"We just saw his mug on TV. There's a manhunt for him," I said carefully, trying not to upset my brother-in-law any worse than he already was.

Noah put the phone to his ear and waited. "Nothing—but the cell reception out there is terrible."

"I talked to Summer at about three o'clock. She was driving back to the shop from running some errands. Let me try her again." Sam followed Noah's lead, and a moment later shoved the phone back into his back pocket.

"We should head over there and check things out in person," Sam said. He was already walking to the door. "We'll take my truck."

I glanced out the window at the darkening sky. In a few moments, daylight would be gone. I still liked the idea about calling the cops, but I didn't suggest it again.

"Hey, I'm coming with you!" I grabbed my jacket off the back of the couch.

When Sam opened the door, a gust of warm, stormy air blew in. A thought occurred to me. "Maybe we should bring a gun?" I called out to them.

They both stopped and looked at each other.

"What, are we now in the wild west?" Noah asked Sam.

Sam shrugged. "I'd say it's better to be prepared."

Noah hesitated in the doorway for a moment. "I'll grab my hunting rifle," Noah finally said.

As we ran down the pathway to Sam's truck, Levi's pasty face popped into my mind once again and a shiver raced through me.

I really wished we each had a gun.

CHAPTER 36

Rose

I pushed the last spoonful of Sarah Ann's baby food into her mouth and wiped her face softly with the napkin. The low rumble of thunder penetrated the walls of the shop and I gazed out the window. A flash of lightning lit up the low-hilled horizon, and the branches of the maple tree right outside the door bent low to the ground with the strengthening wind.

"Ever since the tornado last summer, I really hate storms," Summer said. She peered out the back window with an anxious face.

"I think we all do," Ella added as she cut the cloth that she'd laid out on the measuring table.

I only half noticed the attractive mint green color of the cloth she was working with when the hairs shot up on the back of my neck.

"Oh, you all are a bunch of worrywarts. The chances of there being another tornado in Meadowview are slim at best," Suzanna said confidently. "Summer, come over here and help me move this shelf. I want to put the display with the sewing needles and threads closer to the door."

Summer sighed heavily. After one last glance out the window, she went over to Suzanna, taking one side of the free-standing wooden shelf compartments between her hands.

I set Sarah Ann down in the play pen and touched the velvety soft dark hair on her head. She looked up at me with her lips pressed together. I handed her the teething ring that she liked the most. She immediately stuck it in her mouth. She was content at the moment, so I went back to my sewing machine. Ruth's dress was almost finished. All I needed to do was stitch the bottom seam. I hoped that Ruth wouldn't be disappointed when Summer delivered it in the morning.

"I read in a newspaper article once about a woman who was struck by lightning twice within three years. So I suppose it wouldn't be so unlikely that another tornado might hit the community," Miranda said in a sensible way.

Miranda stood in the center of the room. I smiled at the intense look of concentration on her face as she surveyed the shop, not showing any concern at all for the approaching storm. Her features were pale and her eyes were deep and dark. She was still shy, reminding me of a mouse, but I had noticed that lately, she talked a bit more and she was even beginning to voice her opinion about business matters. It turned out that not only was she a marvelous seamstress, she also had a head for numbers and had taken over the bookkeeping with flourish.

"That is not the kind of talk that Summer needs to hear right now," Suzanna chastised her best friend. "Really, Mirn, can't we think about happier things?"

The pop was so sudden and loud that I didn't even recognize it for what it was at first. The window that Summer had been staring out of a moment before was now broken glass on the floor. The wild wind of the approaching storm blew in through the open space, pushing my hair back.

I saw Miranda's face before she crumpled to the ground. Her expression was confusion. Suzanna and Summer dropped the shelf and it hit to the ground with a crash. The two girls were on hands and knees and I realized with surprise that Ella and I were, too.

Sarah Ann was crying, and I began to rise to go to her, but Ella's hand reached out and grabbed me. She shook her head and pointed to the other two girls on the floor across the shop. Suzanna was closest to the playpen. My eyes met hers and without words, she understood. Suzanna stifled a sob with a strong sniff and the back of her hand. She pushed up onto her elbows and crawled over to Sarah Ann. She didn't dare lift my baby from the pen, but I heard her soft murmurs of comfort from across the room.

My mind could hardly comprehend what had happened. The wind was still blowing into the room and the lights flickered with the latest flash of lightning.

Miranda was completely still. As I stared at her, my heart began pounding madly in my chest. I looked back at Ella and pointed at Miranda. She nodded, and I began scooting over the wooden floor boards toward my prone friend.

Even though I shimmied across the floor, and it couldn't have taken more than a few seconds, it felt as if a lifetime had passed before I finally reached Miranda. I poked her arm and pushed in closer. Her eyes stared blankly at the ceiling and fixed on her face was still a look of confusion. There was a dark puddle beneath her head. With acid rising from my gut, I reached forward and touched the liquid. I snatched my fingers back. They were covered in blood. The back of Miranda's head was mush.

Another roar of thunder bellowed, and louder this time. When the lightning lit up the sky again, the shop's lights went out. The sudden darkness didn't surprise me. Electric lights were only allowed in a few of the Amish businesses, and the wiring was always old and unreliable.

As my heart raced and I struggled to catch my breath, I thanked God for the darkness, feeling that it might actually protect us from whoever shot into the window.

I wasn't able to mourn for Miranda. The threat to my baby and my still living friends was too great. My body was infused with a jolt of adrenaline that stripped away any emotion, other than fear.

"Is Miranda all right?" Suzanna whispered loudly. Sarah Ann's cries were now just agitated *mewings*.

I looked across the dark room in Suzanna's direction. The burst of light from the storm illuminated Suzanna and Summer's faces. In that moment, I shook my head, and Summer gasped. Suzanna's arm went around Summer, pulling her head into her chest. I knew that Suzanna was not only trying to console Summer, but also silencing any outburst she might have been about to have.

When I searched the darkness for Ella, I could see her form still cowering beneath her sewing machine. The next blast of thunder was the loudest yet, and it continued to roll heavily through the flashes of light outside the windows.

I thought I heard footsteps within the thunder, and as my heart stopped beating altogether, I raised my head up and squinted into the darkness below the broken window. I could have sworn that only a moment ago, there had been a large shard of glass sticking up from the window sill. Now it was gone; the board was smooth.

I didn't think. Rushing into a standing position, I lurched forward to grab the scissors off of the table. My foot slipped in the pool of Miranda's blood. I fell backward, hitting the floor with a heavy *thud*.

The room alighted again and a shadow loomed over me. My mind screamed, *no!* It can't be. My nightmare was a reality—or maybe I was actually dreaming. I inwardly prayed that at any second, I'd wake in my bed, sweaty and crying, beside Noah.

"I've waited a very long time for this," Levi's voice echoed in my ears.

The handgun that had killed Miranda was now aimed at my face.

CHAPTER 37

.... Justin ....

S am pressed the gas pedal harder and we lurched forward. I was in the back seat and didn't bother with a seatbelt. As I leaned over into the front seats between Sam and Noah, I began to question the choice.

"The roads are wet, Sam. Don't get us killed," I said.

Sam slowed a notch, but growled out, "I have a bad feeling about this."

"How would he make it all the way here while the police are after him?" Noah breathed out the question in a flurry of words.

"Who the hell knows? He shouldn't have been able to break out of a maximum security prison, either," Sam huffed.

"I would imagine that if he were free, he'd try to escape to a place where he wouldn't be recognized. He certainly couldn't get away with hiding in the community. Father told me that Bishop Lambright went to the prison personally to tell Levi that whenever he got out, he wasn't welcome back here," Noah said. He sounded as if he was trying to convince himself of something.

"Your bishop actually visited him in the prison?" Sam asked Noah, glancing his way. When Noah nodded, Sam said, "Damn, that's just the type of thing that would bring that crazy bastard back here. No one wants to be told what to do—especially not a psychopath."

"I hope you're wrong," Noah said, swallowing.

"Yeah, me too this time," Sam said somberly.

When we came around the bend, I could just make out the dress shop in the distance beyond the tilled up expanse of cropland. Now that it was completely dark outside, I could see that the lights weren't on.

I pointed. "The place is dark."

"The lights were off at the last few houses we passed. It could just be an outage from the storm," Noah said.

"If we're lucky," Sam added.

Sam turned onto the other road, slowing as we approached the shop. Rose's little red truck was parked in front of the building. Besides the trees bending in the wind, there was no movement or activity around the place that I could see.

"I've got a really bad feeling about this," Sam whispered.

I wholeheartedly agreed with my brother.

CHAPTER 38

Rose

The white of Levi's one eye flashed in the darkness. His scarred face was contorted and hideous to look at. The dripping from his rain drenched body mixed with the puddle of Miranda's blood on the floor. Thunder clapped constantly now.

Despite the raging storm, Sarah Ann's gurgles and squeals were loud in my ears. I didn't look in her direction. I knew that Suzanna and Summer were helpless beside her in the shadows. I held my breath, saying a silent prayer that after Levi killed me, he'd run away into the rain. I begged God that the crazed man didn't touch my baby.

"Aw, it looks as if my little sister got her head blown apart," Levi said with a sickeningly sweet voice. "When I saw her through the window, I thought it was too good to be true—the two females I hated most in the world were conveniently at the same location. The Lord guided me to this place, at this moment in time, showing me His purpose."

Levi's ramblings as he stood above his dead sister were pure madness. And yet, his voice was eerily calm, void of any regret whatsoever. Levi was so dangerous because he truly was delusional. There was no rationalizing with a person who believed that he was acting on God's behalf by killing his sister. He would cut us all down on a whim.

"I bet you're wondering how I knew to find you here?" Levi drawled.

My only hope was to keep him talking. Maybe we'd get lucky and someone would drive up to the shop. I swallowed the knot in my throat. "Yes, that was clever of you. How did you figure it out?" My voice was dry, brittle, and not my own.

"Prisons are amazing places. They bring in newspapers from all over the place. We're allowed to read them in the rec hall. There was another man in there from Meadowview. He made some arrangement with the guards to have the Meadowview Plain Talk delivered to the prison on a weekly basis." He shrugged and grinned. "I was able to keep up on things at a distance, you could say. It was brilliant of you girls," he spoke louder across the room and my heart sunk into my belly. He knew the others were hiding. "To advertise the grand opening of your little dress shop in the newspaper."

He laughed and the sound made my skin crawl. I didn't like being on the floor with Levi's form towering over me, but I was too afraid to move a muscle. The gun was still aimed at me. Miranda was still dead, only a foot away.

The storm quieted, and the rumbles began to move away. The wind that had been gusting beyond the broken window softened to a stiff breeze and only a sprinkling of rain fell from the sky. Abruptly, Sarah Ann's babbling could be easily heard. Levi's head whipped to the side. His hawkish features turned into a sick smile.

"Well, well. What do we have here?" Levi took a step toward my baby. "Is this little vermin yours, Rose?"

It didn't matter that his gun was still pointed in my direction. With a strong surge of my muscles, I pushed off the floor and leaped at Levi. I wrapped my arms around his lanky torso and my weight knocked him off balance. We hit the floor together in a heap of kicking feet and flailing arms.

Another flash of distant lightning lit the room for an instant and Summer was on top of us. She was punching Levi in the face, and blood spattered from his mouth. Suzanna had Sarah Ann in her arms and Ella had her arm around them both.

"Bitches," Levi squealed.

I was trying to grab the gun away from him with everything I had, but he was too strong. His arm came loose from my grip and surged upward. The explosion of the gun going off was so close to my ear that the world went silent for a moment. Summer fell backward and Ella rushed forward, dropping to the floor beside her.

Summer was gripping her shoulder. I could just make out the dark smudge spreading out beneath her hand as she clutched the wound. Her mouth was open in a crying scream and Ella was saying something to her, but I couldn't hear anything yet.

Headlights streaking through the windows turned all of our heads. Levi was up, waving the gun. With a loud, rolling noise, my hearing came back with a vengeance.

"I don't care if I die. I knew the moment I jumped on that semi that my days were numbered." Spit flew from Levi's mouth. "This is what the Lord wants me to do," he shouted. "I'll put a bullet in each of your heads before it's over."

He pointed the gun at Suzanna. "I always hated you."

I stood up and cried, "No, wait. Me. It's me you want. I'm the one who cut your eye out. I'm the reason you went to prison."

I recognized the sound of the diesel engine that parked in front of the shop. When the motor turned off, I heard voices and was filled with sudden hope.

Levi heard them too. In a moment of quick decision, he rushed forward and grabbed my arm, yanking me to the back door. I began to struggle but Levi hissed into my ear, "I swear to God, I'll start shooting right now and they'll all die, even your child, if you don't come with me."

Footsteps were stomping across the front porch when I went through the back door with Levi. Drizzle hit my face. Levi jerked me off the back stoop and I landed in a puddle. We ran past several outbuildings before we reached a tractor path running between the woods and an overgrown field that hadn't been bush-hogged in the previous fall.

As we entered the wet darkness beneath the trees, I wasn't afraid anymore.

I was just so thankful that Sarah Ann, and my friends, would live.

CHAPTER 39

······ Justin ······

There was another round of thunder and zigzagging lightning. *Kaboom.*

"Did you hear that?" I asked, looking at the outline of the dress shop in the distance.

"A gunshot—I think it was a gunshot," Sam said. With a jolt, the truck accelerated and I fell backwards. I didn't care this time about Sam's crazy driving. The sound of a gun firing still boomed in my ears.

"This can't be happening," Noah said, pressing a hand into his temple. His other hand gripped the long barreled rifle.

We raced over the roadway without any words between us. I could have sworn that Noah and Sam were able to hear my heart pounding in my chest. I looked with cold dread across the field at the abandoned looking shop. The building sat far off the road, having a long, winding gravel driveway leading to it. There were a couple of trees around the shop and several smaller buildings behind it. The wooden hitching railing in front announced to the world that it was an Amish business.

We turned, lucky to have two wheels on the ground at the rate of speed we were going. The sign that we passed was the one I'd painted, but I hardly glanced at it. I was only focused on the darkened building that Rose's truck was parked in front of. Rose and Sarah Ann were in there—possibly trapped by a psychopath with a grudge, and a gun.

"What's the plan?" Noah said evenly when we parked.

"Shoot him before he shoots us," Sam replied.

With my brother, it was always a Wild West show, but he didn't have the expertise with a rifle that Noah did. As we sprinted up the steps, I worried that Noah didn't have the guts to shoot anyone. Light rain pelted the tin roof. Another flash of lightning lit the sky. I tried to get to a window first, to take a peek in, but Noah was through the front door too quickly. Sam was right on his heels. With little choice, I brought up the rear and burst into the room.

Sam's flashlight illuminated the room. The sight that met my eyes made me instantly want to vomit. One of the Amish girls was on the ground and a puddle of blood surrounded her head. Her dark eyes stared at the ceiling. Her face was still and pale. I had a hard time pulling my gaze away from the dead girl, but when I did, I saw Sam kneeling on the floor with Summer cradled in his arms. She was crying hysterically and there was blood all over the front of her shirt.

Noah swept by them and touched Sarah Ann's face. He began rapidly speaking to the girl that was holding the baby in the Amish language. I thought that her name was Suzanna, but I wouldn't bet on it. It occurred to me that possibly the chaos of the situation had forced Noah back into his native tongue.

Noah kissed Sarah Ann's head and touched Suzanna's shoulder reassuringly. He whirled and bolted for the back door. It was then that I noticed the broken window and felt the rush of wind on my face from the opening.

"Wait," Sam called out. "He's armed. We should call the cops."

"Call them—but we don't have time to wait. Levi has Rose, and he's going to kill her." The panic in Noah's voice was palpable. My own heart leaped into my throat. Just the night before, I'd had a heart-to-heart with my sister in the family room—and now this.

Sam began to rise and Summer cried out again. I thought

about the other girls and my niece's safety. Someone had to stay with them until help arrived.

I held up my hand to Sam. "I'll go. You stay with Sarah Ann and call 911."

For a moment Sam's eyes were locked on mine as he deliberated. But then Sarah Ann began crying, and he came undone.

"Okay, okay—go!" Sam's cell phone was pressed to his ear when I began running.

Noah didn't wait for me to catch up. He sprinted through the door ahead of me. I barely heard one of the girls say, "Be careful," as I jumped outside.

The rain had subsided to a heavy drizzle and my sneakers squished into the saturated ground. Noah ran like a blind man, with no plan or direction. With a surge of strength, I lunged forward and grabbed his shoulder.

"Slow down, Noah, please," I begged.

Noah stopped and turned to me. "He'll kill her—" he rasped.

"Calm down for a minute," I was out of breath, but forced the words out in a steady stream. "Look over there," I pointed at the buildings. "I saw a path going between them. It seems to continue alongside the woods."

Noah nodded, and changed course. This time he moved a little more stealthily and I was able to keep up with him without much trouble.

"We're going to have to sneak up on them," I whispered. At first, I wasn't sure if Noah heard me between the whistling of the wind and our sloshing over the moist ground, but then he visibly slowed. He directed me off of the path. We began climbing a steep hill.

"If we can get to higher ground, we might spot them below us," Noah said.

I followed closely behind him, slipping several times and having to grab onto saplings for support. I was impressed that Noah was able to keep his balance so well with the rifle in his hands. He seemed to be perfectly adapted to running, armed, through the woods on the dark, rainy night. *It must be an Amish hunting thing,* I thought.

Noah pulled up abruptly and I bumped into his solid back. His hand went up to silence me and we both listened.

The sound of muted voices reached me. I held my breath. Noah looked back over his shoulder at me and then bent down. He crept several steps and went to his knee.

I followed suit and stared into the hollow. Rain water gushed down the hillside in a narrow torrent, sweeping away fallen leaves and branches. At the base of the hill, beside the rush of water, stood Levi—and Rose. A gun was raised in his hand, and pointed at my sister's head. They were arguing.

I felt weak. This can't be happening. The dead Amish girl in the shop wasn't real. *This isn't real.*

I looked at Noah in desperation. I was shocked to see calm resolve etched on his face.

He raised the rifle to his shoulder and looked down the barrel.

"Lord be with me," he whispered.

I turned my head away. I couldn't watch.

CHAPTER 40

Rose

*L*evi's breath was sour in my face and I wrinkled my nose, lifting my chin defiantly. By now, Sam should have called the police on his cell phone. Help was on the way, for Summer anyway. My time had run out. I'd already prayed. The only thing I could do now was give Levi a piece of my mind. He'd killed sweet Miranda, his own sister, and one of my best friends. The thought of how her fiancé, Matthew, would feel, made my stomach clench. Levi's fingers twisted in my hair, pulling my head back even further. The gun was closer—almost close enough to brush my forehead.

A hundred thoughts flooded my mind. Sitting on Dad's lap while Mom read a bedtime story, my first bicycle ride, playing in the ocean with Sam and Justin, the dreary day in the cemetery when Mom was buried, the first time I saw Noah in the hallway of our house, our first kiss, and the moment that Sarah Ann was born. All these things came rushing at me all at once.

I was so tired, and so sad. I wouldn't see Sarah Ann walk or run or ride a pony. I'd never feel Noah's warm lips on my skin again or hear Summer's high pitched laughter. So many things I'd never get to see or do. Rain drops fell into my eyes and the gray clouds separated, allowing just enough moonlight to stream through the tall trees, to light up Levi's leering face.

Sadness turned to hot anger. He might end my life, but he wouldn't get the satisfaction of seeing me groveling in fear.

"You're going to rot in hell for this, Levi Zook." I hissed out the words.

"No, God is with me—He always has been!" Levi shouted, and then lowered his voice to a harsh, spitting whisper. "I will punish you for your lies and your promiscuous ways."

Levi's eyes blazed when they met mine. The muzzle of his gun shifted a fraction and his finger began to press the trigger. I closed my eyes.

The gun discharged with an explosion of sound. And everything went black.

Chapter 41

•••••• Justin ••••••

KABOOM, the shot blast echoed through the damp woods and my ears. At the moment the explosion occurred, I could have sworn another one sounded. I swallowed and squeezed my eyes tightly closed. I couldn't look. I felt Noah stirring beside me, and then he was gone.

My eyes popped open and I looked into the hollow. Rose and Levi were both down. Tears stung my eyes and I sucked in a wet breath. Pushing up to my feet, I stumbled down the hill after Noah. He reached Rose first, jumping over Levi's body, and falling to the ground beside her. She was in his arms when I bent down into the slimy leaves. There was blood on his hands.

The sound of Noah's sobs chilled me to the bone. As tears fell down my cheeks, I glanced over at Levi. His face was turned away. There was blood and gore spilling out from his orange hair. The gun was still gripped in his fingers.

Noah's crying changed tone, and my attention snapped back to him. He was laughing now. He'd lost his freaking mind.

Then I heard her voice and I leaped forward.

"My ear. It's only my ear," Rose cried out in triumph.

CHAPTER 42

Rose

I watched from the window as Suzanna and Ella tied the colorful balloons to the dress shop sign. Noah was behind me, sitting on a stool and holding Sarah Ann in his lap. He talked quietly to Timothy, probably about work. It still amazed me how quickly men could get over traumatic events. Or maybe it was just Amish men. Justin and Sam were still pretty freaked out about everything that had happened.

It was three weeks ago to the day that Levi escaped prison and returned to Meadowview with vengeance on his mind. He killed his own sister, and came within an inch of killing me, too. I shuddered and touched my ear. The scabbing was rough beneath my fingertips. A chunk was missing, and my ear wasn't pretty, but I didn't care about that. And I wasn't going to have cosmetic surgery done on it, the way Dad had suggested, either. To me, it was a constant reminder of just how lucky—and blessed, I truly was. Poor Miranda hadn't been as fortunate. The small disfigurement would never let me, or anyone else, forget her.

I swallowed down the knot that formed in my throat.

A hand touched my shoulder. "It just doesn't seem right to have the dress shop without Mirn. And I don't understand how Suzanna and Timothy can go on with the wedding next week." Summer sighed.

She gazed out the window to see what I was looking at. The balloons were floating high above the sign in the sunshine.

Suzanna and Ella were walking side by side, back down the driveway.

Summer's arm was still in a sling, and the bulge of the bandaging on her shoulder was visible through the light blue sweater she wore. She was as lucky as I was. If Levi's shot had been more accurate, she'd be gone, too.

The pain inside of me was still very raw. My eyes watered and I took a gasping breath. Summer turned and threw her good arm around me. She squeezed me tightly as she rocked against my side with her own tears. The scent of vanilla clung to her red hair and the familiarity of it, and the fact that neither one of us had recovered yet, filled me with a little bit of contentment. At least I wasn't in it alone.

When Summer stepped back, she wiped her eyes with the back of her hand. I used the tissue from my pocket to dry mine. My gaze met Noah's for a moment. He looked worried, but didn't approach me. He'd been my psychologist since the attack. There wasn't anything new or revealing he could say. He'd said it all. It was going to take time to heal properly. We both understood that.

The door opened with a jingle and a gust of warm air blew in with Suzanna and Ella.

Suzanna walked over to us, and slightly out of breath, she scolded, "It's too pretty a day to keep these windows closed. Let's open them up a bit, shall we?"

Suzanna stopped when she saw our red, tear-streaked faces.

"You two haven't been crying again, have you?" Suzanna asked, frowning.

I was still pulling myself together when Summer answered her. "Just because you all are so resilient, doesn't mean everyone is."

Suzanna took a step closer while Ella busied herself at the counter.

Her tone was sharp. "Trust me, we're all grieving as much as you and Rose are. But Miranda wouldn't want us to be carrying on that way. More than anything else, she wanted to see this business a success. It had become her whole life, and what better way for us to honor her, than to make that happen. Even Matthew wanted the shop to go on—although, he's still too heartbroken to stop by just yet."

"I get it. I do. I'm just overly emotional today." I sniffed and swallowed.

Suzanna reached out and patted my arm as if I was a child. "I know. But today is our grand opening. Please try to smile—for Miranda," Suzanna said coaxingly. She took Summer's hand and gave it a little shake.

"Look, our first customers," Ella said pointing out the window.

My gloomy thoughts evaporated for a moment, and I squeezed in beside Summer and Suzanna to spy out the window. There were two buggies, followed by Dad's SUV, making their way up the driveway. Several more buggies were approaching on the road.

My heart fluttered with a wave of nervousness.

"I didn't think we'd have such a large turnout," I commented.

I wasted no time, jogging behind the counter and pulling a compact out of my purse. While the girls rushed around with the last-minute details, making sure everything was in order, I wiped any trace of my meltdown away. I even reapplied some powder to my face. This time when our eyes met, Noah was smiling. I smiled back and nodded my head, telling him that I was in fact, okay.

I glanced around the shop and took a deep breath. The window that Levi had entered the shop through had been replaced. The floor boards where Miranda had bled out were new, and stained to match the others. Everything had been vigorously cleaned, and the walls had a fresh coat of white paint. Anyone entering the shop would never guess that a young woman had been murdered here.

The day after Levi's attack, I had really wanted the entire

shop to be torn down or set ablaze. Whatever way to get rid
of it would have been fine with me. But the Amish had other
ideas. The building itself wasn't damaged at all, and the meeting between the bishop, the ministers and many others in the
congregation came up with the consensus that it would be a
shame to destroy a building that couldn't be easily replaced. In
the end, Amish practicality won the day.

For a while, it would be hard to work in the shop, I knew
that. Even now, my gaze was pulled to the middle of the floor
where Miranda had lain, dead. But Suzanna had pointed out to
us right after Miranda's funeral that Miranda had literally shed
her blood here, so in a way, as long as the shop survived, our
friend would always be with us.

It seemed morbid to me, but it still kind of made sense.

I took a steadying breath just as the door opened again
with a jingle. It was Bishop and Martha Lambright, followed
by James and Ruth Hershberger. The women stopped to talk
near the doorway with Suzanna and Ella, while James made his
way over to Noah and Timothy. From the corner of my eye, I
saw James take Sarah Ann from Noah's lap. She instantly had a
wad of his white beard wrapped around her hand.

"May I speak with you, Rose?"

I looked up. The bishop was at the end of the counter. I
nodded and walked over to him.

"Of course. How are you today?" I addressed him cordially,
trying desperately to be businesslike.

He tilted his head. "I've been meaning to visit you—see
how you're faring."

The concern in his voice was genuine. I met his gaze, noting the deep wrinkles around his eyes. At one time, that face
made me tremble with fear, but not today. I began to speak,
but the words wouldn't come out.

"Oh, child," the bishop said. He stepped behind the counter and reached down to embrace me. He was tall, a bit boney,
and his long beard tickled my face, but I clung to him anyway.

"Time heals all wounds. You will never forget what happened, but someday, you'll be able to think on it without crying," the bishop said quietly.

When I pulled back, he smiled awkwardly at me before he joined the other men.

Ruth and Martha stepped up to the counter with kind faces. I'd already been in each of their arms several times since Miranda was laid to rest. This time, when I looked between them, I realized that they were ready to move on from such sadness.

"Do you have my dress prepared?" Ruth asked.

I couldn't help grinning at her forwardness. Bending down, I retrieved the hunter green dress with Ruth's name pinned on it from the shelf behind the counter.

I opened the dress up on the counter for Ruth to see. She leaned in closer, studying every square inch of the garment for what seemed like an eternity. Finally, she straightened up.

"This is fine workmanship. Did you do it all on your own?" Ruth asked.

"Ella helped me a little with the collar, and she inspected it for me. But otherwise, it's my creation," I answered proudly.

"I think you've made your first sale. Of course, I'll need to try it on first."

I beamed at her. Ruth wouldn't compliment anyone or anything unless she really felt it was warranted. She was an honest woman to a fault.

"I'll show you to the fitting room, Ruth," Ella said.

After Ella took Ruth away, Martha handed me a piece of paper. Three of the Yoder women walked through the door, along with Ella's mother and my sister-in-law, Katie. Beyond the window, I could see several more women making their way up the steps. Dad, Tina, Sam, and Justin were at the end of the line.

Feeling a bit flustered, I turned my attention back to Martha. "What can I help you with?"

"I'm here to pick up my sister's order. Abram is taking me

for a buggy ride out to visit her today—" she held up her hand "—but if you girls don't have the dresses ready yet, that's just fine with me. I'll come back for them another day."

"Suzanna and Ella finished the order last night. It was a dress for Miriam and then three dresses for the girls, right?" I said, pulling the bundle with Miriam's name on it from the shelf.

"Yes, that's correct. If they need any alterations, I'll bring them back, but Miriam said that she stopped by last week on her way to town for a final fitting. So they should be the right sizes," Martha said.

She sat down on one of the stools we provided along the counter. I made eye contact with Summer and flicked my chin, getting her to come help me. She'd been standing in the corner by herself, obviously out of her element.

Summer stepped behind the counter with the open expression of a person begging for something to do.

"Can you help Martha check out with these dresses?" I asked Summer.

Summer loved working with the old fashioned cash register. She nodded vigorously.

"Can do," she chirped.

"Thank you for the business, Martha. I hope this helps Miriam out—takes some of the strain off her," I offered.

Martha reached over the counter and patted my hand. "It will definitely help. And it's a start to real dialogue between her and Isaac. He always knew she needed assistance, but he was unsure how to go about getting it for her. Once he sees how thrilled she is with the dresses, he might be receptive to other ways to lightening her load."

"I'm so glad to be able to help her, even in this small way." I fumbled with the words, becoming teary-eyed all over again, but for an entirely different reason.

"You and the girls are doing a good thing here," she told me before turning her attention to Summer.

I walked by Constance Schwartz and several other ladies,

greeting them as I went by, but not interrupting Suzanna and Ella as they conversed with them in German about the shop and its services. Constance smiled at me in a friendly way and I returned the favor. I guessed that she was finally completely over Noah, letting go of her resentment toward him for dumping her right before their wedding. I'd always thought she was a classy girl, and not one to make an enemy of. Now that she was showing interest in becoming one of our customers, I wanted to lay the grudge to rest even more.

Tina was browsing through the fabric shelves, while Dad, Sam, and Justin appeared to be hiding near the door to the storeroom. Dad had somehow wrestled Sarah Ann away from James and was cooing to her.

"Do you see anything you like?" I asked my soon-to-be stepmother.

Tina turned to me, her face beaming. "Actually, I do. I didn't think you'd have such a large selection of printed fabrics."

"We wanted to provide the Amish women with everything they need for quilting, and sewing bedding and curtains. We're going to add even more supplies eventually," I said, admiring the display shelves that Noah and Timothy had built a few days earlier.

"I love to craft, and I see some perfect fabric here for a wall hanging." Tina thumbed through the bolts of cloth. As I was turning to leave her, she looked up. "Are you ready to come stop by my office to chat about everything that happened?"

Tina's voice was low and pleading. She'd been trying to get me in for some therapy sessions ever since the attack, but I'd been too stubborn, and quite frankly, too distraught, to see her. Suzanna's little speech had changed my mind, though. I needed to move on. And I didn't think I could do it on my own.

"Yes, I'm ready. How about Friday afternoon?"

"That's perfect. Text me when you know the time. I'll fit you in," Tina promised. The relief was obvious on her pretty round face.

I left Tina to sift through the assortment of patterns, and finally joined my family.

"Looks like a good turnout," Dad said, glancing around.

Two more women had crowded into the shop. The scene was similar to every other Amish event I'd been to. The men were sequestered to one side, while the women enjoyed each other's company on the other. My partners were keeping busy, but with the social atmosphere in the room, I didn't feel compelled to rush over and begin helping just yet.

"It's more than I imagined," I said honestly.

"The Amish are kind of sick that way," Sam said casually.

"Sam—not now," Dad chastised him.

Sam usually said the rude and inappropriate things that we were all thinking. I gave him a pass and turned to Dad.

"Are you still going to talk to the district attorney?" I asked bluntly.

Dad sighed and shifted Sarah Ann onto his shoulder. He softly patted her back, while she was looked around at all the newcomers with wide eyes.

"I spoke to Amos the other day. He said that the bishop and ministers were already discussing the situation among themselves. He asked me to give them some time to come up with a solution." Dad hesitated. "I told him they had a month. If they don't make some changes to their Ordnung about the teenager's job options by then, I'll go above their heads."

I breathed out in relief. For once, Dad was being reasonable. I hoped that Bishop Lambright and the others recognized the necessity for quick action. But I wasn't betting on it. Decisions were made in slow motion within the community.

"You holding up okay, sis?" Sam asked, dragging my attention back to him.

He was wearing a T-shirt for the community college he attended and his blond hair was messier than usual.

"I'm doing better. Today's been rough. Suzanna had to straighten me and Summer out," I said.

"She's a tough one, that girl." Sam looked over at Summer, and I saw a smile pass between them.

"Things seem to be going really well between the two of you," I commented.

Sam shrugged. "It's amazing how seeing the aftermath of your girlfriend being shot by a lunatic puts everything into perceptive," he said. "I realize now how much she means to me. I'm not going to lose her."

Sam made eye contact with me and I knew that he meant what he said.

"Oh, great. Here comes trouble," Sam said, raising his chin to the window so that I would look out.

Getting out of a buggy were Rebecca and Rachel Miller. Sam was obviously talking about Rachel. Then I noticed Micah tying the bay horse to the hitching rail. I glanced at Justin.

He was also peering out the window. His expression was unreadable, but I thought I saw a spark of jealousy in his eyes. I was suddenly tired. Sam was right. Trouble was definitely on the horizon.

But for now, though, everything was peaceful. I would try to enjoy it while it lasted.

Chapter 43

❧ Rachel ❧

Micah glanced over his shoulder at me. Mother was already through the doorway and I hesitated on the steps. I recognized the Cameron's vehicle and began fretting whether Justin was inside the building. I didn't want him to see me with Micah, even though I knew that it was bound to happen sometime.

Micah's smile was somewhat reassuring, and his green eyes were even lighter in the bright sunlight. The perspiration under my dress made me regret having prayed so diligently for the arrival of warmer weather. It seemed to have skipped springtime altogether and gone straight into summer.

The breeze rustled the leaves on the maple tree and Juniper snorted at the horse he was tied beside. The day was perfect in most ways, and yet, I only felt dread. As much as I tried to push the depression aside, it was always nipping at me, turning a beautifully sunny day into a dark and gloomy one. I hadn't had a drink of alcohol since the night before I'd cut my finger off. It wasn't because I was being a good girl, or just didn't need the numbing sensation any longer. It was because Sadie hadn't answered any of my phone calls. After Levi Zook had killed Miranda and attacked Rose, I needed the liquor more than ever. The entire business had set me on such an edge, I could barely eat most days. The only thing that kept me a little bit sane was the steady flow of books I'd borrowed from the library. Justin was right. Immersing myself in fictional worlds did help some. And surprisingly, both Mother and Father hadn't balked at the type of books I was reading, either. They seemed to accept the fact that I needed something to occupy my always anxious mind while my hand healed.

Micah's smile drooped. He walked back down the steps. "Are you all right?" he whispered.

Micah's gaze was steady and real. He was my last bit of hope for normalcy in the crazy world. Micah offered the wholesomeness of the plain life. With him, I'd have a good husband and a brood of children. I wouldn't have to turn away from the way I was raised, or my people—or most importantly—my family. Micah was contentment.

But then why was my heart in so much turmoil?

"Are you regretting that you accepted my courtship proposal?" Micah asked in a strained voice.

"No, no, it's not that. I wish you could have seen how pleased Father and Mother were this morning." I hesitated. "It's just going in there—doesn't it bother you at all?"

Micah nodded thoughtfully. "Sure it does. I didn't know Miranda very well, but no one should die like that." He glanced at the shop and then back at me again. "From what Timothy Troyer said, the girls think Miranda would have wanted it this way. We should have faith that they knew her heart."

Of course, I couldn't tell Micah that the gruesome crime committed in the shop was only a part of why I was reluctant to go into the building. For once in my life, I had some semblance of direction. I was probably destined to ruin it for myself, but I certainly wasn't going to purposely push Micah away right now.

"Lead the way," I said hurriedly, motioning for Micah that I'd follow him in.

He did so, and he even held the door open for me.

The shop was crowded and loud with conversations. My gaze swept the room. I found what I was looking for quickly. He stood in the back of the room. When our eyes met, he seemed to be looking for me as well.

Butterflies exploded in my belly at just the one quick meeting of our eyes. I glanced away, taking a measured breath. Justin was no good for me. I knew it. He knew it. So why was it both so pleasurable, and so painful to see him, then?

Mother caught my arm and guided me toward the back of the room where Justin was standing with his family. I saw the slight roll of Sam's eyes when he saw me coming, but I ignored him. Mother said hello to the group and then asked to hold Sarah Ann. Dr. Cameron reluctantly passed the baby over to her.

"How is your hand doing?" Rose asked me.

"It's much better. The surgeon let me see it for the first time the other day." I shrugged. "It doesn't look so bad after all. At least the throbbing seems to have finally stopped for good."

I sniffed and looked at the floor. A tingling sensation of unease washed over me. I raised my gaze and hesitantly asked Rose, "How are you feeling?"

"Better," she said briskly.

I lied all too often and immediately recognized hers. Rose still had issues with what had happened. But who wouldn't?

"Rose, I brought Rachel over here because I want to ask you a favor."

"Mother!" I scolded.

"Now, Rachel. Please let me talk to Rose about it. It might be just what you need," Mother said firmly.

I bit my lip and glanced away. When my eyes returned to the group, they settled on Justin. He was staring at me.

"The surgeon told us that since Rachel's finger is healing well, the best thing for it is light use. Amos still thinks Rachel needs a job of sorts, and I was wondering if perhaps she could help out here at the shop. She's a gifted seamstress, and I have faith that given time, she'll be able to sew again. For the meantime, she can iron and fold material and work the register."

Mother's voice was hopeful. I looked for Rose's reaction.

"I think that's a wonderful idea. We might not be able to pay her much at first, but if everyone here today orders a dress, we'll definitely need the help," Rose said solidly. She faced me and added, "I remember seeing some of your drawings of farm animals and local barns. Would you be interested in displaying a few of them on the walls? You can put a price sticker on them and see if they sell."

Her words flashed through my mind. Sell my drawings? Would anyone actually buy them? The thrill of Rose's suggestion eliminated most of the fear of rejection.

"I would certainly be willing to try . . . if it's all right with Mother, that is?" When I saw the broad smile on Mother's face, I had my answer.

Soon, Mother was gossiping with Ruth and Dr. Cameron was chatting with Bishop Lambright. Noah looped his arm around Rose as he bent down to whisper something in her ear. She laughed and they pecked each other on the lips before they moved off to welcome Mrs. Graber when she stepped into the shop. Sam joined Summer behind the counter, leaving only me and Justin still standing there together. I was just about to walk away, when Justin cleared his throat.

"You haven't been playing with any cutting devices lately, have you?"

I looked up to see him grinning from ear to ear. Even though Father and Mother were nearby, and I felt Micah's hot gaze on me from across the room, I couldn't help but chuckle.

I couldn't deny it. Justin could always make me laugh.

Could I really give that up? Only time would tell.

Will the young people of Meadowview finally find their happily-ever-afters? Find out in the stunning conclusion of the Temptation series, as events spiral out of control in the sleepy farming community once again.

The powerful family saga continues with JOURNEY.
COMING IN 2018

ACKNOWLEDGEMENTS

I'm always grateful to my husband, Jay, for serving me breakfast in bed on the weekends, impromptu trips for milkshakes, and for his unwavering support. I love you.

Many thanks to my children, Luke, Cole, Lily, Owen and Cora. You're the best kids any parent could hope for.

Much gratitude for my amazing cover designer, Jenny Zemanek of Seedlings Design Studio, for the beautiful cover image, my hard-working editor, Grace Bell, and my perfectionist beta reader, Heather Miller. I'm very blessed to have the considerable skill of such professionals to help create my books.

Made in the USA
Lexington, KY
04 March 2018